When I Was Jane

When I Was Jane

By Theresa Mieczkowski

Edited by Margo Navage Padala

TTP
Two Touch Press

New York

For Kristin, as promised.

Long, long ago.

∞

We don't see things as they are,
We see them as we are.

~Anaïs Nin

When I Was Jane

~1~

"Stay with us."

Distant sounds break through the silence.

Sirens.

Radios.

Voices.

"Took you guys long enough. She's a goner."

"Ma'am, can you hear me? Can you tell us your name?"

Doors slam. Flickering bursts of red and blue pierce the darkness.

"We've got you, ma'am."

An arm slides behind my back.

"Try to keep still." A woman's voice. "We're going to move you."

Hands grab and lift. Too many hands. Too much force.

"Look what I found. She's been drinking. Perfectly good waste of a Mercedes."

"When will these people ever learn?"

Flying weightless, tight cocoon. Jarring, pulsing pressure.

"Touching down in four. Page the on call."

We drop slowly. Wheels scrape concrete.

"What've we got?"

"Female, DUI…head trauma…femoral injury…"

"Trauma room four. Prep for surgery—"

"Wait."

Hair is pushed from my eyes. Breath on my face. Peppermints, coffee.

"She looks like…"

"We're running out of time, Charles."

My hand is lifted, dropped.

"Oh my God, do you know who this is? *Audrey*. Oh God. Is there another one coming? Is there a little—"

"We gotta move her *now*."

"Right. Page Dr. Gilbert. Tox comes to me only. You hear me? Go. Move. *Move!*"

And then we're flying. His voice above me breathless, begging.

"Audrey, for the love of Christ, stay with me. Jason's coming."

~ ~ ~

In my dream, the day is cold and raw. Red and blue lights reflect off the surface of the dark water onto something bobbing up and down. A bottle. I dive in after it, but it is carried out of my reach.

Someone cries out from the boat. "No! Come back."

I turn to see him drift into the fog.

His pleas blow in on the wind. "Don't go!"

I swim for the bottle, my limbs becoming heavier and heavier. When I can no longer stay afloat, I let myself sink into the darkness below.

"Breathe!" His voice echoes in my ears.

I know better than to breathe underwater, but I'm afraid to ignore his command. Even though I don't understand why he'd want me to, I do as he asks.

I take a breath.

~ ~ ~

"Look again, Patel," a man says harshly. "Run her through one more time."

A heavily accented voice replies. "Keep calm, Dr. Gilbert. We have to treat her like any other patient."

"She *isn't* any other patient."

"You know it is too early to determine the—"

"Did you see that? She blinked."

My eyelid is pried open. Bright light shines in my face. Blurred figures sway in front of me.

"Audrey, it's me. Can you see me?"

"For God's sake, Gilbert, give her a moment."

I see only blinding white.

"Audrey! Audrey!" Rubber soles drag across a polished floor. "Let me go, damn it. She was awake. Let me go!"

He's back on the boat, floating away.

~2~

I wake to the sun on my face. The sky is blue and bright behind the window, so bright I have to blink a few times to adjust my sight. A silver heart-shaped balloon waves in the air, blown by a fan. It dances about, bumping against the glass as if trying to get out and fly. I follow the string down to a shelf overflowing with flowers, cards, and stuffed bears. They sit crowded together, staring.

"Welcome back." A man stands smiling next to my bed. A doctor, judging by the long white coat he wears over his dress pants and shirt. Above his ears, tufts of greying hair frame his bald brown head. "We have been worried about you. Do you remember anything?"

I try to place his accent…Indian, I think.

He raises his eyebrows and waits for me to answer. I shake my head.

"Do you know who I am?" he asks.

I glance at the name tag pinned to his white coat and nod.

"Try to answer," he says.

"Dr. Patel," I whisper, hoping I've pronounced it right. My throat feels like it's been scraped out with sand.

"See? She remembers you," someone says from the other side of the room. "The damage isn't—"

Dr. Patel looks over his shoulder. "Please let me do my job. I don't want to have to remove you again."

He carefully holds a cup of water to my mouth and guides my head forward so I can take a sip. "Do you know my first name?" he asks.

I look up at him, wondering why I'd know that. I shake my head.

"Do you know *your* name? Do you know where you are?"

I remember pieces of things, flashes of time. I remember being pulled from a car. I remember flying in a helicopter. I remember voices. *Female, car accident, multiple injuries.*

"What is your name?" he asks again.

I remember what they called me. "Jane?"

"Tell me what you remember."

I strain to speak. "Jane Doe, possible DUI. Head trauma, femoral damage. She didn't kill anyone at least."

He closes his eyes and nods. "She is echoing what she heard when she arrived," he says over his shoulder. "Charles will concur."

The person behind him sighs. "Elliot, please."

Dr. Patel hesitates and reluctantly steps to the side, revealing a much younger doctor slouched in a chair. Unlike Dr. Patel, he's dressed entirely in scrubs. He looks strung out, eyes glazed and bloodshot, jaw darkened by stubble. One of his legs bounces anxiously.

"Do you know this man?" Dr. Patel asks.

I study the younger doctor's face. He stares back at me like the stuffed bears from the shelf. Frozen, waiting.

"Do you know who this is?" the older man asks, more forcefully this time.

"Yes?" I say with uncertainty, hoping they'll let me go back to sleep.

The younger man jumps from the chair and starts towards my bed. "Let me talk to her privately for a minute."

Dr. Patel puts his arm out to stop him from coming any closer. "Tell me his name," he says, covering the younger doctor's badge.

I struggle to swallow. I whisper the only name that comes to me. "Wyatt?"

The young doctor's eyes harden. "No."

I force myself to raise my drooping eyelids. "Your voice is...familiar, I think."

He again asks Dr. Patel to give us a moment alone, but the older man ignores him, so he turns to me. "You remember my voice? What do you remember me saying?"

I try to concentrate, but there are only pieces of thoughts, sounds of words that slip from my grasp the moment I try to settle on them.

"I think I dreamt you said...come back. You told me to keep breathing." The voice I hear when I talk sounds foreign to me. "I'm sorry, that's it."

Dr. Patel puts a hand on the younger doctor's arm. "She's recalling incidents that occurred after the accident. She subconsciously heard you yelling out to her. Enough questions, she needs to rest."

He shakes the older man off. "Do you remember your age? Where you live? Anything?"

I realize for the first time that I don't know anything at all. My mind is a blank page where thoughts appear and erase themselves before I can see what they are.

The younger doctor snatches the clipboard hanging off the edge of my bed and flips through the papers. "I told them to decrease the Dilaudid—it's going to throw off her mental clarity."

Dr. Patel lowers his voice. "Gilbert, you are not her doctor."

"And what am I supposed to tell Daisy?"

The older man takes the clipboard from him. "We can discuss that later. She's had enough. Go get some sleep; you need it."

"Who's Daisy?" I hear myself ask.

Dr. Patel puts his hand up to stop his colleague from answering, but it's no use.

"Your daughter," Dr. Gilbert says. "Don't you remember her? She's been crying for her mother for the last six days."

The room begins to spin. "I have a daughter?"

"We." He grips the rail at the bottom of my bed. "*We* have a daughter."

~3~

"Blink if you understand me," Dr. Patel says, staring down at me over his glasses. His eyebrows look like fuzzy white caterpillars resting on his forehead. I watch them, waiting to see if they get up and crawl away.

Next to him, Dr. Gilbert stays motionless, a sickened expression distorting his face. "Blink, Audrey."

I blink up at them as I'm told.

The older man puts a hand to my face. "You've had a seizure. It's not uncommon with head injuries like yours. It will take a little time to come out of it."

Dr. Gilbert takes a penlight from his pocket and holds it up to my eyes. His colleague grabs his arm.

"Jason, you were warned," Dr. Patel says, pressing a button by the side of my bed.

Two men dressed in white enter the room and wait by the door with their arms folded.

Dr. Gilbert flares his nostrils. "You can't be serious."

I grasp the corner of Dr. Patel's coat to get his attention but can only manage a garbled *please*.

"Try to keep calm," he says, placing a gentle hand on my shoulder. "It will take a moment before you can speak.

You may feel a little adrenaline rush in a minute or two. That will wake you up a bit." He looks towards the men at the door. "Please take Dr. Gilbert for a walk."

"I can go myself!" he says as they put their hands on his shoulders. He shakes them off and darts to the side of my bed. I notice remnants of a fading black eye and a swollen, bruised lump of skin near the corner of his mouth. "Don't tell them anything, Audrey," he whispers before he's pulled from the room. Metal pans crash to the ground in the hallway. "Don't touch me!" he says over muffled arguing. "She's my wife!"

Dr. Patel closes his eyes and sighs. "I'm sorry about that."

I look down at my left hand. There's a broad line of paler skin around my ring finger.

"They removed your jewelry when you got here. We have it in a safe."

I shake my head slowly.

"Try to speak."

"Are you sure I'm…" I gesture towards the door.

He smiles. "Yes, I am sure. You are married to him. Believe it or not, I have known you for years. Everyone here cares about you. I know you must feel scared, but you need to trust us."

I stare up at the ceiling. His words are sounds and nothing more.

"So who am I?" I speak slowly, concentrating on getting each word out. "And where am I?"

Dr. Patel covers my hand with his. "Your name is Audrey Gilbert. That was Jason Gilbert, a heart surgeon here at the hospital. He is your husband."

"My husband."

"And you are in New York."

"City?"

"State. At St. Genevieve, a large teaching hospital about forty miles from the city. You and your husband live in the next town over from here."

"My husband," I say again, waiting for it to sink in.

"To be fair, he's normally much calmer than that. He's been through a lot. It hasn't been easy for him. You were flown in after a terrible car accident. You weren't expected to make it."

"I wasn't drunk driving. I know they said DUI, but that's not right."

"And you remember this?"

"No. But I just know I wouldn't. I mean, I don't think I would." I realize how stupid I sound. "Never mind."

"Well according to your blood tests, you are right," he says. "But I am not allowed to talk to you about anything other than your injuries and the specific information I need to make my diagnosis."

"Because of the police?"

"Because of your husband."

I want to say I don't have a husband, but it seems useless. This entire conversation is surreal. They could be lying to me. I could have been kidnapped by the CIA and had my memory erased. They could be aliens in human doctor form for all I know. Anything is possible.

"Was he in the car too?" I ask. "His face—"

"No, you were alone. His face looks that way because, like many of our younger staff, Jason belongs to the Jiu Jitsu club down the street. It's how he gets out the stress of having such an intense job."

It looks to me like someone got their stress out on him.

I glance down and survey my body. My left leg is in a cast, and my wrist is splinted and bandaged. The skin on my arms looks like the canvas from a splatter painting; cuts and gashes crisscross bruises of various size and color. I noticed earlier that the side of my face was numb when I tried to talk, and I now realize there are bandages around my head that cover one of my eyes. I touch my face with my good hand. It feels wrong. Lumpy, bruised.

"May I have a mirror?" I ask.

"Not yet." Dr. Patel pats my leg before standing up.

I reach for him. "Wait…can you tell me anything else?"

He sighs. "I promised your husband that he would be present when we discuss personal things. It can be overwhelming to learn your history all at once, and we need to let you rest so your body can handle the stress."

"But—"

"You have very serious injuries, my dear, including minor brain trauma. There may be some damage, but we will need to do more tests before we know conclusively. You may experience periods of extreme fatigue, dizziness, blackouts. And there is the possibility of another seizure, so we cannot risk doing too much for now. Your medications will help you sleep a lot of it off."

I take a deep breath to speak, but a spasm grips my side, and my breath catches painfully in my chest.

Dr. Patel listens to my lungs with a stethoscope. "Give it time. You're alive, and that is all that matters right now. It's very early and you need your rest, but soon we can begin some tests. It may take time, but you're going to be OK, Audrey."

I turn the name around in my head. Audrey. AUD-rey. Au-DREE. It doesn't feel right. "That's not my name."

Dr. Patel leans down and smiles at me the way someone might if they were speaking to a small child. I can see he believes I'm confused. He doesn't seem to understand that they're the ones who are confused. "What shall I call you then?" he asks.

I give him the only name that sounds right. "Jane."

12

~ ~ ~

I have moments of awareness and then gaps of nothing. At times the sky behind the window is black and others it's bright blue, which is the only way I can tell that days are passing. Nurses scurry in to check my pain; aides sit on the bed bending my limbs. They talk to me, and sometimes I respond. The doctor who thinks he's my husband paces around my room, quietly observing everything that goes on. He wants to speak to me alone, but Dr. Patel warns him about tense interactions. Instead, he watches me closely when I talk.

One morning when the husband-doctor is gone, Dr. Patel walks into my room and announces that we're ready for more tests.

"What do you mean *more?*"

"We tried a few days ago. Do you remember?"

"No. Maybe. I thought I dreamt that."

"You are much stronger now. I admit we were a little over anxious to get you up and running again. You're one of our own, after all."

I certainly don't feel like one of them. "How long have I been here?"

"Almost two weeks."

He sits on the edge of my bed and adjusts his glasses. "I would like to tell you about the different types of memory. Within your conscious mind, there is a vital distinction between knowing something and remembering it. Semantic memory is common knowledge of facts, general information acquired over a lifetime. State capitals, for example. Episodic memory, which we will be testing now, employs recollection, which is retrieving information as experienced by you *specifically*. It is completely autobiographical; a summation of your very own thoughts, feelings, and actions. Your semantic memory tells you what a kite is, but your episodic memory holds sensations associated with what it is like to fly one." He looks at me pointedly. "So I'm sure you can understand how episodic memory is a vital part of our identity."

Identity. The word hangs in the air, mocking me.

He leans over and looks me in the eye. "Are you following along?"

"I think so." In truth, I just want to go to sleep. "But maybe you can tell me all that again later, just in case."

"Don't worry; I have been doing this for a long time. I will tell you these things as many times as necessary in order for you to understand. Now let's continue."

We already know I have no memory of my name or the fact that I'm a wife and mother, but we have to start from the beginning. Dr. Patel has a list of information about me that Jason, my supposed husband, provided so we can compare my answers. If I have any.

As it turns out, I know what year it is. I know who the president of the United States is. I know what a dog is and can name a dozen breeds, but I can't describe how it makes me feel to pet one. I know The Rolling Stones are a band, the Titanic was a boat, and how many eggs are in a dozen.

I don't remember personal things from Jason's list such as my favorite flower, but when asked to sniff cards soaked with different scents, I hate the one that smells like lilies, just as Jason said I would. I don't know if I have any hobbies or if I have a favorite movie. I don't know if I have a family other than the doctor claiming to be my husband and the father of a child I've never met. I don't remember my address, my phone number, the names of my friends, or where I was going when I supposedly hit a corner going sixty-eight miles an hour and flipped my car into the side of a tree.

After we finish, Dr. Patel gets up to check my IV.

"What made them accuse me of drinking and driving?" I ask.

"There was an empty bottle of champagne in your car. Your hair and clothes were soaked in it."

"But didn't you say there were blood tests?"

"There were," he says. "And they indicate you hadn't had a drop."

"So why would there be an empty bottle in my car?"

"I don't know. And as I said, this conversation is technically off-limits."

I groan. "How can personal information about *me* be off-limits to *me*?"

"You have to understand, your husband is simply being protective in case you say something to incriminate yourself. But I can tell you that I have never seen you drink. Ever. Not at any of the hospital functions Jason has brought you to over the years. Also, you are a responsible mother; you would not leave a bottle rolling around in the car where it could hurt your child. Or damage someone's head while traveling through the air at almost seventy miles an hour."

"Is that what happened?" I ask.

He nods. "It would appear by your injuries that when you flipped your car, you took a blow to the back of the head in addition to hitting the side of your head on the door before your airbag went off. It is why your head trauma is…unique. They found the bottle, and considering your hair and clothes smelled of alcohol, they assumed you were drinking when you crashed."

I try to push past the emptiness, try to accept that his words are about me. But with no memory to back them up, my mind feels like a black hole caving in on itself.

Dr. Patel puts a hand on my shoulder. "We already know there is brain trauma. Your hippocampus has been affected; we know this because it holds your memories, many of which you have lost."

"Will I ever get them back?"

"Traumatic brain injuries vary from situation to situation. It depends on the impact of the injury and the location of the damage. Not only did you have physical trauma to the head from the impact of the accident, but you also seem to have injury to the tissue in the brain from a sudden acceleration and halting. The contents of the brain continue to move around inside the skull, resulting in damage to some tissue and grey matter."

"And you know this because I've answered a few questions?"

"We know this because you have been through CAT Scans and MRIs. We were able to ascertain the areas of physical damage. But in order to diagnose how it affects you, we need you awake and alert and able to answer questions and process information."

I take a deep breath and exhale. "What if I never remember anything?"

"It is too early to tell. But your level of traumatic brain injury is mild which means you are very, very lucky. You need to be patient. "

"It's not like I have anything else to do."

"You are doing remarkably well just speaking with me for this long. Things could have been much worse. You nearly lost your life."

"But what good is a life when I can't remember anyone in it or what I feel for them? Do people ever wake up not knowing who they are and then successfully return to their old lives?"

He shakes his head. "You didn't just wake up not knowing who you are. That's more of a fugue state, which is a dissociative break and not usually due to physical damage." He folds his glasses and slides them into the pocket of his shirt. "You had your memory knocked out of you. But if there comes a time we think there are any psychological hurdles preventing you from reestablishing your memory, we will need to work that out." He squeezes his eyes shut and rubs the bridge of his nose. "Of course, I will have to get through Jason to do that."

16

I lean back on my pillow and close my eyes, hoping to stop the pounding in my head. I can't grieve the things my memory has lost since I have no idea what most of them are. If I were waking up to a life that had no husband or child in it, things might be different. But how does someone walk into an established life they don't remember and carry on? Do they pretend for the sake of the child? What would I even talk to them about?

Dr. Patel points his pen light at my eye and frowns. "We need to stop for now so you can rest."

"Can I watch TV?"

"Absolutely not. You have a serious concussion; watching TV could cause convulsions."

"Can I read?"

"No. I don't want you focusing on anything for too long. Your brain needs to heal."

"So I'm stuck here with nothing to do?"

He meets my glare with a weak smile. "I'm sorry. We need to see how this injury manifests. Motor ability, cognitive ability. But first, your head has to heal along with the rest of your body. Just try to relax."

"Any ideas on what I do to relax?"

A voice drifts in from the hall. "Maybe I can help with that." The person I now know as Dr. Jason Gilbert, my husband, stands in the doorway, clean-shaven and showered. "Look, even I'm relaxed now," he says, gesturing to his faded jeans, grey v-neck t-shirt, and unbuttoned Oxford with the sleeves rolled to his elbows.

I notice now how tall he is, how broad-shouldered, how lean and fit. Without the temper, he might actually be described as charming. And even more so because of the enormous bouquet of peonies he's holding, elegant white globes with bits of fuchsia staining the tips.

At least I have something else to add to the short list of things I remember: flowers.

17

~4~

"I heard my wife was well enough to answer questions." There is the smallest hint of resentment behind Jason's friendly expression.

Dr. Patel raises his hand in protest. "Now wait, Dr. Gilbert..."

Jason leans casually against the door. "Don't worry, Elliot. I promise to behave. I'm not here as a doctor, just a regular guy coming to see his wife. You wouldn't deprive us of that, would you?" He flashes me a boyish grin and looks to the floor. "Not that I'd let you."

He meets my eyes again and holds the stare. I feel myself flush from head to toe.

"Indeed." Dr. Patel smirks. "Just so long as you follow the rules."

Before I can object, he bids me a formal goodnight and promises to return in the morning, leaving me alone with my husband—the complete stranger. I suddenly feel very insecure about my appearance and wonder if anyone thought to brush my teeth while I was unconscious. I quickly smooth down the sides of my hair and regret not insisting on a mirror.

Jason smiles and hands me the flowers as he slides a large duffle bag off his shoulder. "I brought a few things to make you more comfortable." He pauses and looks at me apologetically. "And about the other day...I didn't mean to scare you. I wasn't myself."

I so hope that's true because I certainly like this guy better than the one who was here earlier. I glance at the bag on the floor. Unless my memories are in there, I can't imagine what he could pack to make me more comfortable.

"Thank you for the flowers," I say. "They're really beautiful."

"They're your favorite." He grabs the plastic pitcher of water from my bedside table and drops the flowers in. "Not bad," he says, assessing his clumsy arrangement. The heavy blossoms droop over the side of the small container, dangling lifelessly.

I pull a few out and snap the bottom of each stem to help them stand upright. "They're from someone's garden, aren't they? June is peony season. It is June, right?" I can't remember if someone told me that or not.

"Yeah. Figures you'd never forget about your flowers. They're from our garden. You fill vases all over the house with these. But it looks like I picked a few duds."

"No, you didn't. They just haven't finished blooming. If we put these buds in sugar water, they'll really open up." I'll have to tell Dr. Patel I remember facts about gardening. That has to be a good sign.

Jason pulls an envelope from his back pocket. "Daisy's coming to see you tomorrow. I thought you might want to see pictures of her first." He takes a long, deep breath. "It would be best if she didn't know her mother doesn't recognize her."

I nod at him and take the envelope. "Are you sure it's a good idea for her to meet me?"

Jason exhales heavily and runs his hand through his hair. "I already told her you're alert enough now. I didn't think you wouldn't *want* to see her. I don't know how I'd explain that to her."

"I'm sure it will be fine," I say, though I don't know if I believe it. "How old is she?"

"Five. Well, almost. Next month." His face softens as he talks about her. "She's named for my grandmother. Her name was Margaret, but everyone called her Daisy. Nobody knew why Daisy was a nickname for Margaret, not even my grandmother herself, until my father brought his French girlfriend home to meet his parents, and she explained to them that *Marguerite* is also their word for the daisy flower."

I look through the photos. Daisy has sandy blonde hair just like Jason. It falls in ringlets around her face which, unlike his square jawline, is perfectly round with full, rosy, dimpled cheeks. She has his grey-blue eyes and thick eyelashes. I find a close-up of her face that takes up the whole picture. She's showing off a large, sweet smile filled with baby teeth.

"That's the before photo," he says proudly.

"Before what?"

"She's been waiting for a tooth to fall out. So far we have no sign of activity, which is a problem because she's the only one in her class who hasn't been visited by the tooth fairy. But she thought she needed a before picture for when it finally happens."

I pick up a photo of her and Jason on a carousel horse and another of her planting in a garden.

"It's her favorite thing to do with you. You've taught her so much. Do you recognize anything?" he asks.

"Yes, dahlias. I can tell by the shape of the bulbs." I feel myself flush, realizing he wasn't asking about flowers.

There are photos of Daisy in a bathing suit building a sandcastle, eating ice cream with chocolate on her nose, blowing out birthday candles, but nothing that provokes any feelings or memories. I sense Jason's hope building as I look at each one. He's waiting for me to recognize something, but I can only disappoint him.

He produces a wooden frame from his bag. "How about this one?"

I recognize the two of them, but there's a woman with them, too. Pretty, laughing. Large brown eyes and long, straight chestnut hair pushed over to one side so her cheek meets up with the little girl's. They're holding on to one another affectionately.

"Is this me?" I assume it must be, though it doesn't seem right. I thought I'd have blonde hair for some reason.

He hesitates for a moment. "This is *us.*"

I look at the photo again and notice how Audrey's hand rests comfortably against Daisy's cheek. I close my eyes and try to imagine what it would be like to do that, but I'm unable to conjure the feeling. It's bad enough that I don't remember her, but I may never be able to act like I love her. It's one thing to pretend I remember being a mother. It's another thing entirely to be a mommy. Seeing them together like this, I can't ignore the responsibility and commitment that I'm accepting by agreeing to pretend.

With shaking hands, I return the frame to him. "I'm sorry. I wish I could remember. I truly do."

Jason stuffs his hands in his pockets and looks down with an indecipherable expression. "Right. Sure you do."

I watch him for a moment, waiting for any hint of something that could explain the awkwardness I feel around him. He must hate me for not being her; the wife he thought would wake up and remember him.

"Who's with her now?" I ask. "Your...I mean *our* daughter." My tongue feels like it's starting to swell.

"My parents. They live nearby. She's their only grandchild, so she's probably being spoiled right now."

"What about my parents? Dr. Patel said you wanted to be the one to tell me about my history." I can sense

21

something strange happening to me, and I squeeze my hand to stop the numbness from creeping into my fingers.

Jason's face darkens as he gathers the pictures into a pile. "Yeah, about that. You don't really have much family."

Without warning, my stomach turns in on itself. A hazy shadow creeps across my eyes. His image begins to blur.

"You grew up in—"

I vaguely hear him swear.

Jason stands over me with a stethoscope and barks orders at a nurse next to him.

"It's OK," he says, but his face tells me it isn't.

When I try to answer my mouth won't move. I stiffen up in panic and kick my leg.

He puts his hand on my cheek. "Let it pass. Just give it a few minutes."

He positions his face over mine so I'm staring into his grey eyes. They're the color of ocean water on a stormy day; I focus only on that and relax into the bed.

When I open my eyes again, the nurse is gone. Jason gently removes the oxygen line from beneath my nose and reaches out to stroke my hair. "Sorry if I upset you. Maybe we won't talk about family for now."

I nod up at him. A part of me doesn't even want to know how many other people are out there waiting to be disappointed by me, by my lack of memories. I don't want to meet them or watch them come in here and realize I'm not the person they think I am. Still, there are so many questions.

I struggle to sit myself up in the bed. "But I was going to ask you this before. Is there a Wyatt in my family? I said the name when I woke up."

"You remember that?" He pauses for a moment. "He's someone you dated before we were married."

"Sorry...that's awkward. If it's any consolation, I don't remember him either."

Jason shrugs. "Don't worry about it. It caught me off guard, that's all. It was just an odd coincidence."

"Coincidence?"

"I saw the staff sheet. One of the EMTs was named Wyatt. You must have heard it when they were tending to you. Or maybe you subconsciously thought of him when the first responders came because he's a cop."

"Is he involved in my case?"

"No, he lives in Maryland. You don't keep in touch other than a yearly Christmas card." Jason looks at his watch and starts to gather his things. "I'd better let you get your rest."

My stomach tightens. "What if it happens again?"

"You mean the seizures?"

I still feel shaky and lightheaded. "What if the nurse doesn't come in to check on me? Could you stay?"

"Yeah, of course," he says.

He lies down on the bed and gently slides one of his arms behind my pillow so his head rests against mine. This isn't at all what I meant when I asked him to stay, but I don't say a word. I'm too tired to care. The man almost lost his wife, and he thinks I'm her. I keep my eyes fixed on the ceiling and remind myself this is normal for him.

A young nurse strolls in with a pouch of medicine in her hand, her long blonde ponytail swinging behind her. "Good evening, Mrs. Gilbert. Time for your painkillers." She stops abruptly in the center of the room and her cheeks flush bright red. "Jason, I mean Dr. Gilbert, I..."

Jason kicks his shoes off the side of the bed. "I'm not a doctor today. Just a regular person visiting a patient."

"Well, I am so sorry," she says sweetly, exaggerating her southern accent. "But in that case, visiting hours are over." She adds a syringe of fluid to the IV bag above my bed.

He cranes his neck towards her. "Morphine?"

She ignores him and leans her adorable face down to mine. "Welcome back, Mrs. Gilbert."

"Thank you." I stare back at her and wonder if I'm supposed to know who she is.

She bats her eyelashes a couple of times. "We're all so glad you're OK. Let me know if you need anything, alright?" She strolls away, turning to look at us with a forced smile on her way out. "Well, g'night."

"Are we breaking the rules?" I ask once she's gone. "She looked upset."

"No. It's fine," Jason says.

"But if visiting hours are over, I don't want people thinking I get special treatment because of you." I yawn, feeling warm and woozy from whatever she just put in my IV.

"They won't. You'll be knocked out in a minute anyway."

I relax into the blankets as a pleasant numbness creeps over me. "OK. But please go tell her it was your idea to lie in the bed."

"Forget her. I'm staying right here. Don't worry, I've got you."

"Why would I be worried?" I ask.

"You're not afraid?"

"Of what?"

"Never mind," he whispers. "Thank God you made it through. I'm going to live up to the promises I made and make sure you're better. No matter what."

"Mm hmm."

"Do you hear me, Audrey? I'm going to do whatever I have to do to make your life perfect now."

The name sounds even more foreign when he says it. I fight to keep my eyes open. "That's not my name."

"Of course it is."

"No, they said my name was Jane." I can't be sure if I've said it out loud or not. The soothing sound of his voice is coaxing me to sleep. I imagine for a moment he's kissed my forehead.

"I'll call you whatever you want if you promise to never leave me again," he says.

Feeling myself slip into the welcoming darkness, I try to rush the words from my mouth. "I'm sure she didn't mean to leave you; they said it was an accident."

~5~

D r. Patel shines his light in my eye. "Things have been progressing well these last few days. Not too bad, Aud—" He purses his lips and puts his instrument down. "Jane."

"It's weird, isn't it? Wanting people to call me that," I say.

"Not if it will help you. A body cannot heal with an uneasy mind holding it back."

"But I'm asking for your personal opinion. Not so much philosophical doctor advice."

He tries to hold back a smile.

"That's not what she would have said, is it? She was more polite than that."

"Who?" he asks.

"Audrey. She would have just accepted your answer, right?" The shock of my situation has worn off, and I've decided the only way to navigate this is to be brutally honest with the people around me.

"Perhaps. But try not to see yourself as a separate person from her. It would be better for you to say I."

"Like *I* wish you could tell me what *I* was like before so *I* can get my memory back?"

Dr. Patel sighs. "There is absolutely no benefit from forcing memories on you. Reminders cannot restore your memory. In fact, giving you information you don't remember could cause you to become frustrated and depressed, which could affect how your mind and memory heal." He makes his way over to the window and looks out at the sky. "You need to remember in your own time and recover your own feelings about those memories. You still have very serious injuries, my dear."

"How long will it take?"

"We can't guess. At least not until we know the full effect of the physical damage. Some people spontaneously remember everything at once; others regain their memory little by little. And some…"

I finish for him so he doesn't have to say it. "Some not at all."

He pats my hand. "Right now we just have to be patient and complete some tests. Brain damage isn't entirely about personal memory loss."

The next round of tests is completely different from the last. I'm moved slowly through one machine and then another and another. Technicians patiently give commands though microphones, asking me to repeat words and phrases or recall patterns of letters and numbers. Once I answer, thumps of motors stopping and starting echo though the walls around me. I wonder how many people have come through these machines and successfully returned to their normal lives—presuming, of course, they had normal lives to return to. I wish one of them had written notes of encouragement on the walls in here, leaving behind words of wisdom, like MRI cave drawings or hieroglyphics or…

"Audrey, please try to focus on what we're doing."

Perched in front of their computers, Dr. Patel and his staff observe and record my brain activity. I imagine how their screens light up when my mind goes off on a tangent about hieroglyphics. To them I'm something to study, a lump of neurons and synapses and grey matter, a lab rat in a thin white gown waiting for the piece of cheese that will bring my memories back and make this entire experience nothing but a story to tell at dinner parties. I wonder if Audrey ever threw dinner parties.

"Mrs. Gilbert, please try to repeat the numbers," the voice in the tunnel says again.

"Sorry," I say into the little speaker near my face. "My mind was wandering. But you probably already know that."

They don't even give me a laugh.

"We're ready to move on," Dr. Patel says once I'm returned to my room. "Procedural memory governs the performance of simple daily tasks that occur below the level of consciousness. It is a variation of implicit or unconscious memory, which calls on past learning without thinking about it."

He checks my eyes, my reflexes, my motor skills. I tie laces on little cards shaped like shoes, over and over again. He has me pull a rope, throw a ball, and give him a high five. I balance a ping pong ball on a spoon fairly well—for a person using only one eye, that is. I'm given a pencil and asked to hold it as one would when writing. I'm given paper and asked to write the alphabet. I take little breaks when my headaches and dizziness come back, which is often.

"When you're able to walk, we will test more gross motor skills like hopping, jumping with both feet, and walking in a straight line. For the time being, we have to rely on what you're able to do today, but even these tests will have to be repeated once your fractures heal."

I'm concerned as to how much brain damage he believes I have, but he will only say we have to do more tests, and my ability to worry about it is a good thing. He asks a barrage of questions: Is a hammer a tool? Which of these things is not a food: a carrot, a bagel, a shoe? Kitten is to cat as seed is to what? After half an hour of that, my head hurts just from the sound of his voice.

Dr. Patel jots some notes on his pad. "You have retained both your semantic and your implicit memory, which tells me the damage is seemingly limited to episodic memories at this point. This indicates that it's actually the parahippocampal cortex, the grey matter surrounding the hippocampus, which has the damage."

"What does that mean for my recovery?"

"It remains to be seen. Your physical injuries prevent us from running the full tests. There are people who suffered traumatic brain injuries and ended up with some episodic memory but no semantic, or the reverse. Last year, we had a man who remembered nothing of his life after a diving accident. He couldn't write his name or tie his shoes, but incredibly, he retained the ability to play the piano as well as Beethoven *and* read music. It is completely subjective."

"How's that possible?" I ask.

"Because your brain stores and interprets information in separate areas. Procedural memory—knowing how to drive a car, or play an instrument, or do normal daily chores—is stored in the cerebellum, a completely different part of the brain from the cortex, which holds the episodic memories. In some cases, information is still present but stuck in a place where it cannot be recalled. We haven't even gone over the psychological effects we touched upon the other day. There can be major psychological ramifications to brain function during a trauma." He looks at me sternly over the tops of his glasses. "And I would qualify nearly dying in a car accident as such a trauma. In addition to all of this, memory is constructive. Previous experience dictates how and why we cling to certain events and how we perceive them, which in turn determines what is stored and what is not."

"What about the fugue state you mentioned the other day?"

"A fugue state is a period of reversible personal memory loss brought on by a traumatic episode or incredible stress. In some cases it can be the result of psychoactive substance use or even injury, but it is very rare and often diagnosed after the fact. An individual may suddenly find themselves miles away from home and not know how they got there, having lost track of several days."

"How come that kind is reversible and mine might not be?" I fold my arms across my chest and sulk. It's the only thing I can think to do since I can't stomp a foot on the floor.

A knock on the open door interrupts us.

"Ready for visitors, yet?" Another doctor, about Jason's age, leans in with a bouquet of pale pink peonies tucked under his arm. The choice of flowers can't be a coincidence; he must have known Audrey well.

He waves a small container in his hand. "Ben & Jerry here. New York Super Fudge Chunk, your favorite." He strides into the room but stops abruptly at the foot of my bed and winces when he looks at me.

Dr. Patel turns and greets him with a nod. "Charles, perfect timing. I was just going."

"Don't let me chase you off, old man. Unless, of course, you're still upset about the little prank from yesterday."

"Yes, very clever. Saran-Wrapping toilets in the doctors' lounge," Dr. Patel says and frowns at me. "This one and your husband seem to think our hospital is a frat house."

I steal a glance around Dr. Patel and begin to suspect that young and annoyingly good looking is becoming a prerequisite for practicing medicine. "Charles" looks back at me, his blue eyes smirking as if we're in on some sort of joke together. He runs his hand along a scruffy beard that's not fully grown in, more of a deliberate five o'clock shadow. I don't recognize him at all.

"Do I know him?" I whisper.

Dr. Patel winks at me playfully. "Unfortunately for you, yes. Thick as thieves, you three." He turns to the other man. "Don't forget that you are on this evening, Charles. Plus taking my on call duty for the next three rotations. Serves you right." He gathers up his supplies to leave and bends down to whisper in my ear. "It's all in great fun. Just don't tell him I said so."

I grasp his arm. "Now would be a good time for a mirror."

Instead of answering me, he strolls from the room whistling, and for the second time in two days, I'm left alone with an unknown man handing me flowers.

He plops down on the bed and carefully nudges my casted leg with his elbow. "So, how do you feel? Other than the fact you have no idea who any of us are, of course." He peels the top off the ice cream carton and pulls two silver spoons from the pocket of his lab coat. "Stole these from the cafeteria."

I take a spoon from him. It's both relieving and off-putting how comfortable he is picking up where we left off—wherever that was.

"I feel OK, I guess. A bit strange." How do you tell someone you just met that you feel nothing? There's no name tag on his lab coat so I can't tell if Charles is his first name or last. "What's your full name?"

"Whoops, sorry about that," he says with the spoon sticking out of his mouth. He lifts my hand from the bed and shakes it jokingly. "Thomas Charles. Pleased to meet you...again."

He has a playful quality to him, a clever sort of mischief that lights up his face. The longer I look at him, the more I feel like laughing. "You have two surnames. I like that."

"You say that all the time," he says.

"I do?"

"Yeah. Weird. Think we should call Patel back in? I hear he's taking notes on every little thing that comes up with you."

"Oh God, no. Please don't."

Thomas carefully moves the hair from the side of my face. "How's that jaw healing up? Looks brutal." He holds up the container of ice cream. "Don't be shy. I've seen you wolf down a whole pint of this stuff during PMS week. Sometimes two."

I feel my cheeks redden. "We sound awfully familiar then."

"I wasn't trying to embarrass you, Audrey."

I wrinkle my nose at him. "It would be OK if you didn't call me that."

"Why?" he asks with his mouth full.

"I don't know. It makes me uneasy, I guess, because I don't remember who I am and Audrey sounds like a name for someone cold and uppity."

"Watch it. That's my main girl you're talking about. The Audrey I know is none of those things. But confusion is pretty normal with a brain injury like yours."

"I don't feel confused. I feel like everyone else is confused."

"Right," Thomas says sarcastically. "Confusion, mood swings, emotional irritability—all normal."

"So you're saying I'm irritable?"

He tries to hold back a smile. "Now you're sounding like yourself."

We talk about him for a while, about his childhood in Chicago and how he's known Jason and me since they started medical school. He tells me that everything I need to know about him can be explained by three simple facts: he's an only child, unnaturally obsessed with college basketball, and he's never had a cavity.

I laugh. "How's that last one relevant?"

"It says a lot about a person. Think about it for a while." He smiles. "At least it'll give you something to do later."

"Yeah, thanks."

"So how are you holding up? Truthfully, I mean. I'm not going to record your answers like Patel."

"Not to insult you, but I'd love to have a visitor who doesn't know that giving me personal information could debilitate me. That way I can see for myself what bothers me and what doesn't."

Thomas sighs. "Poor girl, surrounded by doctors. How about this...I'll give you a few of my own memories and opinions."

"Which are?"

"You're one of the best people I've ever known. You have your flaws like anyone else, but you're generous and compassionate. You think you're hilarious because you make me laugh a lot, but most of the time I'm actually laughing *at* you. You're an amazing cook, an awesome mom, and a trusted friend. What can I say... You take care of us. You're the glue."

"The glue?"

"Yeah, that holds us all together."

"Us?"

"Jason and Daisy and me," he says with a shrug, as if it's obvious information. "You guys are my family."

"You don't have a wife?"

"Nah." He steals a chunk of chocolate off my spoon and pops it into his mouth. "All the best ones are taken."

"We're your family? So we...spend a lot of time together?"

"Yeah, a lot of the doctors here are on seven-day rotations. Seven days round-the-clock here at the hospital and seven days at home. Long ago I decided to start my shift while Jason was on day three or four. That way I get half the week here with him, and I spend the other half with you since he's not home. Then while I'm here, he's home, and you only have three days alone per rotation."

"You schedule your shifts to be with us?" I ask.

"Yup. You and Crazy Daisy."

I look at him suspiciously.

He narrows his eyes and nods slowly. "Daisy…your child? My goddaughter? Sometimes I call her Crazy Daisy, sometimes Lazy Daisy. Depends on the mood."

"No, I mean it's sweet, but…"

"Oh, yeah," he says with a laugh. "Now that I hear myself say it, the living arrangements might sound strange to someone who doesn't know our situation. It works for us, though."

"What situation?" I lower my voice to a whisper. "Are we like all…together?"

He nearly chokes on his ice cream. "Wow, this brain damage thing is gonna be a lot of fun." He smiles and tries to talk without laughing. "No, we aren't *all together*, you lunatic. I have a house, but I stay at yours a lot—in my own room, before you jump to any conclusions. You hate being alone; that's how it started. But now it works for all of us. Jason's the lucky guy who found you first, so I get you as a best friend."

I look at him warily. I know I have a head injury, but that arrangement would sound weird to me regardless.

"Don't worry," he says with a grin. "I manage to control myself. We hang out, watch movies. You bake a lot of desserts that we deliver to nursing homes. I've been teaching you to play golf—which you're terrible at, by the way—and you get me to play board games more than a grown man should. We built you a vegetable garden recently. Daisy and I have been working on a killer scarecrow to keep the deer from eating everything, even though you tell us it isn't going to stop them."

"It won't."

Thomas raises an eyebrow. "Huh. I heard you remember stuff about gardening even though you don't remember being a gardener. That's messed up." He fishes around in his pocket for a peppermint drop, pops it in his mouth, and dramatically tosses the wrapper into the garbage can as if taking a jump shot. "God, I wanna smoke right now. But you've got me chomping these things every ten minutes to stop me."

"I do?"

"Yeah, you gave me until the new year to quit and then you stepped in. Back in March you were doing my laundry and found a pack. That was it. Total healthy overhaul for the last two months. You forced me to exercise and eat better, inspected my car for signs of smoking. I didn't want to say this before, but you're kind of a pain in the ass, kid."

"You'd think a doctor would know how to keep himself healthy."

"That's a common line of yours. You even started packing me lunches since, according to you, all I live on during my shifts are peppermints and coffee."

Peppermints and coffee. As soon as the words leave his mouth, I have a vision of staring up at the night sky, strapped to a gurney. Someone leans in smelling of peppermints and coffee.

Oh my God, do you know who this is? Audrey. Oh God.

A chill runs through me. "You were there. It was you, wasn't it? When they took me off the helicopter."

He looks down at the floor. "Yeah, that was me. I can't believe you remember that."

"You were running and pushing me on the stretcher. You sounded so scared. You thought her daughter was in the car, didn't you?"

"You mean *your* daughter. Yeah. I've seen a lot of things come out of that helicopter in my time, but I sure as hell wasn't prepared for that. I thought we were gonna lose you." He stops and exhales heavily. "If someone hadn't

35

driven by and known to put a tourniquet on your leg, you wouldn't have even made it to the hospital. It's a miracle we still have you. Anyway, I really wanted a cigarette, but I thought if I did what you wanted me to do, maybe it would somehow bring you back. Like if I didn't smoke, there'd be something important for me to tell you, so you couldn't die. Pretty stupid, huh?"

"It's not stupid, it's sweet." Tears fill my eyes. I feel connected to Thomas, even without the memories. There's something very comfortable, safe, and familiar in the air between us. A suchness. An awareness that what I'm part of with him is very rare. I feel almost anchored to something now instead of at the mercy of the currents.

He gathers me into a hug. "All you've gotta do is get better."

"And figure out who I really am."

He laughs over my shoulder. "Does anyone ever know who they really are?"

"But—"

"You're alive, Audrey. That's all that matters."

I pull myself away and look him in the eye. "Why are you so nice to me?"

He leans his forehead against mine. "You ask me that all the time."

"And what's your answer?"

He sits back and looks at me. "How about you tell me when you remember. And do me a favor. Don't put me through this again. I don't ever want to have to track Jason down again and tell him you don't have much time left."

"Track him down?" This hospital can't possibly be that big.

"Yeah, it took me forever to find him. Imagine how hard it was for him to drive all that way thinking he was coming to say goodbye to you."

"What do you mean it took you forever to find him? Drive all what way?" I could swear someone told me Jason had been working at the hospital when they brought me in.

"I think after Jiu Jitsu he went to his parents' old house upstate." Thomas picks up his phone. "Shit. I gotta go. Patient incoming. Get some sleep." He pats my leg and gets up to leave.

"Thomas," I say as he walks towards the door, "is there anything you should tell me about Jason?"

He throws another peppermint into his mouth. "Yeah. He loves you. That's really all you need to know."

~6~

Thomas leaves just before the evening shift change, so I'm not alone for very long. My blonde, ponytailed nurse from the night before has been replaced by an older, stockier version named Dottie, who has a gruff manner and a strong desire to talk. A lot. She continually hurries in for one reason or another, each time bringing a new report of the activity from the nurses' station. From her, I learn two nurses called out sick and the floor will be short staffed for the night, though one of them, she says, isn't actually sick as much as lazy and unreliable.

"They'd call out for hangnail, these dingbats 'round here," she says before sticking a digital thermometer in my mouth. "Nobody's got a decent work ethic anymore. And Lord!" she says, looking up at the ceiling. "It's gonna be a busy night here, full moon an' all. Thank *Jesus* I'm no longer workin' on the seventh floor."

"What's on the seventh—"

"Maternity." She rolls her eyes. "And damned if I know why a full moon puts ladies into labor all the time."

I can't remember going into labor. Or having a baby.

She asks what it's like to not know who I am, but before I can consider a reply, she remarks that a woman in her soap opera had the very same thing happen to her and she ended up falling in love with her husband's father and marrying him.

"But I haven't even met my husband's father yet!" I say in alarm.

Dottie looks down at me and laughs. "Oh honey, you are sweet, aren't you. I used to see you sometimes havin' lunch with one of your doctor fellas downstairs and I always thought you looked like the nicest, doe-eyed little thing."

"One of my doctor fellas?"

"Oh, you know what I mean. Your husband and your friend Dr. Charles. Never saw any boys so devoted to a girl in my life."

"Do you know my husband and Thomas?"

"Honey, there isn't a nurse in this building who doesn't know your husband. Mmm mmm mmm. I wish somebody would bang me on the head and I'd wake up married to a man that looks like him. And Dr. Charles...if there isn't a nurse throwin' herself at him every other shift, then I'm the Jolly Green Giant."

I so badly want to yell out that I actually remember who that is, but I don't bother. It seems a little pitiful that I can remember a man who sells green beans but not the one I've been married to for years.

"Speaking of nurses, who was mine last night?" I ask.

"Let me check." Dottie huffs out to the hallway and comes back with her lips pursed. "That was Leslie." The look on her face tells me there's a strong opinion just waiting to be invited out. "But she won't be back," she says. "She's been reassigned to the other side of the hallway."

"Why?" I wonder if it has anything to do with her seeing Jason in my bed the night before. It obviously made her uncomfortable.

"Who knows why. Maybe there's a man in one of those rooms she has her tramp eye on. Maybe she switched with someone so they'd owe her a favor. Maybe she wants to be on that side of the building because it looks over the fountain. You never know with her. Some of these dumb bunnies 'round here are only out for themselves. There's those who do what we're told and those who do for what it gets them."

I can't focus on anything she says after "tramp eye". It's bad enough that Leslie called Jason by his first name, which I've never heard a nurse do since I've been here, but I also can't get past the look on her face when she left the room. Was she angry? Jealous? I really don't know a single thing about any of these people. Not even the one I'm supposedly married to.

"Do the nurses do that a lot? Throw themselves at the doctors?" I ask, trying to steer Dottie back to our previous conversation.

"Mm hmm." She moves around my bed and straightens the sheets.

I suspect she's trying to make it seem like she's working so she can talk longer, which is perfectly fine with me. Maybe it's because I remind her of a soap opera character, or perhaps her other patients are in comas and she can't talk with them. Either way, she's somebody I want to keep around. If knowledge is power, this one's omnipotent.

"Would you say they throw themselves at my husband?"

Dottie snaps her head up. "Now don't let anything I say get you worryin', honey." She pats my leg. "You just focus all your energy on getting better. Plus, let them try throwin' themselves at your husband. Anybody lookin' at the man for more than a second knows he's off the market, in love, T-A-K-E-N. By you."

"I was just curious." I try to sound nonchalant. If Dottie is as loose-lipped with everyone as she is with me, the last thing I want her telling people is that I'm suspicious of Jason. Because I'm not. Not entirely. But I'd be a fool not to take advantage of her vault of information and get to know everything I can about the man. "It's pretty boring sitting in this bed with no books or TV or company. I guess I'm looking for a soap opera myself."

"Well, honey, why didn't you say so? You're talkin' to the right lady. I can tell you a little bit of something on everybody here. Or I can read you a book. Or the newspaper."

I perk up. "The newspaper sounds good."

Dottie hurries out of the room and comes back with a big pile of newspapers tucked under her arm, a cup of coffee in her hand, and a donut hanging out of her mouth. She pulls a chair up to the side of my bed. "Honey, this is my kinda work, bein' assigned to someone who asks me to sit and read them the paper. These are from the last few days. People always leave them at the nurses' station." She scans the columns. "Let's see…Here's a story about the wheat mill that blew up in Iowa. Killed a whole lot of people. Did you know about that?"

"No. Find something else."

"OK. There's the mayor in California who was just caught with a couple of hookers in his office."

"Why would that even make the news? Doesn't that happen all the time?

"Yeah, well, this one's hookers were only fourteen."

"Ugh…next. That makes me want to cry and vomit at the same time."

Dottie points a finger at me. "No vomiting. I'm the one who has to clean it up you know."

"Then try to stay away from mass killings, underage prostitution, and anything else that might make my concussion worse."

"There's a man dead from a boating accident. They suspect he was drinkin' a little too much and got caught in a rocky area. He must've fallen over tryin' to get himself out and smashed his head on a rock and drowned. Why anyone would drive anything while drinkin' is beyond me." She looks up at me quickly. "I mean, not like he deserved to get hurt. Well, I've gone and put my big fat foot in my mouth again, haven't I."

"I wasn't drinking. There were blood tests, you know."

"Of course, honey, we all know that." She pats my hand and goes back to flipping through the paper.

As soon as she turns the page I see it. A silver Mercedes upside down and smashed to bits in front of a tree. There's a guardrail bent around it. The headline reads, *Police Probe Accident Scene, Local Woman in Critical Condition.* I point to the picture. "Please read that to me."

"Oh, Lord. If Dr. Patel finds out, I'll be back on the seventh floor before the end of my shift. We can't have you gettin' upset, Mrs. Gilbert."

"Please. If anyone finds out, I won't tell them you read it to me."

"Damn, I'm never gonna learn." She shakes her head then straightens the paper and clears her throat. "A Reedville woman is in critical condition following a late night accident off of Wood Vine road in Allenton."

"I don't even know where that is."

Dottie looks at me sternly before continuing. "Police say the driver was traveling at speeds close to seventy miles an hour when she lost control of her car, flipped over the guardrail, and collided with a tree." She reaches up to touch the cross that hangs from her necklace. "Oh, honey. You're so lucky to be alive."

"Keep going."

"The Hills County Sheriff's Department states that police initially suspected the woman was driving under the influence due to evidence obtained at the scene, but hospital toxicology reports indicate the motorist was not impaired. Police have threatened to launch a full investigation into the matter after it was reported the husband of the driver…" She bites the corner of her lip. "Oh, dear."

"Please keep reading."

She continues with her head down. "The husband of the driver, Dr. Jason Gilbert, son of Senator Edmund Gilbert, works at the hospital where the victim was treated and, according to an anonymous tip, was possibly involved in the tampering of lab results."

"What? Wait...who?"

"A hospital spokeswoman stands by the toxicology report and states the victim's husband was not involved in his wife's medical care and had no access to the blood tests or the results. Furthermore, the hospital states that any claims to falsifying information are completely fabricated and go against the ethics of everyone involved."

"Do people here think Jason covered up for me?"

Dottie gives me worried smile and shrugs her shoulders. "Audrey Gilbert, thirty-four, was flown by helicopter to the hospital with life threatening injuries. First responders reported major head trauma, several broken bones including ribs, a collapsed lung, and a forty percent blood loss resulting from an injury to her femoral artery. She is listed in critical condition. Dr. and Mrs. Gilbert are longtime residents of Reedville and have a four-year-old daughter. Dr. Gilbert is the son of U.S. Senator Edmund Gilbert (R, NY) and his wife, Vivienne. Senator Gilbert, a contributing founder of the Confederation for Moral Living, has been a top supporter of stricter penalties for drunk drivers. His office has not commented on the accident other than to say the senator and his wife are praying for their daughter-in-law and wish for privacy at this time. Anyone with more information on the accident should contact local police."

A feeling of dread forms in the pit of my stomach, a sensation not entirely unfamiliar to me, like an old foe coming to call. That's a pretty famous name. I can't believe I didn't connect it before.

"Senator Gilbert's twin brother ran for president, right?" I say. "He's the governor of Illinois? He won an Olympic medal for rowing or something when he was young. And their older sister is a famous playwright. Are you telling me I'm one of *those* Gilberts?" I concentrate on breathing very slowly, feeling the lightheadedness return.

Dottie puts her head in her hands and moans. "You're sayin' nobody told you that part yet? Oh, Lordy. I'm in for it now." She jumps up out of the chair and pours me a glass of water. "You are positively white, Mrs. Gilbert."

"Why didn't anyone tell me? That's pretty crucial information to leave out."

"You had lots of injuries, honey. You weren't expected to make it. Everybody was so worried. They were just tryin' to help you; the less stress the better."

"Why would someone claim that Jason faked my blood tests?"

She paces around the room. "I don't know. Your father-in-law has plenty of people sayin' things about his family all the time. I'm sure it goes with the territory. But don't you worry, the hospital is on full alert. Anyone heard speakin' to reporters will be fired. And damn if I don't get fired for readin' it to you."

"I won't tell a soul, I promise. But leave the papers in here; they need to think I learned it on my own."

"You aren't supposed to be readin', Mrs. Gilbert. Nobody's gonna believe that anyone would be stupid enough to hand you a newspaper."

"Just leave it to me," I say calmly. "So Jason's father is Senator Gilbert. They have no other kids. They lost a son. How do I know that about them?"

"The senator and his wife wrote a book. You must've read it. Sad story," she says, shaking her head. "Your husband had a brother who died when they were young. Tragic."

"He died playing sports, right?"

44

"Mm hmm. Fifteen years old, and he died playin' high school baseball. Just keeled over at his game. Can you imagine? Nobody ever knew James had a heart condition. He overexerted himself, and that was it. Dr. Gilbert was in the stands watchin'. He was only twelve."

"I wonder if that's why he became a heart surgeon."

"That's what they say in the book. Never got over it, none of them. How could they, though?" she says.

It gives me a little more insight into Jason and what he must have gone through. To almost lose another family member must have been unbearable for him. I never considered all the history I'm missing. All the memories, the stories, the little nuances you come to know about people that make you understand them. What if I never regain my memory and have to play catch up for the rest of my life, constantly relearning the things I don't remember?

I can't live in a hospital bed forever. Eventually I'll have to go home, presumably with Jason, and face people who know his family. There will be people in the world who care about whether or not I was drunk when I had an accident simply because it's gossip-worthy, or maybe because it could help them politically by tarnishing the Gilbert family image. I imagine strangers holding their papers and their morning coffee, reading about me, about Jason's family, talking about my accident, thinking I caused it, discussing my situation. I feel so…exposed.

Before I know what's happening, Dottie is next to me raising the back of my bed. "Stop taking so many breaths, Mrs. Gilbert. You have to try to calm down. You're havin' an anxiety attack."

I can't stop my body from reacting. My chest is heaving. Walls are closing in.

She moves to the door to call for help and runs smack into Jason. "Doctor, she's—"

He pushes past her and rushes to my bed. "What have you given her?"

Dottie wrings her hands. "Nothing yet. She had pain meds before the shift change and isn't due for another hour. Seems like anxiety."

My heart dances wildly in my chest. Adrenaline surges through me, flushing my skin. I frantically gasp for air but can't quite get enough. I imagine a balloon inflating slowly inside me, taking up all the room in my chest, squeezing out everything else. I'm unable to stop the breaths from coming faster and faster.

"She can't afford to do this with a collapsed lung," he says to Dottie, motioning her to a machine in the corner. She wheels it over, and he carefully places a mask over my face.

Jason holds my face in his hands. "Audrey, listen. You need to focus on me. Breathe in, one-two-three-four hold."

I concentrate on his stormy eyes—deep grey ocean water.

"Out, one-two-three-four. Again."

Panic strains my neck, tightens my face, stiffens my limbs. I'm in a tunnel, the echo of my heart beating in my ears. I hear Dottie page Dr. Patel over the loudspeaker.

"One-two-three-four," Jason says. "Good. Keep going."

The air reaches down into my lungs, and my arms tremble from clamping him so tightly. When I let go, there are imprints of my nails in his forearms. My heartbeat slows with my breathing, and I swallow hard, feeling satiated by the air I'd been craving. My eyes stay fixed on Jason, whose gaze falls towards the pile of newspapers on my bed. Fury ignites his face.

Dr. Patel hurries in and checks the clipboard at the end of the bed. "What's going on?"

"What's going on is she's having a goddamn anxiety attack. I thought you said we were keeping her off TV and newspapers." Jason snatches up the page with the article of my accident, the veins in his neck tightening. "Where the hell did this come from?"

I push his hand off my face to remove the mask. "One of the cafeteria ladies…collected papers from patients' rooms," I say between short breaths. "When she came for my tray…I took them from her cart…She didn't know…" Before I can finish, Jason forces the mask back on my face. I take a few breaths and push his hand aside again. "I'm sorry…it's really boring here with nothing to do."

"You have something to do," Jason says coldly. "It's called get better."

Dr. Patel listens to my chest and nods at Jason. "It's healing. No damage done. She doesn't need a ventilator yet."

Thomas bounds in breathless. "What's going on? I heard the page for Patel."

Jason hands him the crumpled page from his fist. "She's been reading the newspaper and had an anxiety attack."

"Oh, Audrey," Thomas says, shaking his head. "Reading that garbage will only make you anxious, plus you know the small print can induce an epileptic episode. You have a concussion, remember?" He plops himself down on the edge of the bed and throws a peppermint into his mouth. "Dottie, we may need you to babysit this one round-the-clock."

I look from Thomas to Jason and can't decide who to ask. "Did one of you fake the results of my blood test?"

"Oh, Lord. I told her not to worry about that." Dottie hurries over to the papers strewn on the floor and starts to collect them. "I'm gonna take these to the trash where they belong."

I know she won't be leaving before I get my answers. It's just too good not to stay and listen; she is a soap opera fan after all.

Jason looks at me with contempt. "Of course not."

"I probably would have," Thomas says, "but I didn't need to. It was clean, I promise. That article is bullshit."

"You would have done no such thing," Dr. Patel says. "We are men of our oath, might I remind you, Charles."

"I'm just saying it could've been tempting. If she'd been drinking, that is." Thomas looks at me squarely. "But you weren't. I got the tox screen myself. I can have the lab tech tell you if you don't believe me."

"Then why did the newspaper—"

"Because there are a lot of people who'd like to see my father embarrassed," Jason says. "And I didn't want you worrying about any of that. It would be just like you to worry about what everyone else thinks and not put any energy into getting better, Aud—" He rolls his eyes. "Jane."

Thomas leans over Jason's shoulder. "Who's Jane?"

"She doesn't know herself as Audrey, remember? She heard herself referred to as Jane Doe on the chopper. Thank him." Jason nods towards Dr. Patel. "He seems to think it's a healthy expression for her."

Thomas laughs and stuffs another candy into his mouth. "Well, I'm not calling her Jane. That's just creepy. We'll end up with a regular schizoid on our hands."

Dr. Patel looks at Thomas sharply. "She should rest now. And nobody is to enter this room with newspapers again." He puts a hand on my shoulder. "I understand you have a special visitor coming later...unless your husband agrees now that it is too soon. Otherwise we need to make sure this doesn't happen again while she's here."

"No," Jason says. "Daisy's been waiting for a week. She needs to see her mother. We can order a mild sedative before I bring her if we have to."

"That could help," Thomas says. "And I can stay to distract Daisy. If anything happens, I'll take her down for ice cream."

Dr. Patel leans down towards me. "I'll let it be your husband's call on this one, but if this should happen again, just push the call button for the nurse and she'll help with the oxygen. Charles can deal with the child. Agreed?"

I nod up at him though I'm completely unsure. All I know is if I try to speak I will end up crying. For everything I think I want to know, there's even more that I don't.

~7~

I hear her before I see her. I can hear her all the way down the hallway. Jason scheduled Daisy to come in after dinner so she can stay until her bedtime and then go home with his parents. Since she's having trouble sleeping, he wants me to be fresh in her mind when her head hits the pillow.

"Can I kiss Mommy? Can I hug her if I don't squeeze too hard? Do all of her boo-boos hurt? Should I show her my wiggly tooth or have her guess which one it is?"

I hear the clacking of her tap shoes against the hard hospital floors. Jason said she hasn't taken them off since the accident to preserve the kiss Audrey had placed on each lace when she tied them for Daisy's dance lesson. She's even slept with them on. I sit up straight in my bed and wait anxiously, worried that I'm not a good enough actor to pull this off.

There's a knock at the door. "Special delivery for Audrey Gilbert," Jason announces as Daisy hides behind him giggling.

"Why that's me. I wonder what it could be," I say using the exact words we rehearsed.

"Well, here you go, ma'am!" He picks her up and flies her over to me as Thomas follows behind making airplane sounds.

Daisy kicks her feet in the air and shrieks when she sees me. "Mommy!"

Jason drops her down on the bed. He'd shown her pictures of my injuries so she wouldn't be scared by the bandages or the bruises. "Don't forget Mommy is really sore, OK?"

"Hi, pumpkin," I say, just like he told me Audrey would have said. It feels so strange to see her in person after studying photos for days.

"Mommy, I missed you so much." She crawls onto my lap and throws her arms around my neck.

I feel a pang of disappointment for not remembering her; not her voice or her smell or her curls against my face. I'd secretly hoped that seeing her would be the key to jogging my memory. I remind myself to hug her back and ignore the guilt I feel about lying to a child.

She burrows into me, her little hand slowly patting my back. I imagine Audrey holding her as a baby, patting her softly, and Daisy believing that's what they were supposed to do while hugging. Her soft cheek brushes against mine as she nuzzles closer. Her little body shakes, and I sense that she's trying not to cry. "I want you to come home, Mommy," she whispers into my neck.

And then it happens. An awakening. Her little voice echoes through me, calling out an instinctual ache hidden deep within. An emptiness I never knew existed until the cure for it was right in front of me. The response is primal. My heart remembers her heart, though I know nothing of her. My body remembers her body. My arms rejoice in holding her, as if they knew all along what was missing. I know in my bones that she's mine, even without a single memory of giving birth to her. I fold her into an embrace, burying my face in her hair, and try to hold back the sobs that tighten my throat.

"Are you OK?" She's snuggled in so tight her voice sounds muffled.

All I can do is nod my head before it all breaks free and I begin to cry. I feel like a mommy, a really good one. And for some reason this makes me cry even harder.

"It's OK, Mommy," she whispers. "Don't be sad."

I tighten my embrace, rocking her back and forth in my arms. I spent the hours before her visit obsessing over the things I didn't remember, but I no longer care about the missing years, about not knowing what she was like as a baby, about not knowing what her favorite songs or stories are. I just want to hold her in this moment and revel in the fact that our bond is stronger than the force that deprived me of my memories.

I look up at Jason and open my arms in invitation with Daisy still clinging to my neck. He kneels on the bed and embraces us. We sit like this for a long time, clinging to one another until finally Daisy peers out from under Jason's arm. "Uncle Thomas, too! Family hug!"

As Thomas joins us, Dottie sniffles to herself and mumbles a prayer to Jesus under her breath.

After a while, Jason stands up and wipes his face with his sleeve. "Time to give Mommy her presents."

Daisy untangles herself from my grasp, leaving my arms cold and wanting in her absence. She reaches in her dance bag and produces a stack of pictures which she proudly hands to me. The top one reads *Mommy and me* and shows two stick figures holding hands surrounded by flowers. She pulls another from the pile. "I drew this one because Daddy said you flew to the hospital. I drew *you* flying because I don't know how to draw a hello-chopter."

"Just what I need to cheer me up. I love them."

She beams back at me, her little cheeks pushed as far up to her eyes as they can go.

Jason pulls a roll of tape from his pocket and hands it to Daisy. "Art therapy," he whispers to me as she skips around the room hanging her creations. "I had her meet with the hospital social worker the day after the accident, and she suggested this to help her with the stress."

"Now you can see us every second until you come home," Daisy says.

I'm mesmerized by her every move and sound. It's love at first sight, only so much more. It's the feeling that I've known this little soul in another life—which, of course, I have. I imagine this is how mothers feel when their babies are born. In this case, I'm the one who has been reborn, and it's wondrous to me.

Every so often Daisy returns to my bed and gently touches my wounds, asking if they hurt. She needs to keep hearing over and over again they don't. "When can you take that thing off her eye?" she asks Jason. "I want to see her whole face."

"Should be any day now. Don't worry, Mommy will be good as new." Jason looks down at his phone. "Mom and Dad are waiting for Daisy downstairs. They can't wait to see you. They're coming in a day or two when things settle down."

My stomach lurches. No sooner am I grieving the idea of Daisy going than I'm dreading the idea of the Gilberts coming. My husband's parents. My very famous and powerful in-laws. It makes me wonder what Audrey's relationship with them was like and how I can ever live up to it.

"It's going to be fine. They already love you," Jason whispers, as if reading my mind.

He's changed again somehow; different from the furious man I saw throwing newspapers earlier, different from the unpredictable guy who brought me flowers. He's calm and peaceful and confident. I don't know if I'll ever be able to tell which one is really him.

Jason and Thomas go out to the hall to discuss their schedules, giving Daisy and me some time alone. I pull her in close, memorizing the smell of her skin and the feeling of her hand in mine, grateful to have an actual memory to recall whenever I want.

Daisy's giant eyes peer up at me. "Are you glad that Dr. Patel is a brain man, Mommy?"

"What do you mean?"

"You say it's too bad Daddy's a heart guy when you really need somebody to fix your brain." She wriggles away and twirls around. "Now that you have a hurt head, you get to have a brain doctor."

"When do I say that?"

"You know, silly. When you cry," she says.

"I don't remember crying. There are a few things I forgot since I got a bump on my head. Can you tell me why I cry?"

She shrugs. "Because you're sad."

"And what did I say was wrong with my brain?"

"You said you wish you didn't know some stuff. But I want you to still know me. And Daddy and Uncle Thomas and Otis," she says. Otis, I remember from the photos, is their English bulldog.

"What kind of stuff?" I ask.

"I don't know. It's a secret," she whispers, looking towards the door. "And we can't ever tell Daddy because you said that would make him very sad."

I nod my head and run my hand along her cheek. "Thank you for reminding me, sweetheart."

Jason comes in and scoops her up, promising another visit soon. She doesn't want to go, but Thomas cleverly entices her with an elevator race.

On his way out, Jason turns to me and smiles. "I'll be back up soon. It went really well, don't you think?"

I nod my head. "She's wonderful. I can't wait to see her again. Thank you, Jason."

Daisy's voice trails down the hallway against the clicking of her tap shoes. I'm left unnerved by what she told me. As soon as I'm sure they've gone, I page Dottie to bring me the oxygen.

Jason returns after an hour or so. By then, I'm so exhausted I can barely hold my head up.

"I've been waiting for you. I thought you were going to give Daisy to your parents and come right back up. Did she say anything about the visit?"

"Thomas and I stopped in the cafeteria for a bite. He needed to discuss a patient with me. I've been thinking…now that you're doing better, maybe I should get back to working more."

"Oh…of course. I'm sure you have a lot of things waiting for you," I say. It's going to be a long and awkward road for us if my memory doesn't come back soon. I can't imagine what it would be like to go home with him and pretend that I'm really his wife.

Jason walks to the window and looks out at the night. "I thought seeing her would jog something for you." He can't hide the frustration in his voice.

"Me too."

"I guess if holding your own daughter in your arms isn't enough to bring back a memory, then maybe nothing will."

My stomach tightens at the implication that I'm less of a mother because I wasn't able to remember her. "I did instinctively feel that she's mine, Jason. I wasn't pretending. This is hard for me, too. It's not as if I wanted to forget my entire life."

"Of course you didn't," he says. His hateful expression reflects in the window, and I begin to wonder if he has multiple personalities. One minute he's charming and sweet, the next he seems furious with me. No wonder Dr.

Patel doesn't want us to have emotional interactions. *A body cannot heal with an uneasy mind holding it back.*

"Jason, maybe we should talk about the future—"

There's a knock on the open door, and Leslie leans in. "Dr. Gilbert, you forgot your phone," she says as she pushes a stray piece of hair behind her ear. "Hi there, Mrs. Gilbert. How're you feeling?"

"Fine, thank you." I force myself to sound friendly.

She glides into the room towards Jason, who is frantically patting his pockets. "Your husband is *so* forgetful," she says. "All us nurses tease him endlessly that he'd forget his own name if we didn't remind him."

My cheeks burn. Her comment is a bit rude considering I've just forgotten my entire life. Jason glares at her, but Leslie doesn't seem to notice.

"Well, would ya look at all these presents!" She moves slowly around the room, reaching to touch gifts and smell flowers like she's posing for a photo shoot. She's built like a Playboy bunny, and I have a feeling that's the whole point of this friendly visit. "You sure must have a lot of friends," she says.

As soon as the words drop from her pretty mouth it hits me; I have no idea if I do. It hadn't occurred to me until now. As one of my nurses, Leslie would be well aware that none have visited.

"I'm sure they're all just dying to see you," she says in a sweet tone, though I can tell it's anything but. "I know my girlfriends would be chomping at the bit to see me if I was in a wreck."

"I'm not sure," I say. I study her perfectly made up face and her gorgeous blonde hair pinned in a messy bun, and I touch my own hair self-consciously.

"Leslie!" Jason grits his teeth. "If there's nothing else…"

"Yes, Doctor." Leslie gives me a little wave and bounces towards the door.

"It was nice of you to deliver the phone all the way from the cafeteria," I say, taking the bait to see where it leads me.

Leslie stops and spins around, grinning. "The cafeteria? Oh right, sure. Where he left it. Well g'night, y'all."

When I'm sure she's gone, I turn my attention back to Jason. "I may have had my head cracked open, but I'm not a complete idiot."

"And that means what, exactly?" He looks exhausted. Ready for surrender.

"Are you messing around with that girl?" Not that I care one way or another if he is. "Honestly, it would be better to find out now before I get my memory back and start feeling anything for you."

Jason exhales sharply as though he's been punched. "Wow, that's really nice, Audrey."

"I'm not Audrey."

"No, you certainly are not."

"And since I'm not her, I can tell you objectively if you *are* messing around with that girl, you'd better decide what you're going to do with her because she sashayed all the way in here to make sure I either know it or think it."

He steps back in surprise. "You got all of that from three minutes with her?"

"Of course. Tell me you honestly don't know these things about women."

He shrugs. "I honestly don't know these things about women. I've always had you to translate people for me. You always said I'm not very observant. But I am innocent. To tell you the truth, Thomas is the one who's been screwing around with her. Maybe she's jealous of all of the time he spends with you."

Things would be much easier for me to understand if I had some reliable connections. Friends. Preferably women. "Do I have any female friends, Jason?"

"Don't let what Leslie said bother you."

"You said I don't have much family other than you and Daisy, but you never mentioned friends."

"You're normally very shy, Aud—" He stops before finishing her name this time. "When we moved here you kept to yourself. You like to volunteer with senior citizens, and I'm sure you consider them your friends. But no, you don't have a lot of female relationships."

"But what about the wives of your colleagues? Aren't I friends with them?"

"Not really. You tend to shy away from all that."

"Friends from school? Did I go to college?"

"No. You came with me to medical school. You worked right out of high school."

"OK, how about high school friends? Do I still have any of those?"

"No."

My breath catches in my chest. I can't figure out why this is bothering me so much. It isn't as if I could miss these people anyway. "Tell me about my family then. Anything. I just want to know if there's anyone who can help me fill in the blank pieces of my life."

"Other than me, you mean." Once he says it, he seems to soften. He puts his hands in his pockets and stares at the floor. "I'm sorry. I get it, I do. I can help you fill in a few things. I'm not trying to keep you in the dark." He takes a long deep breath. "Your parents were killed in an accident when you were young. You were raised by your grandmother. She moved you around a lot trying to make a living, so you didn't make many lasting connections with people. She passed away before we had Daisy. I'm sorry. But she loved you very much. She'd want you to know that."

I turn away, trying to hold back tears. "What kind of accident? I assume I have no brothers or sisters."

He lowers his eyes. "No siblings. And I'll tell you anything you want to know about your parents as soon as I know you're ready to hear such heavy stuff without getting a spasm or blacking out."

"It's pretty heavy to find out I'm alone in the world outside of you and my daughter."

"I'm only telling you this because you seem to want visitors. And I'll bring some if it makes you happy. Thomas loves you; my parents love you. All of the wrinkly old people you spend hours a day with love you, and I can bus them in if you want. But if you need me to produce a female friend, a best friend, I'm sorry I just can't do that. Up until now, you've been happy with me in that post."

I lie back on the pillow and check the clock out of habit. The nurses will be in with my pain medication soon, and I'm looking forward to not feeling anything.

"Seriously, are you messing around with that nurse, Jason?" It would explain so much.

He turns back to the window and stares out at the night. "No. I barely know her."

"OK," I say, though I know I've just been lied to.

I finally realize what upsets me so much about not having female friends. It isn't that I don't have any visitors. It isn't that I don't have connections, though that is pretty pathetic. It's that I don't have a single person on my side that can corroborate his facts.

~8~

My in-laws are ushered into the hospital through a private entrance to prevent the reporters who are camped outside from photographing them. Not that there are many left, I'm told, but there are always a few stragglers hoping to sell a photo of the Gilbert family. And truly, what could be better than catching the senator—whose political platform includes stricter penalties for drunk drivers—visiting the daughter-in-law who nearly killed herself while supposedly under the influence?

Jason paces in front of my bed, attempting to talk me out of another panic attack before they come up.

"This is why I didn't want you to know who they were ahead of time. So you wouldn't be doing this," he says.

"You'd rather have me bowled over in shock when they walk in? I see what you mean now about not being a good communicator."

"I assumed you wouldn't recognize them, *Jane*. After all, you didn't recognize me."

"They're pretty well known, Jason. There isn't a person in the free world that doesn't recognize them."

"And I'm supposed to know that someone with amnesia still knows her celebrities?"

"I just want to make a good impression. I'm suspected of drunk driving myself into a tree, and I'm sitting here bruised and bandaged. Can you blame me for feeling a little insecure?"

"They're your family. You refer to them as Mom and Dad. They already love you."

"They love Audrey," I say under my breath. "Assuming that's even true."

"And what does that mean?" Jason grasps the rail at the foot of my bed with enough force to snap it in half.

"Well...it seems I'm being misled about a few things," I say.

He looks away and clenches his jaw.

I wonder if Audrey even possessed a backbone. From what I've gathered so far, she has no female friends, spends all her time at home with either her husband or his best friend, and frequently cries and wishes she "didn't know some stuff" that she keeps from her husband—a man who seems to have a questionable association with a pretty blonde nurse. Maybe sweet Audrey drove her car into a tree on purpose. Or maybe Jason tied a brick to her gas pedal. I'm finding it difficult to trust him; I know he's deceiving me, I just don't know how. I grit my teeth and stare at the window.

"Please don't ask them to call you Jane," he says when we hear the bell for the elevator. "My father won't understand. I get it, I do. But this is a lot for them to digest."

I turn abruptly, hearing a knock. Senator Gilbert and his wife Vivienne stand regally in the doorway. She looks like she fell out of a fashion magazine; raven hair coiffed to perfection, flawless makeup, exquisite, tasteful jewelry adorning her neck and wrists. She'd been a daytime television actress in France when they met, and she looks every bit the part. The senator is as distinguished and handsome as he looks in pictures, in an old-fashioned leading man kind of way. He is tall and athletic like his son, with the same smile; wide and friendly and full of perfect teeth.

Vivienne sucks in her breath and grasps her husband's arm. "Our poor, sweet girl," she says in a melodic French accent. She rushes to my bed and bends down to kiss both of my cheeks and take my hands in hers. "My sweet Audrey, how worried we have been. Thank goodness you are well." She wipes her tears with a beautifully embroidered handkerchief that matches her perfectly tailored cobalt blue sheath.

I bite the inside of my mouth to keep myself from crying, but I tear up anyway.

"Oh, chérie, come here." She hugs me, rocking back and forth.

I realize now how much I crave female contact. It's such a natural urge to want to be cared for by a mother, and she's possibly the closest thing I have to one. And even better, one who loves me not because she has to, but because she chooses to.

She touches my cheek. "My dearest daughter, the worst is over. And when we bring you back to new, we will discover what God wants us to learn from all this. I promise you. Après la pluie, le beau temps."

"Every cloud has a silver lining," I whisper to myself.

She looks at me curiously, cupping my cheeks in her hands. "Est-ce que tu sais quand tu pourras rentrer à la maison?"

"Bientôt, j'espère," I reply. *Do you know when you are coming home? Soon, I hope.* I look up at her. "I speak French?"

"You should," she says with a smile, "because for the last fifteen years you have had a magnificent teacher, if I may say so myself."

I wish I could be happier that I remember what she's taught me, but the things my mind kept hold of and the things it threw away seem so unfair. I turn from her in frustration and wipe my eyes.

She folds her arms around me so gently I imagine I'm wrapped in angel wings. "Je vois, mon amour," she says. *I know, my love.*

I've known Vivienne all of five minutes, and I'm already half drunk in love with her. She's possibly the most charming person I've ever met, which isn't saying much since I currently know only a handful of people, but I'm sure it would still be true even if I knew a hundred. Her beautiful face, the way she smells, the comfort I feel when she holds my hand. I want to be anything she wants me to be, and she wants me to be her daughter.

Over her shoulder I see the senator embrace Jason. "We're so proud of the way you've handled yourself, son," he says, making me wonder how much Jason has shared with them. The senator kneels next to my bed and places his hand over mine. "Audrey, honey, thank God you're OK. That's the only thing that matters to this family, and I want you to remember that." He tousles my hair lovingly. "You went through a lot, kid. You're tougher than I thought."

"Thank you, Senator," I say, unable to meet his eyes. "I want you to know I had blood tests that confirm I wasn't drinking."

He gives me a sympathetic smile. "Audrey, you're my daughter-in-law; you don't have to call me senator. That's a little formal for people who've loved you as long as we have." He puts an arm around my shoulders. "And we know you weren't drinking. Don't concern yourself with that. The truth always finds its way out."

I hope he's right. I so want the truth about everything. I feel connected to Audrey's family in ways I didn't expect, and more connected to Jason because of them.

Senator Gilbert rises to his feet as Dr. Patel enters the room. "Good afternoon, Doctor. We've heard so much about you and the fantastic care you're giving our Audrey."

"Thank you, sir. She is doing quite well." Dr. Patel stands at attention as if speaking to a general.

"Can you bring us up to date on her recovery?" Senator Gilbert asks.

"There is evidence of traumatic brain injury, and her concussion still needs to be observed. The memory loss is related exclusively to her personal history, which we believe indicates that the damage is contained to one specific part of the brain." Dr. Patel pauses and considers his words carefully. "But we will need to wait to see what becomes of it."

Senator Gilbert folds his arms across his chest. "I want no expense spared. Call in anyone you need. If she needs a specialist, go ahead and find one."

Jason looks towards his colleague apologetically. "Dr. Patel is at the top of his field."

Patel raises a hand in reassurance. "Jason, I understand what your father is saying. I'd feel the same if it were my children involved."

Senator Gilbert puts his arm on Jason's shoulder. "We all just want her back to the Audrey we know and love."

Jason steps away from his father and looks out the window. "She's going to be fine. Right, Patel? Maybe even better than before." He says the last part so quietly, I'm certain I'm the only one who hears it. He turns back to them with a smile. "Have faith in her, she'll get there."

Vivienne crosses the room to embrace her son. "Oh, my sweet romantic boy, of course she will."

"I assure you, she's in the best hands," Dr. Patel says. "She has a serious condition and numerous physical injuries. She needs to be able to heal in a controlled environment in order for us to determine if she will regain her memory."

"If?" Vivienne grasps my hand.

"But she is healing miraculously well and getting stronger every day," Dr. Patel says with a reassuring smile.

"When can he break her out of here then?" asks Senator Gilbert. "Surely she'd be more comfortable in her own home."

"She still needs intravenous pain medications, and some of her injuries require the care of our staff. But if things progress well, we can reassess in a few days and see about moving her," Dr. Patel says. "She would need round-the-clock care, of course. A home nurse. Equipment."

"Absolutely," Senator Gilbert says. "Anything she needs. And we will certainly compensate you for house calls."

"Can I choose a nurse?" I ask Jason. "Maybe someone from the hospital I already know?"

"You can have anyone you wish, my dear," the senator says. "And Daisy is welcome to stay with us for as long as you need. Mildred is enjoying her to no end."

"Mildred?" I ask.

"Their housekeeper," Jason says. "She used to be my nanny. You love her, and she's great with Daisy."

Just hearing Daisy's name makes me ache for her. I want so badly to understand the things that are just out of my reach. I don't feel like Audrey Gilbert, whatever that feels like. And I need to know what will become of the person I am now if and when the memories come back. Will I just disappear into Audrey's mind like she has into mine?

Jason continues to talk with his parents about plans for my homecoming. I pretend to follow along, but my concerns are mounting. How am I to go home with a man I hardly know and dive into a life I don't remember? How do I convince a child that I'm the same mother she's always known? And, most important, what happens when Jason finally realizes you can't force feelings that aren't there? Because I can tell beyond a shadow of a doubt that he isn't in love with the person who has replaced his precious Audrey any more than I'm in love with him.

~9~

"Mornin', sunshine." Dottie walks in holding my breakfast tray and grinning like the Cheshire Cat.

"Well whad'ya know? I remember characters from Alice in Wonderland. Call Dr. Patel so he can add it to his random list of nonsense."

Dottie ignores my comment and plops the tray down in front of me. A lit candle sticks out from a pile of mush. "Now don't be a sour puss today. Happy two weeks awake, honey!"

"Is this supposed to be oatmeal?" I ask.

"Just blow out the dang candle. And make a wish!"

I force a smile. As if a person with amnesia would even know what to wish for. It's been over three weeks since my accident, and I'm not any closer to knowing who I am than when I woke up. Dr. Patel and I meet daily to conduct tests that will pinpoint exactly how he'll be able to help me, but so far nothing looks too promising. Bandages have been removed, cuts and bruises will mend and fade, and my concussion will heal. But any attachments I had to being Audrey Gilbert show no signs of returning.

I have become what Dr. Patel has referred to on numerous occasions as "depressed". How could I not be? I'm trapped in a hospital room with no contact with the outside world. I have a few visitors; Thomas and Daisy, Jason— though he's gone back to work as a heart surgeon, and I don't see him as much as I did when I first woke up.

I spend my days wondering. Wondering what my favorite color will be, where I will go on vacations, and what style of clothes I will choose to wear. Dottie keeps me company and occasionally sneaks in with news or gossip from the nurses' station, but all in all I'm very much alone. My in-laws were called away on urgent business the day they came to see me and promised to return by the end of this week. I'd love to see Vivienne again; I suspect she'll be the key to my survival.

I'm now able to get out of bed with help and hobble back and forth to the bathroom. Sometimes Dottie will prop me against the windows so I can look down and watch people in the parking lot coming and going. I pass time by making up stories about their lives, and I'm actually a decent storyteller. At least Dottie says so; she's entertained to no end by the tales I invent about people.

There's been talk of releasing me, and I can only hope it's true. A week ago I thought I'd rather stay in the hospital than go home and share a bed with a man I don't feel married to, but now I'm so stir crazy I'd sleep with him right here and now if it meant getting out. I dream about walking in the grass or sitting by a stream or running through a field. It's a frantic craving that makes me angry at the people who get to feel sun on their faces and come and go as they please. I don't even remember what the sun on my face feels like. I'm a captive trapped by a jailer who fled her own body and left me here in her place. I'll put up with any test and answer any question Dr. Patel asks in order to bust myself out of here and start putting the pieces of my life together. Whether or not it's Audrey's life I repair remains to be seen.

Hours tick by. Physical therapists visit to massage and bend my limbs and ask me to squeeze a ball. The social worker stops in to chat. I know most of her life story now, since there isn't much to say about my own. I act as friendly and optimistic and Audrey-like as I can, but inside I'm plotting and planning, skeptical of everyone. All of these people are bricks that make up the path that will lead me back into the world.

At some point during the day, Dr. Patel decides I'm ready to see my reflection. He feels that my injuries are healing, and the sight of them isn't likely to induce further anxiety.

"You sure you're ready?" Jason asks as Dr. Patel hands me the mirror.

"Of course," I say, though I'm not altogether sure. I close my eyes, take a deep breath, and slowly bring the mirror up. I'm not really that shocked. I know what Audrey looks like from the pictures Jason brought. I look like her, just quite a bit more beaten up. I refuse to let myself cry and stare at the face I don't believe is mine. It's harder for me to see Audrey as someone else when I'm looking at her face in a mirror which is probably why Dr. Patel wants me to see my reflection. I suspect he's trying to dispel the idea of Jane.

There's still swelling around my eye from the corneal scratch, and the part that should be white is stained red, so dark I can barely make out my iris. My nose is swollen and heavily bruised, as is my jawline, which I expected since it's been painful to chew and talk since I woke up. I slowly study one side of my face and then the other. A clear length of tape stretches over one of my eyebrows, and I can see the black threads of the stitches underneath. My eyes are tired and sunken. My hair lays limp on my shoulders, shaved close to my head over one of my ears where they treated my injuries. I have a long narrow neck and slender shoulders. I imagine Audrey wearing a single strand of pearls everywhere she went, even with t-shirts. No trace of pearls now, just yellowing bruises that stretch out from under the collar of my hospital gown. My skin is pale and sallow.

I stare at the reflection interested, but completely detached. She looks back at me and blinks.

I hate you, I want to say, but I know better than to do it out loud. The woman who did this to me left me high and dry to deal with her mess. I wonder if she'd be crying about the damage to her face. I notice that my mouth is turned down at the corners, and I make a conscious effort to straighten it out.

"Well?" Jason asks.

I shrug. "Not as bad as I thought."

"Really?" He exhales in relief. "God, you're handling this well. Everything is healing up nicely. It'll be back to its normal state soon."

"It's the normal state I'm talking about," I say, tilting the mirror so I can see him behind me.

Dr. Patel nods as if he'd been expecting this exchange.

"What?" Jason asks.

"She's not remarking on her injuries, Gilbert," Dr. Patel says. "She's a smart girl; she can see past them. The problem she's having is that she doesn't accept this as her own face. It can be very difficult for some people."

"But imagine how many women would want to wake up looking like her. She has the face of an angel. Once she's healed she'll see it," Jason says, as though I should feel lucky to have woken up in a pretty package.

Dr. Patel rattles off data about amnesia sufferers and their reactions to seeing themselves, but I barely hear him. I recall Dottie's comment about Audrey looking like "the sweetest little doe-eyed thing" and I see now what she means. Large brown eyes—huge really—with long lashes. A bit Bambi-like. Her essence behind these eyes would seem sweet and innocent. In contrast, I'm jaded from spending days in a hospital bed, stripped of my identity. I stare back with hardened eyes and fierce determination. With my current attitude at the helm, she doesn't seem so doe-like anymore. Even though Dr. Patel has explained the physical brain trauma thing to me over and over again, I can't help wondering if Audrey had just been too fragile a person to handle the accident. Maybe that's why she checked out of our brain and left me here holding the scrambled pieces.

"Can you tell me what you're feeling?" Dr. Patel asks. "Just one word, perhaps."

"Pissed off," I say.

Jason puts his head in his hands.

I look up at Dr. Patel with exaggerated remorse. "Oops, that was two words."

"What are you pissed off about?" Dr. Patel asks.

"I'm pissed off at Audrey. She should come back and face her own problems."

"It would be better to start joining your ideas of Jane and Audrey," Dr. Patel says. "To try to see yourself as some of both."

"But who is Audrey, really?" I toss the mirror onto the bed. "I can barely stand to look at her."

I suspect Dr. Patel thinks I'm having some kind of a psychological breakdown. Although he played along in the beginning by calling me Jane, he now addresses me only as Audrey, and his questions veer towards what I think and feel about becoming her again. As if he believes an alter ego has emerged and is taking over her life like some stupid comic book anti-hero.

Dr. Patel pats my shoulder. "That's enough for now. I think it's time for your bath."

"Great. Sponge baths. I will never, ever tire of those."

Ignoring my sarcasm, Dr. Patel turns to Jason. "Gilbert, may I speak to you privately?"

They walk out to the hallway whispering. I've been growing tired of so many things, but at the top of the list is the fact that multiple conversations are conducted without my involvement. I strain to hear what I can from their discussion in the hall.

"A psychiatrist?" I hear the anger rise in Jason's voice. "Don't you think it's a little early for that?"

Dr. Patel keeps his voice low. They continue in hushed tones I can't make out.

"No," Jason says. "I want her home where she belongs. That's an invasion of our privacy."

More whispering.

"Just give her time. I don't think we need that yet." Jason sounds furious.

Dottie strides into the room holding the plastic container of water that's been my "bath" for as long as I've been trapped here. She collects the soap and washcloth from the cupboard next to my bed, humming to herself happily.

"Shhh!" I pull myself up by the bed rail, grunting and heaving.

She puts a hand on her hip. "What in the name of glory are you—"

"Quiet," I whisper, leaning my torso over the edge of the bed. I can see the corner of Jason's lab coat. I know if he gets angry enough he'll yell again, and I'll be able to figure out what they're saying about me. A trickle of sweat drips down my temple, and I shake from trying to hold my own weight on arms that haven't lifted anything heavier than a spoon in weeks.

Jason's voice gets louder. "I don't want her studied like some freak!"

"Aw, hell no." Dottie stomps off to close the door. "The last time you got wind of something you weren't supposed to know, you almost stopped breathin'. And the last thing I need is you fallin' outta bed on my watch."

I struggle to catch my breath. "How would you feel...if people were discussing you...behind your back? And what century is this anyway? They need permission from my husband...before they can talk to me about anything?"

71

"If I were you, I wouldn't be admitting I don't know what century it is. With that amnesia thing you got goin' on, they're likely to believe you." Dottie laughs as if she just told the joke of the year.

"Hilarious," I say.

She laughs again and gathers my hair in a ponytail so she can wash my face and neck.

"Dr. Patel thinks there's something wrong with me," I say.

"More wrong than not remembering who you are and having severe injuries that almost killed you?"

"Yes. He thinks I'm not getting better because I don't want to or something."

Dottie scrubs my neck and takes one of my arms out of the gown. "Now, honey, why would he be thinkin' that?"

"I don't know. I was trying to figure it out before you closed the door."

"Well, I'm sure whatever it is, your husband and Dr. Patel are takin' care of it."

And that's what I'm afraid of. I haven't been around that long, and it already seems like they want to exorcise me from poor Audrey's body.

"Dottie?" I say.

She wrings water from the sponge. "Mm hmm?"

"Why do you think I don't have any friends?"

"Oh, c'mon now. You have lots of friends. Look at all these cards and things people sent you."

I shake my head. "Those are from people who know his family, people who work here in the hospital. I'm talking about friends. Did you know that I don't have any friends? Other than senior citizens apparently?" My voice breaks.

"Honey, don't be sad. You have a whole full life out there just waitin' for you. Don't let this confinement get the best of you. What about all them doctors' wives? They all go and take day trips together and hang out while their husbands are on rotation. Some of them volunteer here at the hospital and work on all the fancy events for the board. They're comin' and goin' all the time. You're probably good friends with some of them."

"No, I'm not. If I had girlfriends, they would've come to see me by now. And besides, Jason told me I shy away from those groups."

"Hmm."

"Something doesn't feel right to me about Jason. I need help figuring it out, from someone who knows us both." I smile at her and bat my lashes.

"Oh, honey, I don't wanna go diggin' into anyone's business."

"But I heard Dr. Patel tell Jason earlier that when I go home, I'll need round-the-clock care. I'll need someone for a month at least." I gaze up at her, making my eyes as doe-like as possible. "I'll ask for it to be you. Just think…no seventh floor, no nurses calling out sick last minute."

"Sounds tempting," she says. "What would I have to do?"

"I need someone I trust to help me put my memories back together. To find out a few things about Jason and me. Maybe get some clues about the accident?"

"Oh, no. You heard Dr. Patel. Forcin' memories on you isn't gonna help you recover," she says.

"You wouldn't be forcing memories on me. And besides, these things will be going on with or without your help. I'm sure Leslie would take the job. Do you think she'd feel comfortable sleeping in a doctor's house?" There's no way I'd let Leslie anywhere near my recovery effort, but the threat of it might be enough to hook Dottie. She has to know by now that Leslie is not to be trusted within five feet of me or, more specifically, Jason.

Dottie huffs and pretends to mull it over. "OK, fine. I'll do it."

"Just talk to people. Ask questions. I'll tell you everything I want to find out. In the meantime, I need to get closer to Jason to find out what's going on with him—any way that I can."

She scrunches up her face. "And what does that mean, missy?"

Before I can answer, Jason walks in. "Oh, sorry," he says and turns his back to give me privacy.

"It's fine," I say casually, unlike the last few times when I had Dottie pull a screen around me. My gown is down around my shoulders, but everything is covered. "Jason?"

He turns to face me with his eyes lowered. "Yeah?"

"Can you get Dr. Patel's permission for me to take a real shower? I think it would make me feel much more...alive."

"I don't need Patel's permission to order a shower for my wife. If you feel up to standing, we can try it. Dottie, can you help us with that?"

I smile at him lovingly. "Maybe you can help me, too?"

"Uh, yeah. Of course," he says.

Dottie looks at me with narrow, judgmental eyes. I know exactly what she's thinking, and she's right. There's very little I have to use to my advantage, but what I do have, I plan to use. Just as any woman would.

She peers in one of my gift baskets. "Might as well break into these presents. Boy, did somebody wanna pamper you! Caviar shampoo? I didn't even know there was such a thing."

Jason smiles. "That's from my aunt in California. She likes to spoil Audrey." He brings the walker over to the bed and cuts the feed to my IV catheters so I can stand up.

I slide to the side of the bed and pull myself up to stand. Dottie helps me balance as I place the walker a few inches in front of me and hobble to it, using my heel as a stand. The cumbersome leg cast goes all the way to my thigh and is difficult to maneuver.

74

"See how good she's gettin' at this?" Dottie says, and then hurries ahead to turn on the shower.

"I was hoping you could ask Dr. Patel this afternoon about arranging my home care," I say to Jason, trying to catch my breath between steps.

Jason raises an eyebrow skeptically. "You sure you're ready?"

"I think so. I'd like to get it settled today and leave in a day or two. It'll be good for Daisy, don't you think?"

"Absolutely. I had no idea you wanted to come home so soon."

I stop to look at him and do my best to keep eye contact, making a conscious effort to smile. "Won't it be good for us, too?"

He hesitates. "Yeah, of course."

When I reach the bathroom, Dottie takes the walker and I lean on her to support my weight. "Do you mind if he helps me in?" I ask.

Dottie rolls her eyes. "Of course not, Mrs. Gilbert."

Jason takes her place under my arm and holds me up while she fits a protective bag over my cast. I tighten my grip around his waist. When she's gone, I take a few shaky steps towards the shower, holding on to the handicap bars for support.

"Don't leave me in here, OK?" I say. With my back to him, I nudge the gown with my chin and let it slide it down to my waist. "Thanks for helping with this. I feel a little weird having Dottie do it." Losing my nerve to completely strip in front of him, I close the curtain behind me and hobble into the shower, pulling my gown off and throwing it over the curtain rod.

The hot water washes over me and soothes every muscle in its wake. I forget all about Jason or going home or Dr. Patel thinking I'm an alternate personality and become so relaxed I need to hold the walls to keep myself up. This is the most intoxicating experience so far in my short life as Jane,

75

and I realize that one of the few perks of losing my memory will be having a lifetime of "firsts" to look forward to. I hold my face under the stream and laugh as it tickles my skin. It takes a while, but I'm able to turn myself by grasping the bars on the side and propping my casted heel against the wall. As soon as I'm steady, I ease back in and gather my hair up to let the water massage the back of my neck and melt away the knots left behind by the flimsy hospital pillows.

"Oh my God," I whisper in pure exhilaration. I reach for a shampoo bottle and it slips through my drowsy fingers and drops to the floor.

"Audrey, what was that? Are you OK?"

Before I can respond Jason throws the curtain aside, but I'm too relaxed to care.

"Jason, you've got to feel this." I grab a fistful of his shirt and pull him into the shower, too carefree to worry about being naked in front of someone who has already seen my body more than I have.

"Audrey, what the hell?" he says as the water soaks his scrubs.

"Is this not the best thing you've ever felt in your whole life? Why didn't anyone tell me this was in here?"

I tilt his chin down to get his attention, but he keeps his eyes respectfully fixed on the wall above my head. Water streams off his nose onto mine, which for some reason strikes me as hysterically funny, and I begin to laugh. He stands in silence, hair matted to his forehead, and his lack of amusement only makes me laugh harder.

"I'm sorry," I say, trying to stifle my giggles. "It just feels really, really good. I don't remember having done this before." I clutch the sides of his waist to keep my balance.

Jason's face softens. "I hadn't thought about it like that."

I notice flecks of gold and green in his grey eyes that I haven't seen before. Droplets of water hang off his thick eyelashes before trailing down his face and falling off the sharp edge of his jaw. I trace the shape of his lips, the small scar on his chin, and I watch his chest as it rises and falls.

I raise my eyes to meet his and see that he's watching me. There's pain in his face, and it knocks me off course. I no longer know what I'm doing or why; I can only stare up at him, paralyzed by uncertainty. What was I thinking dragging a man I barely know into a shower? What was I thinking trying to exploit what he feels for his wife? He breaks our stare first and pulls me to him, nearly crushing me in his embrace, cradling my naked body against his soaking wet scrubs and burying his face into my shoulder. For a second I think he's laughing, until a deep moan rises from his chest.

"Oh God, I don't know what to do," he whispers between sobs. "Forgive me."

"It's OK." I pat his back, unsure of what to do. I don't know how, but I manage to hold us both up, trying my best to soothe his grief, which builds and builds until he is limp and shaking.

He cries into my hair. "I'll give her up if it will make us happy again."

"Everything's going to be fine," I say, only because it's all I can think to do.

We stay under the water for a long time, holding on to one another as I wait for him to work out whatever it is he's dealing with. The sound of Dottie coming into the bathroom brings Jason back to his senses, and he lets go of me with the most heartbreaking expression torturing his face. He looks, *really looks* at me. Probably for the first time since I woke up. His eyes grow cold and indifferent, telling me he finally sees me as a stranger. With that, my last shred of confidence runs down the drain, and I instinctively shield myself with my arms.

"I'll bring you home, Jane. Tomorrow."

Before I can respond, Dottie clears her throat outside the curtain. "You alright in there, Mrs. Gilbert?"

Jason backs out of the shower. "She needed help standing up. We need to get her ready for discharge, Dottie. I assume you'll be coming with us."

"What about Dr. Patel? Will he allow it?" I ask.

"Let's see him stop me," he says. With that he walks away, leaving me reeling in confusion.

I pull the curtain aside and use it to cover up. "I don't know what just happened," I say to Dottie.

She puts her hand on her hip. "What happened is you are one quick worker, honey. Sounds like you're gettin' outta here."

~10~

I've felt Jason watching me the entire ride home, waiting to see if I recognize anything. Unable to look at him, I focus on the scenery, still full of regret for having dragged him into the shower. I'm beginning to believe that my brain damage causes psychotically carefree behavior one moment and complete self-consciousness the next.

I adjust my casted leg on the back seat in a futile attempt to get comfortable and lean my head against the partially opened window to let the breeze cool my face. Though Jason's offered to turn the AC on several times, I prefer the open air. I've grown so tired of the synthetic hospital, the paging intercoms and beeping machines. At least now I'm free of that stagnant environment, though I have no idea what I'm headed towards.

For now, all I want is to experience sounds and sights and feelings away from the white walls and stiff bed where people knew me only as the woman who doesn't remember anything. Out in this world I can be anyone. I can go to a store and talk to a clerk and carry on a complete conversation about the weather without anyone knowing I have brain damage. Once I can actually walk, that is.

Jason breaks the silence by telling me about the house. It belonged to his great-grandparents and was passed down twice before it became Jason's after his grandparents passed away. His parents renovated part of it, though they never intended to live there, and he and Audrey moved in and took over the project soon after Daisy was born. Apparently they only have a few more rooms to go before it's finished. Thankfully, Dottie is already there waiting for me, having set up the solarium as my temporary living quarters. Jason asks if I'd rather he stay down there with me or up on the third floor in the master bedroom, but I don't respond.

I watch the houses go by and notice that they get bigger and farther apart the longer we drive. Finally, the car begins to slow, and we turn onto a cobblestone drive and follow it around a wooded patch of yard and up towards a sprawling brick house presiding over beautifully manicured gardens. Two large wings bookend an enormous central section, and several chimneys poke out of the roof. Black iron window boxes explode with brightly colored blooms and cascades of ivy and vinca. On a grassy island in the center of the driveway, Otis runs in circles, barking and whimpering.

Jason opens the back door and leans in to help me out of the car. "You ready?"

"Wow." I crane my neck to look at the top of the house, trying to wrap my mind around the idea that I live here. "What's in the dormers?"

"The master quarters take up the entire third floor. One dormer is in your dressing room, one is in our bedroom, and one is in my study," he says.

I nod my head. "So you spent a lot of time here as a child?"

"Yeah. See those?" He points to the brick steps leading to the front door. "I busted my bottom lip trying to skateboard down them when I was seven." He sticks out his chin to show me the scar.

"And I carved my first girlfriend's name in that tree over there." He gestures towards a massive weeping willow in the corner of the yard. "I wanted to redo it when we moved in and put yours...Audrey's I mean, but she wanted us to have our own tree."

He hands me my crutches and leads me to a young cherry tree in the center of the yard surrounded by flowering hostas. A faint heart is carved into the bark with J&A etched inside, and a smaller heart is carved underneath with a D in the middle.

"That's sweet." I trace the outline of the carving with my finger. "You did this?"

He looks at me as if he's about to say something but just nods.

"Mommy!" Daisy runs barefoot across the yard wearing a two piece purple bathing suit with a tutu bottom, her wet hair stuck to her face.

I do my best to bend down and hug her, but with the full leg cast, I can't get low enough. She climbs up on a garden bench and throws herself around me in a hug, and I smother her in kisses.

"Wanna watch me in the sprinkler?" she asks.

"Whoa, careful now." Jason laughs and peels her off of me. "Sorry about that, she's really excited," he says, already forgetting to act normal in the first few minutes home by treating me like a guest she's accosted. He whispers something in her ear and smiles. Whatever he says sends her shrieking excitedly into the house.

He puts his hand on my back and leads me across the driveway, explaining that Daisy understands that because of the bump on my head, I might be confused about where things belong in our house, so it's OK to let her know if I can't find something. He helps me maneuver up the steps and through the grandiose front door.

"Surprise!" Daisy stands under a huge paper banner taped to the wall behind her. WELCOME BACK MOMMY is scrawled across it in crayon, surrounded by stickers and hand drawn pictures.

"Oh, Daisy, I love it!" I stop to admire each detail she's added, oohing and ahhing as she describes each sticker and names every color on the banner, one letter at a time.

She proudly points to the Y in Mommy. "That color is fruit punch pink. Fruit punch is what we drink at fancy parties, but Daddy gives it to me at dinner when you're not home."

Jason smiles and tickles her under the chin. "I don't think Mommy forgot what fruit punch is…and thanks for ratting me out."

I can tell he's trying to act relaxed, but his anxiety is palpable. If I were Audrey, I might be able to absorb some of it. But since I have no idea what part of bringing me home is bothering him so much, his uncertainty just bounces right off me. It knocks around the room for a bit like an errant ping pong ball, only to land back on him.

I try to survey the house without making it obvious to Daisy that I've never seen it before. The foyer is spacious and open with a three-story cathedral ceiling. Above us, polished wooden banisters frame the second and third floors. A staircase leading to the second floor winds gradually up one wall. "How do you get to the top?" I whisper to Jason so Daisy can't hear.

"There's a staircase in the back of the house that runs from the second floor to our suite and another that goes all the way up from the kitchen to the third floor through the butler's pantry."

"You have a butler?"

He laughs. "No, but my great-grandparents did."

"That's a lot of stairs for someone on crutches." At least now I have a solid excuse not to share a bedroom yet.

"You won't be on crutches forever." He leans on the railing and points up the stairs. "Daisy's room is on the second floor. And Thomas stays on the main floor off the kitchen near the exercise room. You'll get to know the exercise room soon enough once your physical therapy begins."

I try to imagine myself feeling at home here. Doing laundry. Walking in with groceries and knowing where they belong. For a fraction of a second I regret leaving the hospital.

Daisy runs back in the room and tugs on the bottom of my skirt. "I want to go in the sprinkler."

Dottie lumbers in after her, fanning herself. "I may go in the sprinkler with you, Daisy. And welcome home, Mrs. Gilbert. I think this job change is agreein' with me already, don't you? Miss Daisy is keeping me busy." Dottie models a plastic crown and strands of fake pearls and dress up necklaces.

I smile, relieved to see her. Things would be much more awkward without her here as a buffer. I follow Jason across the foyer, past a library tucked behind glass French doors, and down a hallway adorned with oil portraits.

"All the Gilberts, from my great-grandparents to Daisy," Jason says, pointing to the paintings. He guides me towards the back of the house to a kitchen and living area. Skylights and glass doors surround the entire space, showcasing the wooded backyard. Outside, a large balcony wraps around the back of the house with steep stairs down to the garden below.

Antiqued cabinets with customized nooks for dishes wrap around the perimeter of the kitchen, encircling a huge island with a professional stove in the center. A large wooden pot rack hangs over the island, displaying expensive looking cookware and hanging herbs and dried flowers. Off to one wall are double ovens next to a small beverage sink and a food prep area lined with mixers and knife blocks and walls of tools. Daisy emerges from one of the doors chewing on a cracker; behind her is a huge walk-in pantry.

On the opposite side of the room, a long breakfast bar lined with stools stretches out from the main sink. Countertops vary from butcher block to tile to granite, and baskets filled with fresh fruit and vegetables and old metal pitchers full of flowers are spread out across them, giving the room a farmers' market feel. Several of the cabinet doors are covered in Daisy's drawings suggesting Audrey didn't need her space to look like a professional showroom. I can hardly wait to get my hands on the tools and gadgets that must be hidden in those cabinets, and I try to imagine how it feels to push a rolling pin over a mountain of bread dough or chop vegetables from my own garden into a salad.

"This kitchen makes me want to cook," I say.

Jason gives a half smile. "Please start soon. The take-out places are sick of me." He sees me studying two weathered, whitewashed plaques hanging on the walls. *Je fais mes courses. Ouvre pour déjeuner.* "Gifts from my mother," he says. "She spent a lot of time in here guiding Audrey through family recipes. She considers her to be the daughter she never had. I'm sure in time she'll feel the same about you."

Jason speaks about Audrey in the third person more frequently now, and on a few occasions he's even called me Jane without sounding resentful. Whenever Daisy is within earshot, he says *Mommy* for her benefit, but he seems to accept the idea that for now, I'm not her.

He guides me into the adjoining living room. "Would you like to sit?" He pauses and sticks his hands in his pockets. "This is weird, right? Do you feel weird?"

"Kind of. I feel worse for *you* actually," I say.

He helps me into an oversized chair draped in a white slipcover and lifts my casted leg onto a matching ottoman. The coffee table next to me is also white, as is almost every piece of furniture. There are accents of green from the leaves of white hydrangea blooms gathered in hurricane bowls all over the room. They pick up the light green stripes in the mostly white area rug and the pale green mats of the framed black and white prints on the wall. All the pictures are beach scenes; a few landscape shots, one of Jason and Audrey kissing as a wave crashes into them, one of Jason and Daisy sitting in the sand, one of Audrey and Daisy from the back walking down the beach holding hands. A large mirror with a distressed white wooden frame is propped against the white mantle. All the woodwork is white. The lamps, the afghan thrown onto the sofa, the candlesticks on the end table; all white.

"It's so subdued in here," I say.

"Audrey has a thing for white. She finds it soothing."

"It reminds me of the hospital."

"We can add a little color if it makes you more comfortable. I'm sure Daisy would be happy to get out her markers," he says.

I laugh. "No, that's probably not a good idea. But you're lucky you have such a pristine little girl. Imagine if you had a boy. I'm sure this room wouldn't stay white for very long."

Jason shifts in his seat. "So tell me why you feel worse for me."

"It can't be easy to bring someone to a home they don't remember. To try to live comfortably with a virtual stranger."

He smiles. "You aren't exactly a stranger. I've seen you naked."

"First of all, you're a doctor and you see plenty of people naked; that hardly defines who's a stranger. But you have to admit, it's going to be even more awkward for us now that we're home." Unless I point these things out to him, unless I state the obvious up front, he'll either just wait around for me to remember who I am or try to pick up where Audrey left off.

"Perhaps. But maybe having Dottie here with you and having the place to yourself every other week while I'm at the hospital will make you more comfortable." He looks at me for validation, but I don't respond.

"Also, they'll be sending counselors over from the hospital to meet with us to develop coping strategies," he says.

"Us?"

"You alone, me alone and on occasion, us together. Then maybe once or twice with Daisy to make sure she isn't interpreting anything negatively."

"So a psychiatrist, you mean? To see if I'm progressing correctly?"

"Nobody's judging you. There's no way to do this correctly." This must be how he sounds when he's trying to deliver news to one of his heart patients. "Dr. Patel wants to make sure that you have adequate coping strategies so you don't become disconnected," he says.

"How can I be any more disconnected than I already am? I have absolutely no memory of my life."

"He's concerned that you still insist on being called Jane. He thinks it would be better for you to accept that you're Audrey."

Jason doesn't need to tell me what Dr. Patel thinks. I'm perfectly aware he believes I've commandeered Audrey's brain. I take a deep slow breath and exhale. My lung still hurts. Any time I have this conversation, I feel like I can't catch my breath.

"I understand, I think," he says. "But he doesn't. Maybe you should just tell him what he wants to hear so you don't feel pressure to conform and he doesn't feel pressure to get you more psychiatric help."

"I guess so. You mean lie?"

"Not lie, exactly. Just try to lay off the 'I'm so angry at Audrey' stuff. Then maybe you won't have to talk to the counselors right away."

"And how do you feel about it? Do you want me speaking to those people?"

Jason looks at the floor. "These are my colleagues, Jane. I don't want them to know personal details about our private life."

I stare at him. He appears so ordinary, dressed in plaid shorts and a golf shirt. He should be outside playing with his daughter or on a picnic enjoying the summer day. But instead, he's talking about psychiatrists and showing the stranger who woke up in his wife's body around the house she doesn't remember.

"See, this is why I feel bad for you. You should be out enjoying your life and not going through this," I say.

"You are my life. This is what people do for one another; this is marriage. We have to work this through for our family."

Fed up with the conversation, I rest my head on the pillow behind me and stare up at the ceiling, pressed tin tiles with impressions of fleur-de-lis. "Cool ceiling."

"Thanks."

"Did you pick this out or did she?"

"I did," he says impatiently.

"I don't know what to say, Jason, and that's why I feel worse for you. I'm the one who doesn't remember and therefore has no connections." The words just slip from my mouth unprotected. There's no use in trying to sugarcoat anything at this point. "But you still have all the feelings associated with everything. You see the big picture; I can only see my own small piece. I don't know what I feel about having to keep a family together, because I don't remember having a family."

A disturbed expression passes over his face. "So what are you saying? You want a divorce?"

"No. I'm not making any decisions. We're not supposed to be doing that yet."

"Fuck the goddamn rules. Patel doesn't get to manage my marriage. Do you want a divorce? Do you want to start over in a new life?"

"I don't know what I want."

"Well you'd better make up your mind soon," he says, "because I have a daughter to worry about, and she needs a mother. We can't have you come home only to get up and leave again. She's been traumatized. She's wetting her bed. She's been through too much for someone her age."

"I wouldn't do anything to hurt her," I say.

Jason throws his hands in the air in frustration. "Then you need to decide if you're going to give this a fighting chance. Not just pretending you belong here, but actually keeping your mind open to believing it."

"But if all you're worried about is Daisy, then you should know I'll always try to be a mother to her."

"Maybe I'm worried about myself too. Maybe I'd be willing to take you as someone else, as Jane, just to not lose you entirely. Can't you even entertain that possibility?"

"Of course I can. But let me get to know you first. Let me see for myself if I can feel something for you. Let me learn to trust the things you tell me," I say.

"Such as?"

"Tell me why I drove my car into a tree and where you were when it happened."

"Jesus," he says, closing his eyes. "I was at the hospital."

"Well according to Thomas, it took him quite a while to find you, and you had a long drive to get to me. So unless you were driving around the hospital parking lot for hours, then we appear to have a discrepancy in the stories."

Jason clenches his jaw. "The problem here is that you *want* to think the worst of me. I did have a long drive. I was called to the hospital upstate because a patient of mine had a heart attack while on a business trip. I got the call about your accident while I was there. And I don't know where you were going when you had it."

"Funny, you'd think Thomas would know that," I say.

We're interrupted by the sound of little feet running through the kitchen.

"Mommy!" Daisy bounds in completely soaked and out of breath. "There's a bunny in the yard! He hopped all the way over to the vegetable garden! He's gonna eat all the tomato plants!"

I laugh and try to get up from the chair. "It's fine."

Before I can stand, Jason scoops her up like a football and runs out to the yard to see the bunny—or maybe to get away from me.

Dottie surveys the scene from the doorway with a hand on her hip. "How's everything in here so far?"

I look back at her and sigh. "Really, really white."

~11~

The foundation level solarium is as spectacular as the rest of the house; one large, open room lined with glass doors that lead out to the patio and back gardens. My hospital bed is arranged next to the couch, facing the back yard where I can enjoy the view. An impressive entertaining kitchen and a full bar hug the inside wall next to a stone fireplace. Dottie has a bedroom off to the side, and there is a large bathroom down here for us to share. The only other rooms are a wine cellar, which I'm told Audrey had no use for, and a large storage area that spans the remaining footprint of the house. There's a sound system so I can listen to music, but I'm still forbidden to read or watch television until I'm cleared by Dr. Patel.

Thomas slides open one of the glass doors. "Knock knock. Came by to say hello."

"Oh thank God," I say, thrilled to have a visitor, and even happier that it's him. "I don't suppose you brought anything for me to do."

"Sorry, just me."

"Will you play a game with me?"

"Depends. No Scrabble." He nods towards a pile of games Daisy had dragged out from a cupboard behind the bar. "Or anything else that requires you to concentrate on letters, numbers or shapes."

"No cards then? I was hoping you could teach me gin."

He laughs. "No. And you already know how to play gin, but you suck. Daisy could beat you." He walks over to the bar and gets himself a beer from the fridge. "Want anything? He's got the flavored seltzers in here that you like. And iced tea."

"No thanks. They're up there eating dinner. Did you see them?"

"Of course, I just left there. Think I'd miss out on Jason Gilbert's famous fish sticks? I heard there was an intruder in the garden today. Daisy made me check the tomato plants. Since I was out there anyway, I figured I'd come check on you."

"She's coming down in a bit to put on a show for me before she goes to bed. So that's something to do at least. Will you stay?"

"Stay? I'm in the show. Who do you think is playing the rabbit? We're recreating the incident from this afternoon," he says.

"Does she do this a lot?"

"All the time. And I have four days home until my shift starts, so I'm sure you'll see me in a few more productions before then." Thomas sits down on the sofa next to my bed. He picks up a plastic tube attached to a fat straw with a mouth piece and hands it to me. "Let's see what you got."

I roll my eyes and reluctantly suck on the tube, trying to get the stupid red ball to float up. Dottie already made me do it four or five times earlier. It barely lifts off the base before I give up. The little red ball torments me; I have half a mind to take the thing apart to see if it isn't stuck to the bottom.

Thomas holds it back up to my mouth. "Give it another go, Audrey."

"Don't call me that," I say.

"I already told you I'm not giving in to this bullshit of calling you Jane. It isn't healthy. I don't like it."

"Why not?"

"I just don't, that's why. You need to at least try to return to who you were."

I don't answer him. There's no point, and I have more important things I want to discuss. "Did you know that on the night of my accident Jason was at another hospital treating a cardiac patient of his?"

"Yeah, he does that sometimes."

"I thought you told me you couldn't find him. That he was checking on his parents' old house upstate."

Thomas takes a sip of his beer. "I think he checked in on the house because he was up that way anyway. Honestly, that night was a blur and I don't remember every detail. Does it really matter where he was?"

"To me it does. If I'm expected to live with him, I should be able to trust the things he tells me."

"And you don't?"

"No. On several fronts."

"All I know is that he checked in on the house and was visiting a patient," he says.

"He checked in on a house while one of his patients was having a mild stroke because he happened to be in the area? Or did he check in on the house after he got the call that his wife was in a life threatening car accident and was on his way home?"

"Wait, what?"

"Neither scenario looks good for him," I say. "Either he's a bad doctor or a bad husband. Which is it?"

Thomas sneers. "I don't know what's going on inside your brain, but you're way off."

"Let me tell you what I think. I think he was upstate, possibly at his parents' house, and probably with one of the nurses from the hospital. You told me that when you found him, he had to drive all the way home to get to me in time. Only neither of you realized what the other had said, and now both stories can't be true. Jason couldn't have been tending to a patient *and* checking on a house upstate. Unless he was doing it while either his patient's life was in danger or mine was."

Thomas sits back on the couch and stares at me. "I don't even know why I'm arguing with you. You have a head injury. Something in there is scrambled, and now you're suspicious of someone who doesn't deserve it. How about instead of inventing scenarios to entertain yourself, you focus your energy on getting better and reclaiming your old life?"

"Well can you blame me for being suspicious? Ever since I tumbled down this rabbit hole otherwise known as the life of Audrey Gilbert, I don't know which way is up, and I certainly don't know who to trust."

Thomas is silent for a moment. I can see in his face how my words have wounded him. "You know what?" he says. "Part of being a friend is helping someone even when they don't want it. It's loving and supporting them no matter how many mistakes they make because you know that they can and *will* do better. I'll do that for you because I'm your friend." He takes a deep breath and exhales slowly. "But you need to know you're making a huge mistake right now."

"Or you are," I say quietly. "I'm not rejecting your friendship, Thomas. I know you believe everything you're saying. But you're forgetting about women's intuition, and mine is telling me something isn't right with that husband of mine up there. So before you start thinking I'm the problem, just make sure you can fully trust everything Jason has been telling *you.*"

Thomas sits back and scratches the side of his face. "He *has* been under a lot of stress lately. But you have to consider everything he's been through and that he's afraid he could still lose his wife after all. It's not easy for him."

"I know. But how were things between them before the crash?" I ask.

He shrugs. "You mean how were things between the two of you? That's not for me to say."

"Then you just told me what I needed to know. If things were fine, you would've said so."

"Don't put words in my mouth, Audrey. Before the accident you knew us, so your intuition was usually dead on. Now you don't have the facts or the faith in us to back up your hunches, so you shouldn't jump to conclusions."

"Something's not right, and I can't trust that man until I know what it is. But I'd like to trust you."

Thomas tilts his head and smiles. "You *can* trust me," he says, linking my hand with his.

I'm completely disarmed but manage to hide it. "That was a pretty nice speech you gave before about what it means to be a friend."

"Well I can't take credit; I was quoting someone."

"Who?"

He arches an eyebrow. "You, of course."

After Daisy's performance, Thomas and Jason bring her up to bed. After having her father to herself for so long, it's going to be hard for her when he returns to his long shifts at the hospital.

Dottie helps me to the bathroom and waits outside the door while I get ready for bed. I look at my reflection in the mirror. My eye is healing, and most of the redness has faded. The swelling on my face has gone down considerably, and some hair has even started to grow back where it was shaved over my ear. I may eventually think of us as pretty if I can ever forgive her for sticking me in this situation.

"What was going on with you, Audrey?" I ask into the mirror.

She looks back at me silently.

I narrow my eyes, and she does the same.

"You do realize we're completely insane," I say to my poor reflection since she can't think for herself.

Dottie calls through the door. "What was that, Mrs. Gilbert?"

"Nothing. Just talking to myself."

I brush my teeth and dab some of the cream Jason's aunt sent me under my eyes. "*La Mer*...Well let's see if it works on these bags of mine."

"Who?" Dottie asks.

I turn off the bathroom fan so she might recognize when I'm talking to myself and stop yelling at me through the door. As soon as I do, I hear Thomas and Jason talking through the ceiling vent. I imagine they must be in the food pantry directly above me.

"I didn't ask you to lie for me," I hear Jason say angrily.

"What did you want me to say? I didn't know you were gonna tell her you were at another hospital."

"Why did you tell her anything at all?"

"Are you kidding me? It was right after she woke up. We were talking about how I watched her come in on a goddamn stretcher and how you drove all that way in agony, knowing she may not make it."

"Christ, Thomas. Why would you tell her that?"

"Why wouldn't I?"

So Thomas is just as much in the dark as I am. Their voices lower to a whisper, and I strain to listen for more. If it weren't for my cast, I'd climb up on the vanity to put my ear to the vent.

"She made a good point, though, Jay. Did you stop at the house on the way to see a critical patient or on the way home when you thought she was dying?"

"Neither."

I hear a huge thump.

"Jesus, you're gonna put a hole in the wall," Thomas says. "What the hell is going on? I'm telling you, Audrey knows something isn't right. She doesn't trust you."

"No kidding."

"You know what? I don't even want to know what it is. That way I don't have to lie to her, too. Just tell me if you're in trouble."

"Not yet," Jason says.

"How bad are we talking?"

"Pretty bad."

Dottie knocks loudly on the bathroom door. "Mrs. Gilbert, you OK in there?"

"Yes. I'll be right out," I say quietly, listening for more. Their conversation abruptly stops and is replaced by the sound of Jason's footsteps thumping down the stairs. I quickly flip on the bathroom fan.

Dottie knocks again. "Dr. Gilbert is here to say goodnight."

I open the door slowly and smile. "What? I was just washing my face. Sorry, I can't hear anything with this fan on in here."

Jason stands behind Dottie and peers in at the vent. "I just wanted to check in on you and say goodnight. If you're not awake tomorrow when I leave for the hospital, I won't see you till next Tuesday."

"OK, goodnight, Jason. See you next week," I say. Out of the corner of my eye, I see Dottie slink away to give us privacy.

He surveys the cotton night slip his mother bought for me to wear while I have the cast on my leg. "You look really beautiful. It's going to be hard to be away all week. You sure you're OK with me going back to work? I could stay…"

"No, you should go." I try not to sound too eager. "We need to get back on schedule so I can see what normal life is like, right?"

"Right." His eyes settle on the scar that stretches across my chest under my collar bone. "One day soon everything's going to clear up, and this will all be nothing but a bad memory." He shifts uncomfortably. "Can I hug you?"

"Of course," I say, only because I can't think of a reason to say no.

He steps closer and hesitantly puts his arms around me. I manage to hug him back, even though I really don't want to. He pulls me in so forcefully my breath catches. I try to squirm from his grasp, but he holds me tighter.

"I know you think I'm not to be trusted, Jane," he whispers, "but you're very, very wrong. I'm only trying to protect the best interests of my family. Remember that." He kisses me on the cheek and steps away. "I'll see you in a week. I hope you're a little more...healed by then."

"I'll bet you do," I whisper.

"I'll grow to love you, Jane. In so many ways I already do. And you'll grow to love me, too." He turns and walks out, leaving me alone and trembling.

When Dottie returns, she takes one look at me and sucks in her breath. "We gotta get you into that bed, Mrs. Gilbert. You're shakin' like a leaf." She supports my weight across the room and tucks me in, piling the blankets on top of me.

I don't know how to tell her that I'm not the least bit cold, and no amount of blankets will be enough to melt the ice between Jason and me.

~12~

I'm in a bathroom. I have no idea whose it is or how I got here. Large, white ceramic tiles stretch out endlessly beneath a vintage clawfoot tub. As the water runs, thick clouds of steam rise slowly towards a giant stained glass skylight in the shape of a daisy. A boiling tea kettle screams in the distance, echoing off the walls. But it isn't a kettle, it's a woman. Her screams get louder and louder. I feel something flowing under my feet and strain to see if the tub is running over, but the drain stopper hangs on its chain by the faucet. I glance down and see that it isn't water, but blood. It spreads in a thick pool across the floor, slowly covering every tile until there's no white left. Only then do I realize that I'm the one screaming.

"Wake up, Mrs. Gilbert." Dottie shakes me by the shoulders. "It's just a dream. You're OK. Take a deep breath." She places a mask over my nose and mouth and flips on the oxygen machine, then picks up her phone and begins to text someone.

I grasp frantically, trying to wrestle the phone away from her.

She yanks it back. "It was just a dream. You gotta breathe for me, honey."

Behind her, Thomas appears rubbing his eyes.

"Third time this week, Dr. Charles. Sorry to wake you, but you said to let you know if it happened again," Dottie says.

Thomas looks down at me. "Audrey, listen, you have to calm down. You were having a nightmare again."

Desperate to get away, I push his arm off mine and struggle to get out of the bed. Dottie restrains me while Thomas holds the mask over my face. I flail my legs and claw at their hands, trying to free myself.

He touches my cheek. "It's me. Thomas. I'm not going to hurt you. Stop holding your breath."

I hadn't realized I was doing that. I take a deep breath and feel my chest open up immediately.

"Atta girl," Dottie says.

Thomas wipes the tears from my face and lays a damp washcloth over my forehead. "It's OK, we've got you. You're home, Audrey. It wasn't real."

I try to keep myself from shaking, but that only makes it worse.

He turns to Dottie. "I've got this under control. You can head to bed."

He stands above me listening to my lungs with his stethoscope while I take in air from the mask. "If we can't get this lung under control, we'll have to admit you again. I'm calling Jason and Patel in the morning."

I cover his hand with mine and shake my head, feeling the tears sting my eyes.

"This is getting ridiculous," he says. "Jason's been gone for four days, and you've had nightmares for three of them. He needs to be back here with you."

I turn away from him. I haven't spoken to Thomas about anything significant since the night I heard him talking with Jason through the vent. We've eaten together a few times, and he's started reading me *Sense and Sensibility* from Audrey's book collection, but I haven't confided in him about anything important—not that I have anything important to say.

"Try to get some sleep now," he says.

I put my arm out to stop him. "Don't go."

"OK..." He rubs the side of his face as though he's considering it. "I'll take the couch."

"No, please stay with me," I say, reaching out for him. "I'm so scared."

"C'mon, Audrey. There's nothing to be afraid of. It was just a dream." Thomas lies down on the bed next to me, and I lean my head on his chest and cry into his t-shirt.

"Aw, man...not my lucky Bulls shirt. Female tears will jinx us for the entire season."

I want to laugh but I can't. Instead I just breathe in the scent of him and concentrate on that to stop the shaking. He smells really good, like soap and saddle leather.

"Jesus. You have to calm down." He tightens his grip around me. "Was the dream about the accident?"

I wish I knew.

"Don't go, Thomas. Don't leave me here, OK?" I say, catching quick breaths as the last of my tears dry.

"I'm not leaving. I'm staying right here."

"I mean you need to stay in the house with us. Don't go back to your house—even after he comes home, OK?"

"You can't honestly tell me you're afraid of Jason," he says.

I can't answer him. I don't know what to say. Soon I hear his rhythmic breathing and feel myself drift into sleep again, comforted only by the awareness that he isn't going anywhere.

~ ~ ~

Vivienne has taken Daisy for a few days in case my breathing condition puts me back in the hospital. She's going

100

to teach her to make crepes, which Daisy's thrilled about. I'm selfishly relieved that she'll be gone for a while. I need a break from pretending to be Audrey.

Thomas shows up with fish tacos from his favorite local food truck and entertains Dottie and me with stories of his surfing adventures in Baja. He mentions that Dr. Patel is aware of the stress being put on my lung from the nighttime screaming, but aside from that, he barely looks at me.

Later that night, Thomas returns to check on me after Dottie has gone to her room. "Are you OK?" he whispers, sitting on the side of my bed. "There's a storm rolling in."

I keep my back to him. "I will be if you stay with me."

He climbs into the bed. "I don't like knowing that you're down here terrified, but I can't make a habit of this."

"Because you're worried about Jason?"

He lies behind me and drapes his arm over my stomach. "I'm not half as worried about Jason as I am about myself. What you don't understand is that Jason would want me to be here taking care of you in his place. I'm like a brother to him. He trusts me with his life, and rightfully so."

I don't know why, but hearing him say that disappoints me. We lie in the darkness, listening to the rain coming down outside. I've so needed to feel someone's arms around me. I gather my hair up on top of my head so his face is right up against my neck, and I find his hand to intertwine my fingers with his.

"Thank you, Thomas."

"I must be out of my goddamn mind," he whispers into the darkness.

~ ~ ~

Dottie and I eat breakfast on our stone patio surrounded by limelight hydrangeas and bright patches of

101

salvia. "You must have some green thumb, Mrs. Gilbert," she says through a mouthful of blueberry crepes, a special delivery from my in-laws to show how well Daisy is doing with Vivienne's cooking lessons.

"I guess so. I don't remember doing any of it, but the flowers are beautiful. I wish *I* could plant something."

"Don't you go gettin' any ideas. It's gonna be a long time before Dr. Gilbert lets you carry a purse, let alone a wheelbarrow." She nods towards one leaning upside down against a small garden shed, still untouched from the day before the accident.

Audrey had apparently been adding to the large garden that wraps around the foundation patio. Several holes sit unfilled, waiting for the flowers she was going to plant. I wonder what Audrey was feeling that day. I wonder where she was going when she had the accident or where she was coming from. I wonder so many things about her these days.

"Dr. Gilbert is comin' home today," Dottie says, flashing me a wide smile. She couldn't be more relieved. The woman nearly had a heart attack after she saw Thomas in bed with me one morning, the two of us lying like spoons in the silver drawer, as she put it. *Oh, Lordy* was all she said before Thomas jumped up, babbling about me having another bad dream, and smacked his head on the door frame on the way out. If he hadn't acted so guilty she may not have considered it again, but he could barely look at either one of us after that and went back to work at the hospital without as much as a goodbye.

Dottie pours herself more coffee. "You need to start workin' on this marriage of yours. No more of this snuggly time with Dr. Charles and bein' all suspicious of Dr. Gilbert. You gotta try to get back to the way things were."

"I have no idea how things were," I say, cutting a grapefruit in half. "How could I go back to them? And my *snuggly time with Dr. Charles* is not at all what you think it is. I just needed someone to hold on to me. The nightmares have been terrible."

She clicks her tongue at me. "I'd be more than happy to hold on to you. And you should see the look on your face right now. It says, 'Oh, no…I want a handsome man to hold me, the one with the piercing blue eyes.' Humph. You already got yourself a handsome man to hold on to you, so don't go thinkin' about anything else."

I laugh. "You're literally having a conversation with yourself right now and just doing my parts. I never said anything like that."

"You listen to me when I tell you to get back to the way things were." She waves her fork at me. "No good's gonna come from you tryin' to get closer to Dr. Charles."

"What makes you think—"

"Because I know you now. I know you're lookin' for answers, and I know that Dr. Gilbert isn't givin' them to you. I know Dr. Charles is practically made of mush on the inside. He's such a softie, especially when it comes to you, so you're tryin' to cozy up to him to see what's what. But you don't even realize you're gonna to end up with feelings for him if you don't stop that."

"I didn't keep him here all night to use him for information. But speaking of that, what have you found out?"

"Well, it is bizarre," she says shaking her head. "They say it's Dr. Gilbert who won't let you join their groups. They told Florence from the E.R. that you were invited to be in a book club with a few of the ladies, and after you went one time, he didn't want you goin' back. He didn't like you out at night drinkin' and gossiping, and that's what they do at those book meetings. They even have a name for themselves…the 'Carpe Tinis.' Why would anyone wanna name a book club after a fish?"

I have to put a hand over my mouth to keep myself from spitting out my coffee. "Carp-*ay*," I say once I've recovered. "Carpe Tini…like 'Carpe Diem', but instead of '*seize the day*' they switched it to *seize the martini*. Clever. Too bad I don't know them; they sound pretty cool."

"Humph." Dottie rolls her eyes. "I'd like to seize me a martini. Anyway, here's the strange part. I heard from Angie…" She stops buttering her toast and points her knife at me. "You remember Angie—the one who brought you your tray in the mornings? Well, she said that when some of them book club ladies were volunteering in the kitchen, they were sayin' Dr. Gilbert told you not to get on any of those committees to plan the hospital fundraisers because he liked to keep his work life and his home life separate and he didn't want to mix it all up."

She stops talking to take a much needed breath. One of these days she's going to talk until she turns blue. "But that doesn't make any damn sense," she says, "so I think whoever started that rumor got to everyone with the same stupid story."

"Oh, it makes plenty of sense." I sip my coffee and try to imagine Jason telling Audrey not to be friends with the other doctors' wives. "I think Jason didn't want Audrey to know what he was doing behind her back, and with those women always hanging around the hospital, they were bound to hear rumors. He was probably afraid that if Audrey became friends with them, they'd tell her what they were hearing."

Dottie opens her mouth but doesn't say anything for a moment. "What in the name of holy hippos leads you to believe he was foolin' 'round on you and that the other ladies knew it?"

I fold my arms across my chest. "Are you going to sit here and tell me that you haven't heard a single thing about Jason and Leslie?"

"I heard that trashy little thing threw herself at him, but to no use. And I heard he turned her bony little ass down flat."

I look at her warily. "We'll see."

"We'll see nothin'. That Leslie is a sly little nobody. If Dr. Gilbert paid her any attention, any real genuine attention that meant anything, she'd be on top of the building crowin' about it for the whole world to hear. It isn't enough that he's a good lookin' doctor. Think about it. Think about his family. Leslie would want everyone to know that she snared herself a Gilbert. There'd be no hidin' it. He was raised with people tryin' to get close to him because of who his daddy is, and that's the reason he'd never go for her. I'm tellin' you, you're wrong."

I nod my head begrudgingly; she has a point. After meeting the senator and his wife and seeing their interactions with Jason, it would be hard to believe he'd jeopardize the family name by having a fling with a nurse. Then again, I don't really know him. Maybe he couldn't help himself.

"There's something I need you to do for me, Dottie. I need you to call the hospital upstate and ask them about the night of my accident."

"No." She drops a sugar cube into her coffee. "No way, no how."

"Please. I need to know if he was there."

"Why? What difference does it make?"

"If they tell you he was there, I'll have no reason to be suspicious. I'll try to get back to normal life."

She folds her arms across her chest. "And what am I supposed to say?"

"Tell them you're in the medical records department and calling to check because of insurance paperwork or something. Say that the wrong hospital got billed. I don't know. Just verify that he was there."

She snorts. "This is a fool's errand, that's what this is."

"But what if I'm right? I should know if something was going on behind Audrey's back. There could be so much more I haven't even considered yet."

Dottie shakes her head. "I can't believe you're gettin' me into this, but fine. Now you got me wonderin'." She pushes back her chair and helps me into my walker.

I smile at her, grateful that my condition still requires a nurse. It seems that for now, at least, my injuries are working for me. Once they're gone, Dottie goes with them. And then I'm completely on my own.

~13~

Dottie and I search online and come up with a contact in the medical billing department of Davenport Hospital, where Jason claimed to be the night of my accident. She also jots down the cardiac unit number to double check in case he never officially signed in as a visiting surgeon. "Darn doctors don't even bother with formalities these days," she says as she reaches for her phone.

I chew the side of my thumbnail, unable to stand the suspense.

"Yes, hello. This is uh...Charlotte Baker." She covers the mouthpiece and whispers to me. "I use my cousin's name for everything. Even my passwords."

I poke her in the arm. "Keep going!"

"Yes, I'm with Stateline Insurance," she says. "I need to check on a treatment date we were billed for that belongs to your hospital. But, uh...the bill went to another hospital by mistake. Yes, mm hmm."

She's such a hideous liar. I should have called myself.

"The patient's name? Well...I don't have that information here. We're just tryin' to see if a Dr. Jason Gilbert was documented in any of the charts for the night of June fourth. Possibly in emergency or in the cardiac unit."

She covers the mouthpiece again. "She's checking in the personnel office to see when he was on duty," she whispers before bringing the phone back to her ear.

She sings along with the music while she's on hold. "Raspberry Beret. Mmmm...I love me some Prince. Brings me right back to summers on the Jersey Shore. Don't you just love when you hear a song and—" She stops herself, probably realizing that for me, songs mean nothing. Even the ones I remember the words to.

"Yes, I'm still here," she says into the phone. "What? Are you sure about that? Maybe you should call up to the unit and speak to the...no, I understand. Of course." She gives me a panicked look. "What department am I in? Uh..."

I quickly grab the phone and disconnect the call. "What did they say?"

"Well...they said that Dr. Gilbert hasn't attended to a patient in their hospital since February."

"Ha! I knew it."

"But she also seemed pretty confused why I'd have the doctor's name and not the patient's name if I was callin' from an insurance company." She wrings her hands. "I'm gonna be in for it now. What if they traced the call?"

"Dottie, it was medical billing you were speaking to, not the FBI. I'll call in a while, tell them who I am, and warn them that reporters may be calling local hospitals to drum up more dirt on my accident. Then they'll just think you were a reporter."

Dottie narrows her eyes. "For somebody with brain damage, you sure think quick on your feet."

I shrug. "Probably because I don't have anything in there slowing me down."

She softens with a laugh. "So Dr. Gilbert wasn't at the hospital upstate the night of your accident. Now what?"

I hand her the phone. "I need you to make another call."

"Oh, no." She backs away with her hands up.

"Just call anyone you trust in the hospital and have them check if Leslie was on duty the day I was brought in. If she wasn't there, we'll know they were together."

"That's a big jump to conclusions, missy. But fine, I'll do it." She takes the phone into her bedroom. "Nope," she says when she comes back. "You're wrong. She was on a double shift that day. Seven a.m. to eleven p.m."

"Unless someone else punched her in," I say.

"Not only was she punched in, she was given a citation that night by the floor supervisor and had to report it to HR. It's all documented in her file."

"For what?"

"I don't know. She's already gotten two for talkin' back to patients. Smart ass, that one." Dottie falls back onto the sofa and sighs. "But now you know wherever he was, they weren't together."

"Damn. But I should still warn the hospital upstate about the reporters."

"What reporters?" Jason's voice startles me.

"Jason...you're home." I limp over to my bed trying to buy time. "There was a phone call earlier—someone asking questions about the night of my accident. I mentioned that you were working in another hospital. I figured I should call Davenport to warn them not to speak to anyone in case they tried to check that story."

"Why would you tell anyone anything? I told you that reporters are always trying to dig up dirt on my family." He walks outside and paces around the patio, yelling and gesturing into his phone. When he hangs up, he gives me a weary look and slides the glass door open.

"Davenport got a call from someone claiming to be from an insurance company. Must have been right after you did. They won't be taking any more calls about us." He sits down on the bed and runs his hand through his hair. "You can't speak to anyone about that night, understand? People think I faked a blood test for you, and that could ruin my career and my father's in one swoop. I know you don't remember being in this family, but you have to help us protect ourselves by being smarter than that."

I look away from him. "I'm sorry."

Dottie jumps up from the couch, runs into her bedroom, and slams the door. If I know her, she's on her knees praying to Jesus that the Gilberts won't fire her when they find out she helped me do something this stupid.

"What's with Dottie?" Jason asks.

"She told me not to take the call and I didn't listen."

"It's good to know we can trust her," Jason says, "but I don't like this. People shouldn't be calling here asking questions while you're trying to recover." He walks to the glass window and looks outside. "I won't be taking any more long rotations for a while. I need to be here with you. Thomas told me about the nightmares."

I should probably be worried that they're sharing information, but I can't imagine Thomas telling Jason that he spent two nights lying next to me until dawn. He would have spared Jason's feelings, which are already confused when it comes to me.

"I'm fine. It was just a bad dream or two," I say.

"That's not what Thomas said. Patel's coming later to see if you need a breathing tube."

"Jason, no. I'll do the lung exercises every hour, I promise. No more poking and prodding."

"Will you tell me about the dreams you're having?" he asks.

"I'm in a bathroom and the floor is covered in blood and there's a woman screaming and then I realize it's me and I wake up." I rattle it off casually without going into detail. "Sounds stupid, I know."

"It isn't stupid. I'm glad you weren't alone, but I'd rather be the one to comfort you. Do you think if I were here you'd have let me?"

"It's hard for me when I know you're deliberately withholding—" I grasp the bedrail and wince in pain. I lean back into the bed and hold my breath until the clenching in my chest subsides.

Jason grabs a stethoscope from the drawer and listens to my chest. "Look at you…this is why we can't talk about certain things. It's too much for you. I need to have you admitted; your lung doesn't sound good."

"I don't want anyone else to touch me."

Jason lowers his eyes. "Believe me, I know. I'm sorry to be the bad guy here, but you have no choice. You're going."

I glare at him, hoping he feels how much I dislike him.

"If it makes you feel any better about me, just know that Thomas would intubate you himself right here and now if he decided you needed it. He wouldn't be worrying about what you wanted."

I suddenly realize how selfish I'm being. I can tell by the look on his face that he doesn't like this any more than I do. And he clearly thinks I see Thomas as a playmate and him as my warden. "Fine," I say quietly. "I'll do what you want. But in exchange I need you to answer a few questions."

He nods in defeat.

"I know you can't share sensitive information with me because you think I can't handle it, but your lies are just as bad. I'm trying to figure out what kind of a person you are. Was there something going on before the accident that was affecting your marriage to Audrey?"

He puts head in his hands. "Not this again."

"Jason, answer me. My intuition tells me something isn't right. Were there problems in your marriage?"

He sets his jaw and barely moves his lips as he answers. "Yes."

"Are these problems ongoing?"

"No. Are we done here?"

"Was it the nurse from the other night?" I ask.

"No. For the last time—"

"Then explain to me why she acted the way she did. Say something, *anything* so I can have faith in what you tell me. I don't even care; I wouldn't blame you. Please just give me some shred of honesty so I can see how it feels to get it from you."

Jason lowers his head. "OK. Audrey and I went through something last year; we were working some things out. Leslie was constantly coming on to me. She throws herself at a lot of doctors, but especially me. I usually ignore her. The week before the accident, I was pulling longer shifts than usual. I was dead on my feet, and Audrey was acting distant. I was in the break room trying to sleep off an eighteen-hour day, and Leslie came in offering to rub my shoulders, trying to comfort me. I kind of broke down."

"Broke down as in slept with her?"

"No, jeez. I mean broke down emotionally. I was overwhelmed. She kissed me and I didn't stop her. And then I kissed her back. Longer than I should have."

I almost laugh. "That's it?"

Jason scowls. "Some people would consider that an indiscretion, Jane."

"I'm sorry, but I can see how it could happen." Having my feelings and memories severed from him makes it easy to be objective. "So you didn't have an affair with her?"

"No. I loved Audrey too much to do anything,"

"I'm not sure that has much to do with it. It isn't hard to understand, really. You can love someone and still—"

"What's the matter with you?" He hurls his words indignantly, but then softens a bit. Perhaps once he remembered it isn't his actual wife he's talking to. "Yeah, I guess I know what you mean. I was lonely. And confused. And liked the attention. I may have wanted to for a moment, but I eventually pushed her off me and left. After that, I couldn't shake her loose. She followed me everywhere, left

112

notes on my car. On the night of your accident, she followed me all over the building trying to console me, saying that she would take care of me if anything happened to you. I finally had to report her. There was too much going on that night already, and I just had to keep her away from me."

So that explains why Leslie was written up the night of my accident. At least some of what he says seems to follow actual events.

"And there's one more thing I should tell you," he says, his leg bouncing up and down. "I think Leslie called in the anonymous tip about me faking your results to get back at me for rejecting her."

"Were you afraid to tell me that?"

"I guess so. And also ashamed that it got my father involved. I was raised to know better than to give some woman a reason to blackmail me."

"She wanted me to think you were involved with her. When she brought you your phone that night in the hospital, she made it seem like you two had been alone together."

Jason nods. "She stopped me while I was on the way back up with Thomas. She said she was sorry for the way she acted and asked if we could be friends. Then she hugged me. I think she did it to take my phone just to confuse you."

"Why would she want to confuse me? I have brain damage for God's sake."

"Because if you and I don't find a way to mend our relationship, or if she can drive a wedge between us, then she believes she'd have a chance with me," he says.

"I guess you know more about women than you think."

He shakes his head. "Not really. Thomas explained it to me the other day."

"Thomas knew about this?" I'm surprised to hear that. I'd thought he was more loyal to me than to keep something like that secret.

"I only told him two days ago. He said if I didn't start explaining myself to you, things were going to get weird."

My cheeks grow hot. In Thomas's mind, "things getting weird" probably involved me inviting him to stay with me all night.

Jason studies my face. "What's wrong?"

"Nothing. I assume there's more to the story, though. Do you think Audrey knew about you and Leslie and was upset?"

"No. Audrey would have understood that better than most people. She was incredibly open-minded about relationships and the reasons we all have for doing things. I'm not as compassionate as she is. I think what I did was completely wrong."

"Then why was she was acting so distant before the accident?"

"We shouldn't discuss that right now. Even Patel agrees that certain things could affect your healing."

"And Dr. Patel knows these *certain things?*"

Jason nods. "He does. Think you can trust me for now?"

"I guess so. It's just hard for me to blindly accept what's handed to me."

"And that's why I'm not handing it to you all at once," he says.

I believe his story about Leslie; I doubt he could be this good an actor. His eyes are watery and bloodshot, and he looked like he was going to be sick when he told me he didn't stop a woman from kissing him—and I'm not even the wife he cheated on, not that I even consider what he did to be cheating. But if Dr. Patel knows there are incidents in our history and felt it was safe to send me home with the same man he once called a hothead, maybe things aren't as bad as I thought.

Jason takes my hand. "Can we try to start over? Get to know each other as we are now? Without you feeling like you have to be Audrey."

"But I don't. That's the whole point. I just pretend for everyone else."

"Don't worry about my parents. My mother will take you in any form; she'll understand this. And my father just follows along with what she does. He takes all emotional cues and parenting advice from her anyway." He spins my wedding band around my finger. "And I want to spend more time with you, quality time, when I'm relaxed and not constantly worried about your safety. I know I didn't behave like someone you'd want to know, but I nearly lost everything. And still could…"

I'm back to feeling sorry for him. Every time I'm alone with this man, I'm either suspicious of him or feeling terrible for having been. There has to be a way to settle in to a normal routine of getting to know him. I have a feeling I'll need to know myself first, and that's hard to do when you're two completely different people. At least that's one thing Jason and I have in common.

~14~

Vivienne Barteau-Gilbert sits on a kitchen stool with one leg tucked beneath her and the other dangling towards the floor like a teenager, her designer sandals lying lazily on the tile below. Daisy is nestled in her lap, cutting pieces of dough into triangles for the chocolate croissants we're making. So far I've remembered and replicated two of the dishes I learned from Vivienne as her apprentice.

After spending the entire afternoon with her, I've decided I'd follow her in just about any subject. Everything she does fascinates me; every gesture, every look, the way she holds herself. The best word I've come up with to describe her is statuesque, but I need to find a new one because that implies something made of stone. In contrast, she's so full of life, so warm and lovely I'd be perfectly content just to sit and bask in her glow.

It feels odd to be so enamored of Jason's mother when I haven't yet been able to warm up fully to him, but there are just so many things preventing us from moving forward. Things I can't see or touch but I know are there. Sometimes he looks at me, and I sense he's holding back, resenting me for not being Audrey, trying to read my thoughts to see if anything is coming back to me. He seems to be walking on eggshells, treating me like a guest in his home. Even if I remind myself that his intentions might be good, I still sense his uncertainty and it escalates my own.

Daisy holds up a mangled piece of dough. "Regardez ce que j'ai fait, Mamère." *Look what I made, my mother.*

"C'est marvellieux," Vivienne says. "It is marvelous, my sweet." She repeats everything she says to Daisy in English after she says it in French, which is probably how she taught her to speak fluently. It's probably how she taught Audrey as well.

"It's so sweet that she calls you 'my mother,'" I say. Apparently Daisy couldn't say grandmother in French and made up her own version of the word.

Daisy throws her dough to the dog, who gobbles it up and waits for more.

"But the poor thing will have a stomach ache, ma bichette," Vivienne says for the third time. She looks at me knowingly; Otis has devoured several chunks of dough already, and I realize that's my cue to say something as the mother.

"Daisy, please don't feed the dog any more dough. He'll get sick, silly. And then we'll need to take him to the doctor."

Daisy pushes out her lower lip. "Can Patel give him a look?"

I laugh. "No, I don't think so. But it may make Otis feel better to go outside and run around for a while in the grass."

"Is that what makes you feel better, Mommy?"

"Oui." I tickle her under the chin. "Just as soon as I get this thing off my leg." Though most of my injuries are healing, I'm still burdened by my bulky cast. I'm feeling better since I was ventilated at the hospital. Luckily, the process didn't take longer than a day, and now I'm back home under Dottie's careful observation.

Daisy runs out to the yard with Otis, and I'm selfishly happy to have my mother-in-law to myself.

"You are doing well," Vivienne says as she flattens the mounds of dough that Daisy handled.

I carefully lay the croissants on a cookie sheet. "I can't believe I remember how to make everything."

"No, my darling, I mean with Daisy."

"Oh," I say, feeling incredibly stupid for thinking she was talking about food. "Do you think so?" I've been trying to act as Audrey-like as I can for my daughter.

She smiles. "It is amazing the instinct that kicks in for us, is it not? Though you have no memory of being her mother, you are able to mother her well."

"Thank you. I just hope she sees me as her mother."

"I think she realizes you are a bit different after being in the hospital, but she understands it is because you were injured and are trying to get better."

"I hope so." I'm disappointed to hear that Daisy may notice I'm a bit different. I so badly want to ask Vivienne what she means by that—different as in not as good as the old Audrey, or different as in better?

Vivienne moves from her stool and floats across the floor to me. She holds my cheeks in her hands. "You are worrying for nothing, chérie. I did not mean to offend."

I hadn't realized I'd been so transparent. "Oh, I…"

"I know, my sweet daughter." She kisses each of my cheeks. "I know how your face falls when you are sad. I know you worry about what we are thinking of you at every moment."

"Was Audrey that way, too?" I ask.

"Sometimes." She breaks a corner from a cooling croissant and pops it into her mouth. "Mmm…perfection."

"You two were very close, weren't you?" I glance at my reflection on the oven door and push my hair over to the side to cover the patch that is now growing straight out in a lump. Standing next to Vivienne makes me feel like a toad.

118

"Yes we were, and we will be still," she says.

"But doesn't it bother you that I forgot who I am? That I forgot who your son is? That I lost all my memories?"

She returns to her stool. "Of course it bothers me. But what does that knowledge do for you? Having you know that I am bothered for my son and for you, does that help you to feel better?"

"I guess not. I just feel bad that any of this is happening."

"Of course you do, but it is not your fault. You did not ask for this."

I open my mouth to counter, but she holds up her hand.

"Even if you are going to tell me that you could have caused the accident or that you are responsible somehow for your condition, I will still say that you did not, with malice, intend to hurt anyone around you by hitting your head too hard. And that is all I need to know."

Part of me wonders if she's just saying these things because she wants to excuse Jason of something. "But then no one is ever accountable for anything," I say.

She tries to hide a smile. "I do not know if that is completely true. But I decided long ago that I can move in only one direction, and that is forward. I cannot go back and say, 'what if Audrey didn't get in the car that night,' or 'why did my son die at a baseball game,' because I will spend the rest of my days waiting for answers that will never come. I will miss the laughter of my granddaughter because I will be distracted thinking about the answers. I will miss the way my husband still looks at me, even though we have been married nearly as long as you have been alive," she says with a wink. "I will miss the smell of my favorite foods, the sight of the flowers in front of me, and then what do I have? Nothing at all. I can ruin my chances at making new memories if I am giving my attention to things that are over with.

119

"You want to be Jane because you do not remember Audrey? So that is fine for now if it gets you through the sadness of not remembering." She stands up and puts her hand on my chest. "But you have her heart; you have her spirit. I feel it when I look at you. I hear it in your voice.

"And look at the honor she has given you. You have been left in charge of her family. Perhaps you are here for a purpose. Have you ever thought of that? Perhaps Audrey called you in to help her in some way, to help one of us, to make some sort of difference that would not happen otherwise."

"Is that what you think? That Audrey couldn't handle her life and fled?" I ask.

"Not exactly. Let us not judge Audrey any more than we would judge you. I just think that maybe you can try to see your time with us as something that we can all grow and learn from instead of a curse set upon you."

I think about her words. I *have* felt cursed. "But how does someone just let it all go?"

Vivienne stares out at the yard. "When I was faced with my son's death, these ideas did not come to me so easily. I was tormented by grief and nearly driven mad with anger for a long, long time. But then one day my other son said to me, 'Maman, we have all died but only James was allowed up to Heaven.' And I realized that in his eyes I *was* dead. I needed to try to find a way to live, to not miss out on what was in front of me or deprive Jason of a life.

"And so I asked myself, 'Can I put this heavy thing down for a day? Just one day so I can show Jason how to live again?' And then I asked myself that same question the next day and the next. And then one day I asked myself if I could put it down for a week, and then two weeks, and then a month. And sooner or later I realized that I had not asked myself that question in a long time."

I blot my eyes on my apron. "Is that what I should do? Take one day at a time and enjoy whatever that day brings me?"

"Every day does not always bring joy, my daughter. I would be a fool to tell you that. There are many things to be noticed and experienced without searching for joy all the time. As for what you should do, it is not for me to say. I would very much like to see you learn to live again. To keep your heart open for others to enter it again. I think the answers you seek will come to you when you are ready for them."

I lean on the counter and take a deep breath to compose myself.

Vivienne folds her long arms around me. "Oh, chérie, I am sorry; I did not mean to make you cry."

"I feel so sad," I whisper. "Audrey was sad, I know she was. Daisy told me Audrey cried a lot. Is that why I feel sad? Because it's who I was? Or do I feel sad for myself, the person I am now? I don't even know."

Vivienne grasps my chin in her hand and stares into my eyes. "Audrey, *who I still believe is you*, was sad sometimes. Audrey forgot who she was once in a different way than you. Like many women, she started to lose herself in her life. When there were ups and downs, she did not remember who to call on for strength.

"I sat with her in this very kitchen and she cried into my lap, and I told her what I am going to tell you now. Who you are depends entirely on who you want to be. The grass is not greener anywhere but the place you decide to water it. We all get sad, we all cry, and we all pick ourselves up and move on. We are not men." She laughs and hugs me tight, guiding my head onto her shoulder. "But there is nothing, *nothing* that can take your strength away from you unless you let it. I know that Audrey was strong when she needed to be, and I would love to see how strong Jane can be if you let her."

What am I to say to this? I feel like an ant standing in front of a giant. She's so firm and wise and elegant in her beliefs. And all I want is to believe I can become what she is. "What would you do if you were me?" I ask.

"My dearest, you forget you are asking this question to a French woman. I would put on something lovely and lacy and make passionate love to the person who prayed to every saint he knows for..."

She looks at me, startled, and her eyes fill with tears. "Mon Dieu, I just thought of something beautiful. My boy prayed for his love to return to him, and it was *you* who came. Perhaps you should think about that."

~ ~ ~

"Audrey, it's me," Jason says, pinning me down by my shoulders.

Dottie holds a mask over my face. The air makes its way up my nose and down into my throat and lungs. I look around the room, trying to remember where I am. Trying to see if the floor is covered in blood.

"Jane, it's OK. You're home and I'm here," Jason says. He's slept on the sofa bed next to me for the last two nights, and each time I've woken up screaming and fighting. "This is getting ridiculous," he says to Dottie. "Get Patel out here in the morning."

She nods and looks at me with concern. "You OK, honey?"

I nod my head under the mask.

Jason sticks his tongue in his lower lip to show me a cut. "You got me good. Classic right hook."

"I'm sorry." I slide the mask from my face and hand it to him. "I don't need this anymore."

Jason looks down at me, and for a moment our eyes meet. He reaches out to touch my cheek, then pulls his hand back and turns his head. We're back in our dance of not knowing who to be or how to act. As long as I'm a patient, he knows what to do with me. Otherwise, we're strangers bound together by a daughter and a history that only one of us understands.

"We're looking good, Dottie," he says. "Why don't you go back to bed? Daisy will probably be getting you up early."

"You're gonna be OK, sweet thing," Dottie says as she walks towards her room. I imagine she's overjoyed that he's here with me now instead of Thomas.

Jason sits on the side of my bed. "Was it the dream with the blood on the floor?"

I nod. "But it wasn't a tile floor anymore; it was a wooden floor, like a deck. What do you think that means?"

He shakes his head. "I don't know."

"I feel like Audrey's trying to tell me something."

"It's probably post-traumatic stress from the accident. You lost a ton of blood."

"In a bathroom? On a wooden deck?"

Jason runs his tongue over his fat lip. "Who knows what the unconscious mind holds on to. God, now I sound like Patel." He gets up and reclaims his spot on the sofa. "Think you'll be able to go back to sleep?"

"No." I roll over to my side and stuff my body pillow under me to support my leg. Part of me wants him to stay in my bed like Thomas did, but another part keeps me from asking. With Thomas, things are easy; he's a trusted friend. But if I ask Jason to come into bed with me, it will set a precedent for future nights. It will imply I'm ready to act like a wife. I sigh in frustration, forgetting he's next to me.

"What is it?" he asks through the darkness.

"Headache," I say, because I can't tell the truth.

"You're still nursing one hell of a concussion."

"Startling diagnosis. I guess that's why they pay you the big bucks."

123

"Was that a joke?" His voice lifts slightly in amusement.

"I think they call it sarcasm."

"Huh."

I turn towards him. "What's huh?"

"Nothing. You're kind of funny, that's all."

"Am I not supposed to be funny? Was Au—" I stop myself; we promised not to do that to one another. We're trying to get to know each other as we are now so I don't always think he's looking for Audrey and he doesn't always wonder if I'm pretending to be her.

We lie in the darkness listening to each other breathe, and I decide he must be thinking the same thing I am. He has to be wondering how we're ever going to make this work. What becomes of two people when everything that bound them together has been washed away?

"Can you tell me a story, Jason?" Once I've said it, I can't imagine what prompted me to ask.

"What kind of story?"

"I don't know. Tell me a story from your life. Tell me how you met Audrey."

"OK …since I'm not going to be getting much sleep anyway." He stands up, walks over to the bar, and opens the fridge. "Want anything?"

"No," I say, covering my eyes. "God that light is blinding. You better watch out going through the dark now."

He grabs a soda off the shelf and makes his way back to the couch, stubbing his toe on the coffee table. "Damn it!" he says as he doubles over.

I have no idea why it's so funny, but I can't stop myself from laughing.

"Shit, that hurt. Why do women always think it's so funny when a man hurts himself?"

I have to push my face into the pillow to stifle my laughter. "Because it is. And keep going when you can."

124

For a moment he sits quietly rubbing his foot. "Well...Audrey was living in Georgia at the time, one of the places her grandmother moved her to. I was in college and it was spring break. She was on a church retreat with a bunch of teenagers she volunteered with, and I was with my parents as they were taking a break from my dad's campaign. We stopped for gas at this hole-in-the-wall mini-mart and the church bus was broken down in the parking lot. Audrey was talking with the driver as he looked under the bus, and I could see she was really upset."

"You noticed all this while you were getting gas?"

"Well, they were hard not to notice. There were teenagers running in and out of the mini-mart to buy junk food and sodas. There was a giant tow truck next to the bus, and the two drivers were arguing. And then there was Audrey, in a little sundress and sweater, with her hair up in a ponytail. She offered the tow guy all of her money, but he refused because he couldn't pull a bus with his truck. I heard them say they were going to have to call for another bus, but they didn't have enough money to rent one, and nobody from their church was picking up the phone. My father and I went over to see if we could help. Dad offered to pay for the new bus, but Audrey wouldn't even consider taking his money.

"I talked to her about what kind of a church it was, where they were going, and pretty much anything I could to extend our conversation. My father later told me that he could see I was a total goner, and he decided to step in before I made a complete fool of myself. He introduced himself to the driver; they talked a little about politics, and Dad convinced him to let us pay for the bus if they'd agree to take me along on the church retreat. He told them I was a lowly college kid who needed a little religion and that he and my mother would pick me up in three days on their way back home."

"Your parents let you drive away with a bus full of strangers?" I ask.

"It was a church group led by a young girl who looked like an angel fallen from the sky; it hardly seemed a threat to my safety. And I was twenty-one years old, for God's sake. My father was trying to help me meet people. That was hard for me. After my brother died, I kept to myself, spent a lot of time with my parents. They wanted me to get out and experience life. Until that point, I'd always resisted."

"So what made you go?"

"Well...Audrey in that sundress was a pretty convincing argument for getting out and living a little."

I laugh. "So that was it? You just hopped on the bus?"

"My father's driver arranged for another bus to pick us up and I climbed aboard, the last minute chaperone of the Sugar Creek Baptist Church weekend revival. The kids sang the entire way. For hours. I never knew there were so many Bible songs. I sat behind Audrey and tried to talk to her, but she was too distracted with the kids. One was crying because her boyfriend was talking to another girl, another was upset because she'd lost her sunglasses. Eventually, I gave up and went to sit in the back with a bunch of boys who'd apparently only gone on the trip to be with the girls. We were all in the same boat, hanging on until we got the chance to sit with the girl we had our eye on. Audrey was the chaperone, so I didn't have any competition there.

"Anyway, when we got to our destination, a little lakeside camp, I stayed in one of the boys' cabins and she stayed with the girls. There were chaperones that worked at the campsite and activities for the kids to do all day. Swimming, boating, fishing. It took Audrey a while to warm up to me. She was painfully shy, and I was just some random guy who hitched a ride on their bus from the middle of nowhere; I could have been a serial killer."

"Right. Because most serial killers travel with their famous parents during college break," I say.

"Well, that's the thing...she didn't know who my family was. Her grandmother didn't follow politics and never watched the news. They didn't even own a TV. That's how I knew she liked me for me."

"Did that happen a lot? People liking you because of your parents?"

"Yeah, of course. It's still a problem. There are sycophants everywhere. And people who want to cause trouble for us. It's hard to know who's genuine."

"I know the feeling."

"But Audrey was real." Jason continues with his story, oblivious to my implication that I can't tell if he's genuine or not. "And I finally got her to talk to me. I'm pretty sure it was my macramé skills that did it," he says with a laugh. "We took a canoe out one day and talked the entire time. That night, she sat next to me during the bonfire and we roasted marshmallows. She let me walk her back to her cabin, and when I kissed her, all the girls were cheering in the window. It was pretty awesome."

I have to admit, it's a good story. He's a different person when he's talking about something precious to him; he sounds alive, animated.

"And then you just parted ways?" I ask.

"God, no. I was hooked," he says. "I was ready to forget medical school and stay on that church bus with her forever. But my parents were waiting in the parking lot of the mini-mart, and I left with them. My mother, the romantic that she is, decided we should take an extra day or two in Georgia, and we followed the bus back to where it came from. After Audrey handed the last of her campers off to their parents, we took her out to dinner so they could get to know her. My mother knew right away that you were the one."

For the first time ever, I don't correct him that it's Audrey he's talking about.

"My parents and I stayed in a hotel and took Audrey and her grandmother out for lunch the next day. Her grandmother was unimpressed by who my father was, and it was so refreshing to him. Eventually, we had to go home, but Audrey and I kept up a long distance relationship for over a year. Once I went to Chapel Hill, she moved there to be near me, and the rest is history."

"That's a sweet story." Sweet. Everything about Audrey sounds sweet. Too sweet; saccharin, almost. "Is it true?" I ask.

"What? Why would I make that up?"

"Because you can," I say into the darkness. My eyelids are getting heavy.

"Well it's up to you at this point whether you want to believe me or not."

"That's what your mother said."

"Then you should listen to her," he says with a yawn.

"So when did Audrey date Wyatt?"

"She and I took a break once. I was too busy in my residency and dropped the ball. We weren't spending much time together, and in the little spare time I had, I was hanging out with other resident doctors—some of whom were women. We needed to see what we wanted, and that's when she dated him. I wasn't too happy about it, so I decided to win her back."

"But you met him? He and Audrey remained friends?"

"Yeah. If exchanging yearly Christmas cards counts as friendship. It bothered me for a while, but now that we're married, I'm OK with it," he says.

There's something tugging at me ever so slightly, a pull just below the surface that keeps me from wholeheartedly embracing this life with Jason. I wish there were a way to either figure out what it is or shake it free.

"Thanks for sharing your story with me," I whisper, but by the sound of his breathing, I can tell he's asleep.

I close my eyes. I can picture all of it; his parents, the bus driver, the scene by the lake. I can almost smell the wood from the cabins and hear the crackling fire as they roast marshmallows. I drift off to sleep imagining Audrey and Jason holding hands, walking back from the dock where they tied their canoe, and I wake up shaking when I realize the dock is covered in blood.

~15~

"Are you ready?" Dr. Patel runs the blade along the length of my cast. "It's going to look a bit odd for a while."

"Just get it off. I can't wait anymore." I kick my feet like Daisy does when she's waiting for her dessert. The thought of spending any more time in that contraption is torturous to me, especially because we're in the midst of a late July heat wave.

"You're still going to have to take it easy." He cracks the plaster open and peels a piece back. The skin underneath is pale and covered in hair.

"Ew!" I say, hiding it with my hands.

"Audrey, please. I am a doctor."

I pull my dress down to my knee. "It's disgusting."

"Do you mind?" He looks up at me, holding the scissors carefully. "I have to get to it to remove it." The giant glasses he's wearing make his eyes look three times larger. He cuts another long section and lifts up the plaster.

The smell hits me hard. "Oh my God, it stinks!" I lean towards him to pull the mask he has around his neck up over his nose.

He swats my hand away. "Lie back, Audrey. I think you got some water in here, maybe from one of your showers." He takes out another tool to slice through the section around my knee, pulling and tugging small sections at a time. "Straighten out, please."

Dottie marches in with a basin of water and some towels. Every inch of my leg that's pulled from the cast gets covered in a warm washcloth. "Ahh, that's so much better," I say, relaxing into the bed.

"Some pressure here." Dr. Patel holds my foot as he cuts through the bulk on my ankle. It feels like I'm being smashed with a hammer.

Dottie smiles. "Almost there. You're gonna need a suntan, Mrs. Gilbert." No matter how many times I ask, she won't stop calling me that. Probably because I don't answer to Audrey, and she thinks I'm "batshit crazy" for wanting to be called Jane.

Dr. Patel mumbles to himself on the floor, and with one final tug, I'm free from my bondage. I pull myself up using the bars on the bed and stare down at my leg. Dr. Patel was severely underestimating the appearance when he said it may look odd for a while. It isn't odd, it's absolutely grotesque. The leg looks small and withered compared to my other one, and the skin is a sickly, grey color. A long, barely healed wound runs down my thigh, wider in some places than others, and involves stitches or staples of some kind. The skin surrounding the wound is purple and puckered. An odor from the cast hangs in the air, and for a moment, the bed appears to sway in front of me.

"I'm going to be sick," I say, just in time for Dottie to grab the basin of water and hold it under me before I throw up.

She rubs my back. "It's OK, honey."

When I think I'm done, I give her the thumbs up, only to see my leg from under the basin. I grab the basin and heave again.

"Gilbert said she has a weak constitution," Dr. Patel says. He places a sheet across the bars on either side of my bed to cover me while he examines my leg. His hands feel cold and foreign on my skin.

Jason comes in through the sliding glass door. "How's it going in here?"

Dr. Patel answers without looking up. "The incision is healing, but it needs more time. It will need to be cleaned out three times a day." He throws a giant piece of orange stained gauze into the bucket.

"What was that?" I swallow to keep myself from gagging.

Dottie pats my hand. "The antiseptic pads under your cast to stop infection. It's lookin' good, honey, real good."

"We couldn't have been looking at the same thing then," I say as a sharp pain rips through my thigh. I pound the bed with my fist.

Jason clamps both of my hands in one of his and uses the other to lift the sheet and peer under it.

"What are your thoughts, Gilbert?" Dr. Patel asks wearily, as if he's expecting them anyway.

"Atrophy. And we need to watch for infection. Dottie, make a note to call the plastic surgeon and the physical therapist. See if they can come out together. I want a temporary removable cast for now. And up the meds to reduce the swelling."

"Yes, Dr. Gilbert."

"She can have ginger ale but no medication until she can keep food down. Keep this covered during the day, and let it air out at night. I'll bring down a few long dresses and skirts so she won't have to look at it. She needs to be supervised in the shower in case she gets dizzy or tries to put too much weight on it. And no shaving for a few days."

"What?" I say. "You've got to be kidding me."

"You need to let the skin heal," he says.

I open my mouth to argue, but Daisy bounds down the stairs with Vivienne following close behind. As she runs towards my bed, Jason quickly throws the sheet back over my leg and motions for Dottie to take the basins out of the room.

"Is it off yet?" Daisy peers over the railing to take a look. "Can you go in the sprinkler now?"

Her little voice soothes my soul. I reach out and push one of her thick curls out of her eyes. "Not yet. But I can still watch you go in, and we can play our new game."

Jason leans down so he's nose to nose with her. "You girls have a new game? How does it go? Can I play?" He's so animated when Daisy's around he seems like a cartoon character.

She hops from one foot to the other. "Yes! I run to the sprinkler and right before I get there Mommy says, 'favooorrrite.'" She draws the word out really slowly.

"Favorite?"

"Yep. Then she says something like 'movies', and I have to yell the answer when I jump through the water."

He nods his head. "I get it...I think."

I reach out and tousle her hair. "I get to hear all her favorite things. We're running out of categories, though." Because of the game I invented, I already know her favorite foods, colors, books, holidays, and friends.

Jason bows his head and whispers so Daisy can't hear him. "Brilliant."

Vivienne places her hand on my shoulder. "How is she healing, Dr. Patel?"

"Very well. She will need physical therapy of course, and Jason would like to consult a plastic surgeon about the scarring. But it will all be as good as new in time."

"Wonderful news. And when you're ready, Daisy and I have set out lunch for everyone on the patio," she says.

Jason hoists me from the bed and hands me a pair of crutches. I'm disgusted by the sight of my leg and can't imagine it ever looking normal again. My legs are like Audrey and me. One is shriveled and broken, the other is just fine. And yet the bad leg has to do all the work to get better while the fine one gets to do nothing. Seems unfair to me.

"So when is Thomas coming back?" I ask.

"In a few days. He's been really busy at the hospital," Jason says.

I wonder if he's staying away on purpose. If asking him to stay with me at night was too bold. All I know is that I miss him and want to see him again.

I place the crutches under my arms and hobble outside. Jason puts his hand on the center of my back and guides me to the garden patio. It feels strange to be without my cast, but the bandages Dr. Patel applied to my leg feel sturdy and supportive. Another small taste of freedom.

Vivienne claps her hands together as I navigate past her. "Audrey needs a celebratory gift for being such a good sport."

Jason pulls a chair out and helps me into it. "What did you have in mind, Maman?" he asks.

Vivienne smiles at me. "What would you like, Audrey? Would you like for Jason to take you away someplace? Edmund and I can watch Daisy for the weekend."

Dr. Patel clears his throat. "It would be better if she could wait to travel."

"Well something pretty then. Jason, you must pamper our girl. She has been through so much." Vivienne gets up from her seat and takes my hands. "Would you love some new flowers for your garden, chérie?"

"Maman, you know her," Jason says. "If I buy her flowers, she'll be out there kneeling in the dirt. I'll take her anywhere and buy her anything as soon as she's healed up."

Vivienne's eyes widen. "Oh! I have a lovely idea. It will be a surprise. I have the perfect gift for you, darling. Just give me a few days to prepare."

"I'd love a nice long bath. That would be a great present," I say. And even better if I happen to forget my doctor's orders and shave my legs while I'm in there.

Jason smiles at me. "That we can manage. I don't even want to know what my mother has in mind for her surprise. If we give her too long to plan, we'll have Cirque de Soleil in the backyard." He leans over and puts his arm on Dottie's shoulder. "Can you handle her in the bath?"

I don't even bother to wonder why he's requesting her help. We've come to a place where we don't need to pretend we're comfortable with one another anymore.

After dinner, Jason helps me up the stairs. It takes me so long to go one step at a time that when I reach the second floor, he gets impatient and throws me over his shoulder to carry me the rest of the way.

"I put fresh flowers in the bathroom for you," he says as he tries to catch his breath. "Holy crap, I'm getting out of shape. It's been a while since I worked out."

He guides me into the bedroom, which is as elegant and gigantic as I imagined it would be. It has more of a masculine feel than the other rooms, and its dark mahogany walls and thick wooden trim look original to the home. In the center of the room is a huge four-poster bed draped in billowy white linen. A suede chaise flanks the end of the unmade bed, and a copy of Time magazine lies open next to a man's robe. Piles of white throw pillows litter the floor beneath the large front windows. Across from the bed is a large fireplace with a stone mantle. The mahogany wall above it has been opened up to reveal a large TV.

Jason points to archways that bookend each side of the fireplace, explaining that one leads to his study and the other to Audrey's dressing area. "And over here is the bathroom," he says, walking me past the bed to a door. "I gave Dottie instructions on where everything is. She's in your closet getting your robe."

As if on cue, Dottie strolls into the room whistling. Jason hurries out, wishing me a relaxing time.

Dottie grips one of the heavy posters at the corner of the bed. "This is some bedroom. I could get used to this."

I start to take off my clothes. "I wonder if I could."

"You'd have to be crazy not to." She struts into the bathroom to fill the tub. "Oh, sweet Jesus," she says with a gasp.

"Is it that good? I can't wait to see. What is it about us girls and our bathrooms?" I take the ponytail out of my hair and slip my robe on. "Even with amnesia I know how important a girl's bathroom is. Are you stunned to silence, Dottie?" I ask as I limp through the door.

She's frozen, staring straight ahead.

"Dottie, you look like you've seen a ghost."

I suddenly realize what's wrong. Large, white ceramic tiles stretch out beneath my feet, covering the floor and most of the walls. Directly above me, a flower-shaped stained glass skylight illuminates the room. A daisy. Giant, yellow petals surrounded by mosaics of reds and oranges against a deep blue background. In the center of the room, raised up on a higher level, looms a vintage clawfoot bathtub. I can almost hear the screaming from my dream, and I'm afraid to look down for fear of seeing a pool of blood.

Dottie grabs my arm. "Is this what I think it is?" She's probably got the scene memorized, she's heard about it so many times.

"Yes." I nod in case I haven't actually gotten the word out. "This is my nightmare."

~16~

"I think you should go in," Dottie says as she tries to pull me off Jason's bed.

I cling to the headboard and refuse to move. "I'm not going in there."

"The man planned a nice treat for you. He brought flowers in there. You're gonna go back down and tell him you decided not to take the bath you've been beggin' for?"

"Doesn't this seem a little strange to you? That I dreamt of that room without ever seeing it?"

"No. Of course you remember that bathroom. You lived here. I don't think it's all that weird now that I've had some time to think about it logically."

"Oh, right. Logically," I say. "You mean after you ran from the room with every hair on the back of your neck standing straight up."

She puts her hands on her hips. "Look at you, a grown woman hangin' on to a bed, afraid to go in the tub. I may as well be tryin' to bathe a golden retriever."

"You know I've been terrorized for weeks about that very room."

"It's all part of that collective subconscious of yours. I've been readin' up on memories. I got a whole stack of books so I can understand you. Your brain is tryin' to let go of little pieces of memories, and they can get stuck to other little pieces that are floatin' 'round in there. You obviously remember that bathroom, but you also remember all the blood from your accident."

I push my face into the pillow, wanting to scream. It smells just like Jason, and for some reason that stops me.

"Ok, let's assume you're right," I say, sitting up straight as I realize the advantage being handed to me, "and my mind is letting little chunks of memories just float around and stick to other memories."

Dottie eyes me suspiciously. "Mm hmm."

"Then in order to sort things out, I'd need to investigate these chunks so I can toss them aside and find new ones, right?"

"Why do I feel like I'm gonna be makin' prank phone calls again?"

"No more phone calls. I'm saying we should explore the memories as they float through and then dismiss them if we think they're junk."

"Maybe. Is that gonna get you in that tub any faster? If not, I might as well get in."

"I'll get in." I stand up slowly trying to keep the weight off my leg. "But you're staying with me."

She smiles. "I'll stay if you promise to relax and enjoy yourself."

Moments later I'm submerged in bubbles. The bathroom doesn't seem so nightmarish now. Light filters through the stained glass above me, projecting a kaleidoscope of shapes and colors onto the water and my skin.

"Promise me you'll take a bath later, Dottie. You need to experience this decadence," I say.

She sits on Audrey's vanity stool. "I'll take a bath in my own house. Dr. Gilbert doesn't need some nurse floatin' in his tub."

I peer over my shoulder at her. "You aren't *some nurse*; you're our friend." I'd assumed she felt the same way. She's really the only friend I have other than Thomas. But then again, she's being paid. "I hope at some point you'll feel like we're friends."

"I already do, honey," she says. "I'm just gonna get some fresh air in the bedroom. It's so steamy in here I can barely breathe."

I lay my head back on the cushion and melt into the soothing water. It really is a spectacular bathroom. Jason and Audrey each have a massive vanity area on opposite sides of the room flanking a huge shower built for two. Beside each vanity is a door labeled *Toilette*, a separate one for him and her. Everywhere I look, plants fill large containers, even at the ceiling where trails of ivy spill from their hanging baskets and creep down the walls to the floor. The entire place feels like an oasis. I stick my toe into the antique faucet and wonder how many generations of women in Jason's family have sat in here soaking their cares away.

Without warning, a scene begins to unfold before my eyes. Audrey bathes a baby, but I'm her. I know I am; I feel I am. A small inflatable tub full of water sits inside the one I'm in now. Daisy slaps the bubbles and giggles until her belly shakes. Her amusement fills me so completely, I can't help but laugh too.

Do it again, sweetie, I hear myself say.

Daisy slaps the water and sends it splashing over the side. The echoes of her laughter hang in the air so tangibly I want to reach out and collect them as treasures. But just as quickly as it came, the vision slips away.

"No!" I frantically grasp for them, but they dissolve into the air with the rising steam. For one brief moment I felt something real, only to have it stolen before I could make it my own. I grieve the memory as if a piece of me has been taken away.

Dottie crouches next to me and pulls me into her arms. "What is it, honey?"

"I saw something." I know I won't be able to explain how I feel without sounding like a lunatic.

"The nightmare again?"

"No. Something lovely," I say though tears. "I want it back."

"What?"

I punch the water. "I don't know. I saw Audrey bathing Daisy and laughing. They were so content, and I felt like it was me. I felt... happy."

Dottie claps her hands excitedly. "Oh! You had a memory! Maybe things are comin' back to you now."

"I don't know," I say.

I want that feeling back so badly, even if it means becoming her again. I just need to find a way how.

"Damn you, Audrey," I whisper. "You could have at least given me a little more."

"Dr. Gilbert! She's remembered something!" Dottie calls down to Jason and prances around excitedly, proudly sharing the news as if I'd given birth to the memory and she's the grandmother.

I slowly make my way down the stairs. Jason stands up from the couch and rubs his palms on his shorts.

"What do you mean?" he asks.

Dottie claps again. "A memory! In the bathtub! Should we call Dr. Patel?"

"A memory of what?" He comes to the landing and watches me navigate the steps one by one. It's impossible to tell if he's happy or not. With all the nightmares lately and the difficulty we've had getting to know one another, I'm not surprised. He's probably braced for anything.

I try to catch my breath from maneuvering the stairs. "I think it was a memory of you and me bathing Daisy."

Jason stuffs his hands in his pockets and exhales heavily as if he's relieved. "Oh."

"Oh?" I say. I'm surprised he isn't happier about me remembering a piece of our life together.

"Yeah...Oh. I thought maybe it was another nightmare." He runs his hands through his hair and looks over his shoulder into the kitchen where Daisy is coloring and singing to herself. "Listen, Jane, something's happened. There's been a bus accident on the freeway. The driver went off the road and flipped the bus. It caused a ten-car pileup and there are a lot of people hurt...fifty-seven on the bus alone. I have to go to the hospital to see how many they bring in for surgery. I could be there for a few days. Can we talk about this when I get back?"

I realize now his tone may have had nothing to do with me. "Of course," I whisper.

He kisses me on the cheek and heads towards the door.

"And good luck," I say awkwardly. "I hope you can help a lot of people." I don't know what Audrey would say when sending him off like this, if she would have any eloquent words of motivation to offer as he goes into this kind of battle. As his car screeches out of the driveway, I realize there's a whole other world that waits for him outside of our house. One I'm not at all a part of. I've monopolized his time and energy for too long. A patient living in his home.

I find Dottie a few inches from the TV, watching the coverage of the accident as though she'd like to crawl through the screen and set up triage.

"You should go," I say. "They'll need all the help they can get."

"But what about you? Dr. Gilbert won't like—"

"I'll call Vivienne. I can get around a bit on my own now, and I need to start doing more for myself anyway. Please go, Dottie."

She pauses, pretending to think about it. "If you're sure…"

"I'm sure." As soon as I say it, I realize that this is my chance to spend time with Daisy without anyone watching over us. I make the decision to call Vivienne only if I must.

"So it's just you and me?" Daisy asks excitedly, bouncing on her stool in the kitchen.

"Yup. Total girl time."

"What are we going to do?"

"Whatever you want. I'll make dinner and then maybe we can watch a movie together."

"Daddy said you can't watch TV because you whacked your noodle."

I can't help but laugh. "My noodle will be just fine as long as you know how to work the TV."

I heat her usual fish sticks and serve them on her favorite plate, a dolphin shaped plastic dish with a little compartment in the tail for her ketchup and separate spots for her carrots and apples. "I thought people were supposed to eat fish sticks with tartar sauce," I say teasingly as she licks ketchup off her fingers.

"Tartar sauce looks like chunky bird poop," she says with a stone serious face and then laughs so abruptly I'm afraid she's going to choke. She points to her mouth and giggles. "Did you hear what I just said? Bird poop!"

"Can I assume that Daddy taught you that?"

"Uncle Thomas. He talks about poop a lot." She smiles. Her mouth is missing three teeth now. She puts her hand up in the air dramatically and rolls her eyes like a sixteen-year-old. "Sooooo much. Seriously."

I want to scoop her up and kiss her face but I manage to contain it. "Yeah, boys are gross. So what movie would you like to watch?"

142

She shrugs. "You can pick. You haven't picked in a while."

While Daisy washes her hands and face from dinner, I sit in front of the wooden armoire and go through their movies. "How about *The Parent Trap*?"

"Is there kissing in that movie?"

I look over the back of the box. "I don't know, maybe. Maybe this mommy and daddy kiss," I say pointing to the pictures of the actors.

"You and Daddy don't kiss, do you?"

I don't know how to answer. "Do you want us to?"

"No."

"Why not?"

She pretends to lock her lips and throw away the key.

"OK," I say with a sigh, allowing her to keep her secret. "Couch or floor?"

"We can put all the pillows on the floor and put a blanket down and pretend it's a movie picnic," she says, already starting to remove couch cushions bigger than she is.

"Are we supposed—" I stop myself, realizing I sound like someone who has no idea what she's doing. "Sounds like fun."

We watch the movie surrounded by cushions, which works out for me because I'm able to rest against the couch and keep my leg elevated on the pillows. It takes a long time to get through the entire thing because she pauses to go to the bathroom every ten minutes. I paint her nails while we watch, and she somehow talks me into painting Otis's nails, too, though it's hard to keep him still while they dry.

Towards the end of the movie, Daisy turns to me. "Is that how you did it?"

"Did what?"

She tilts her head. "Do you have a twin sister like the girl in the movie? So you could switch places with my other mom?"

"What?" I say much louder than I intend, and struggle to sit straight up without falling over.

She bites her lip like she's trying not to cry.

I open my arms to her. "I'm so sorry I yelled. Come here. I was just surprised, that's all. I'm really interested in what you're thinking about."

She looks up at me with wide eyes. "My Audrey-mom got in a bad accident. And then you came here, but you aren't the same as her." She stops and scratches her nose. "I mean you look the same as her, kinda, but you aren't the same as her inside."

"Because I don't do things as well as she does?"

"No, you're just different."

There's nobody here to tell me what to do or say. I could lie to her, but that doesn't seem to be working as well as we thought. "Wait…is this why you don't want me to kiss your daddy? Because you think I'm not your same mom?"

She nods her head.

"First, I love you just as much as your Audrey-mom did. And I really am just the same as her. It's just that when I whacked my noodle, some of the thoughts in my brain got a little mixed-up and that made me forget a few things."

"Like where our dishes go and where we buy the strawberry milk. I know, Daddy told me."

"No, more than that. Like how to be exactly like myself. I kind of forgot how to be me, the Audrey me. So I seem a little different. Do you understand?"

She nods. "I think so."

"I'm not another person or a twin sister. See this birthmark?" I pull my shirt up and show her the jellybean-shaped patch on my side. "Your Audrey-mom had this too, right?"

She nods again.

"So you know I'm the same person. It's just that the bump on the head makes me act funny."

144

"You are funny," she says shyly. "She was really sad. You aren't sad."

"I remember you told me that. Do you know why she was so sad? Everybody has bad days once in a while."

She shrugs. "I don't know."

"Lots of people get sad. Some people get sad, some people get lonely, some people get angry. That's just the way things are sometimes."

She widens her eyes. "I know. Daddy used to get *really* angry. But not anymore."

"He did?"

"Uh-huh. Like this." Squeezing her face into a scowl, she balls up her fists and holds her breath until she turns red. The look in her eyes makes my blood run cold.

"What was he so angry about?" I ask.

"I don't know. But he said if we didn't have a mommy anymore we'd be OK. It would be me and him and Mamère and Monpère and Thomas and Otis and we would all love each other so much."

"Oh. He probably said that to you because your mommy got really hurt in an accident and he didn't know if she was going to be OK."

"No. Daddy didn't say that to me after Mommy had an accident. He said it to me before. He said to me the day the ice cream truck came. Then the next day I went to Mamère's house for the night and that's when Mommy crashed her car."

My stomach drops at hearing this. Audrey was sad, Jason was furious, judging by the demonstration Daisy gave of his anger, *and* he was talking to her about not having a mother before the accident. But I can't interrogate a five-year-old about the night her mother nearly died in a car accident. She's just a little kid—there's no way I can put too much faith in what she says. "Will you still love me like your Audrey-mom until I remember everything again?" I ask, hugging her.

"Of course, silly." Her muffled voice squeaks out from where she's smothered in my bathrobe. If only it could be as simple to talk to adults as it is to talk to children.

I let Daisy sleep in the living room since I can't navigate the stairs alone. I lie on the couch and hold her like Thomas held me during my nightmares. Every so often her little leg jumps in her sleep and she mumbles or purses her lips. I love her so much I could lie here forever and watch her sleep. Nuzzling my face into hers, breathing in the smell of her hair and skin, I close my eyes and drift off.

Soon I'm back in the bathroom, watching the blood spread across the floor. I wake up sweating and breathless, but I'm somehow able to keep myself from screaming out and scaring Daisy. I peel myself out from under her and head to the kitchen.

I flip open the laptop computer and go right to Amazon. I access Dottie's account, remembering that she uses her cousin's name for her passwords.

"Thank you, Charlotte Baker," I whisper and type *Luminol* in the search box. I check the expedited delivery option before placing my order. If all goes well, the box will arrive tomorrow afternoon. I'm tired of waiting for answers to come to me. It's time to seek them out.

~17~

"What on Earth?" Dottie carries the Amazon box into the kitchen, having beaten me to the door when the bell rang. I'd expected her to be at the hospital for at least another day helping out with the bus disaster, but she was sitting in the kitchen when I woke up the next morning. Now she stands before me with a confused expression, holding the box like it's a bomb. "Who'd know to send me a delivery to your address?"

"Oh, yeah. Well, I ordered something and couldn't remember my account information so I sort of...used yours."

I grab one of the checkbooks Jason keeps in the kitchen drawer and write the amount for twice what I paid, scribbling Audrey Gilbert on the bottom line like a perfect forger. I hold out the check and smile at her cautiously. "This should cover the cost and the trouble."

She puts a hand on her hip. "What trouble? The trouble of me goin' to the door or the trouble I'm gonna get in for whatever's in this box."

"I can explain."

She grabs a letter opener to slice the top open. "I'm listening."

I lunge for the box. "Dottie, let me—"

147

"It's my mail, isn't it?" She yanks the top open. "What in the name of mercy! Luminol? Are you crazy? Honey, you must've watched too much CSI. What're you gonna do? Sprinkle this all over the bathroom and see if the whole place glows blue from the blood you keep dreamin' about?"

"Yes, actually that's exactly what I'm going to do. Thank you for explaining it so well." I grab the supplies and line them up on the counter. Rubber gloves, safety goggles, spray bottles and containers of Luminol. All I need to add is peroxide, which we have plenty of down in the solarium, thanks to my injury.

"You know, when I took this job I thought I'd be nursing somebody tryin' to recover from an accident. Not be the accomplice to a paranoid lunatic tryin' to squeeze a mystery out of something simple," Dottie says.

She's trying to make herself look angry, I can tell. She has to because she's employed by Jason's family. Otherwise she might actually be enjoying this.

I point a finger at her. "How's this for simple? I dream about a strange bathroom and see it fill with blood every night. Then it turns out it's *my* bathroom. My daughter tells me that not only did Audrey cry every day, but that Jason was angry a lot. Furious, if you could have seen the face she made imitating him. And he apparently told her *before* my accident that if they no longer had a mommy, things would be OK."

"You mean you sent me outta here last night so you could get information from a baby?" She grabs the box and tosses all my purchases back inside.

I look away from her. "Well, no. It just happened to come up. I didn't *try* to get her to talk. We were having fun together." I realize it sounds terrible.

"So your motives are good, but Dr. Gilbert's aren't? Do you hear what you're saying? I'm sure he has his reasons for everything, too."

148

"Well, I'm not hearing any explanations from him. Or from anyone else for that matter. I'll tell you what," I say as persuasively as I can. "If you let me do this—this one stupid CSI project—and it looks like I have nothing to worry about, then I'll drop it. I'll even let him call me Audrey again."

Dottie pauses to consider it. I can only hope the soap opera fan in her is intrigued.

"This house is as old as dirt," she says. "You know how many people could've bled in that bathroom up there?"

"The blood needs to be recent within the last few years to make the chemical glow. The more blood and the more recent it is, the brighter the glow."

"And what kind of weirdo is selling this stuff online anyway?" she asks.

"I read that it's used for kids' forensic science fair projects. Also, realtors use it sometimes before they sell a house."

Dottie purses her lips. "Mm hmm. You *read* all of this?"

"Surprise!" I say, realizing I've just confessed to doing something else I'm not supposed to. "No convulsions! I think my head is healed."

"I think your head is screwed on backwards, that's what I think. You have to be the worst behaved patient I've ever had, and honey, that's sayin' a lot."

"Really?" I try not to let my disappointment show. I'd always assumed that Dottie truly cares for me and she just likes to talk tough. But there are times like this when I'm not so sure.

"Oh, I'm just kidding. You don't follow directions too well, but I like you. You're a good egg, I can tell. Just a little too mischievous for your own good." She shrugs. "Fun, though."

I give her my giant doe-eyed Audrey look. "So fun that you think you'll help me?"

149

"Fine. But remember your promise. When it turns out to be nothing, you're gonna forget all about this nonsense."

"Gotcha."

"And when I say turns out to be nothing, I mean we aren't goin' crazy over a little spot of blood left by somebody cuttin' their leg shaving."

I salute her. "No going crazy. Got it."

Dottie folds her arms in front of her chest. "And how the heck did you even sign in to my Amazon account?"

"I've heard you say your email address a hundred times for one reason or another. And when we called the hospital in Davenport, you told me you use Charlotte Baker as your password for everything."

"Is there one dang thing you don't pick up on like Sherlock freakin' Holmes?"

"It's amazing the things your mind can do when it isn't full of anything else."

Dottie clicks her tongue at me. "You scare me, lady."

"I scare myself. You can't imagine the things I've considered."

We wave goodbye to Daisy. Lucky for me, her weekly sleepover with her grandparents happens to be the night I need for our project. As soon as the car is out of sight, I lay out the supplies in the kitchen and anxiously wait for the sun go down so the bathroom skylight won't hinder our progress. The room needs to be completely dark.

I open the spray bottles. "We have to mix the chemicals and use them quickly. Once the solution reacts, it'll only glow blue for thirty seconds before it fades."

"You mean *if* it reacts," Dottie says.

"Right. Of course."

"Wait a second," Dottie says slowly. "It says here on the bottle that other things can cause the blue glow. Copper, horseradish—"

"Well then, let's hope no one was bathing themselves in horseradish," I say with a smirk.

"And bleach. How about that one?"

"I read that. And I already looked in the housekeeper's closet. No bleach, only products that contain it. If the Luminol reacts to a cleanser that contains bleach, the glow will be evenly distributed throughout the bathroom on faucets, toilets and counters, and it won't be as bright. But if someone poured straight bleach onto the floor, to clean up blood maybe, then it would be concentrated in one area."

I mix the Luminol solution with the peroxide and swirl it around in the container. Then I pour the solution into the spray bottle and hand it to her. "Let's get to work."

I hadn't accounted for how long it takes me to get up the stairs. By the time I get to the top, I'm completely winded and stop to catch my breath. Sweat drips down the side of my face.

Dottie narrows an eye at me. "I better see this same effort from you when your physical therapist gets here next week."

We continue to the bathroom and start at the front of the tub. We work side by side, walking backwards towards the door so we don't step on the chemicals. I spray the solution as evenly as I can, following the directions about proper coverage.

"Ready?" I ask.

She rolls her eyes. "Ready. And try not to sound so excited."

I slam the door and flip the light switch.

"Sweet Jesus," Dottie whispers.

Neon blue illuminates the room, glowing from a large puddle that runs parallel to the entire length of the tub. Stretching out from that, a vibrant stripe about eight inches wide travels towards the door, smudged in spots with what looks like the imprint of a shoe. I hobble quickly to the vanity and spray the sink, the faucet, and the floor in front of the

151

shower in case Dottie tries to use the bleach argument. Nothing. I spray in front of the toilets. Nothing. By then, the illumination from the tub to the door is vanishing.

"Did you see that?" I whisper to Dottie in the dark.

"I'm about to pee my pants I'm so scared," she says softly.

I turn the light on and look at her. "Now do you understand how I feel?"

"Uh-huh. I get you now," she says.

The sight of the Luminol jolts us into action, and we race to work in the bedroom. "See if you can find anything," I whisper, even though we're the only people in the house.

Dottie searches the inside the TV cabinet over the mantle, and I look through the nightstand drawers on either side of the bed. When I enter Audrey's dressing room, I nearly choke. "Oh my God, look at all these shoes!" I say as I peek behind tidy rows of hanging clothes, sections of formal dresses, small shoe cubbies that go on forever, shelves of bags and scarves. "I can't wait to try this stuff on."

Dottie turns to look at me in the mirror disapprovingly. "Are we lookin' for clues or playin' dress up here?"

I move to the vanity in the center of the room, a large antique dressing table with bottles of perfume and cosmetics set out on top and little drawers lining each side of the lower half. I quickly open the drawers and rifle through. Toiletries, small cosmetic bags, a sewing kit. Loose photographs and birthday cards from when Daisy was a baby. Stationery, hair ties, bobby pins. I pull a long drawer from its spot in the center of the vanity and there it is, sitting on top of a pile of papers.

"Bingo. She kept a journal." I sit on the vanity stool and flip through the pages.

We went to the store today. You're practicing talking to strangers. I asked you to choose somebody who you thought looked kind.

You walked up to him and said, "Excuse me sir, my name is Daisy Gilbert, and I'm named for my great-grandmother who was a French flower." It was the cutest thing ever. We ate ice cream and discussed how you felt talking to someone you don't know. I hope when you get older you'll be able to judge for yourself who is worth your attention and who is not. For now I can only teach you to be confident in yourself and not afraid of the world.

"Letters to Daisy," I say with a sigh. One after another after another. Little notations about what they did together or memories Audrey wanted to save. She documented the things Daisy said.

March 13th, 4 years old
You still say valinna instead of vanilla, and we don't correct you because it's so cute.

I want these memories for myself, but I don't have the time to keep reading. Jason could be home at any moment if he gets a break from the patients in the bus accident, or he could end up sleeping at the hospital for days—I really have no idea. I push the drawer back in, planning to come back to it later.

"There has to be another one here. If she kept a journal for her daughter, she probably kept one for herself."

Dottie shakes her head. "This feels wrong."

I point to Jason's dresser. "Go through those drawers."

"Uh-uh. No way."

"Fine. Look under the bed then. I can't get down that far anyway." I open Jason's dresser drawers and feel around inside under the clothes. I find a few postcards and a bag of golf tees, and I imagine him taking them from his pocket at night and carelessly tossing them in.

Dottie hurries over to the bed. "Oh, I can't believe I'm doin' this. I'm in a doctor's house. This is just askin' to get fired now." She lowers herself to the floor carefully, her face growing red as she balances on her stomach and reaches under the bed. "I have *got* to get into shape," she says with a groan. "Got somethin'."

When she finally gets back up, she places a rectangular hat box in the middle of the bed. We stare at it for a moment and then look at one another. Before she can come up with a reason for me not to, I snatch the lid from the top and toss it aside.

"Jackpot!" I say. This could be exactly what I've needed. Inside the box are at least a dozen journals. I flip through the first one in the stack, noticing right away there are sections missing. Audrey wrote a lot; the pages left intact are filled completely, front and back. I set the journal down and take another and find the same thing. Every so often a page has been torn from each one. I look up to see if Dottie is as confused as I am.

She puts her hands on her hips. "Now why would she be rippin' pages out of her own diaries?"

"Maybe she wasn't the one who did it. Maybe Jason doesn't want me to find something."

"Then wouldn't he just burn them? Why keep them at all?"

"I don't know. His memories are in here, too. Maybe he wants to save them."

"But he could've just hidden them someplace," she says. "Why would he rip the pages out and then put the diaries under the bed where anyone could find them?"

"I'm not supposed to be up here yet, remember?" I flip through the pages of the journals. Audrey wrote about lunches with Vivienne, how grateful she is for her life, her husband, and her daughter. She wrote positive affirmations about letting go of negativity and living in the present. I feel voyeuristic reading it. "I don't understand. What could be in the missing pages? We need to keep looking."

Dottie gets up off the bed. "You know, there could be a perfectly good explanation for all this. Don't you think we oughta give him a chance before we go pokin' through their things tryin' to find proof of somethin' that we don't even know happened?"

I slam one of the journals down on the bedside table, startling her. "There's evidence in there that someone bled. A lot. And did you see those trail marks? It looked like someone was dragged through the bathroom. Jason had already told Daisy that they'd be OK without a mommy in their house before Audrey's accident. What if—"

She shakes her head. "Don't say it."

"What if he couldn't divorce her because of his family or the publicity and he tried to murder her and make it look like a car accident?"

"That's crazy. I was in the hospital that day, you know. When they flew you in. I'm tellin' you that man was completely out of his mind. Do you know it took Dr. Charles and three other doctors to physically restrain him while they were revivin' you after surgery?"

I stop what I'm doing. "I was revived after surgery?"

Dottie puts a hand to her mouth and averts her eyes. "Well, see this is part of that 'lettin' you recall things in time' idea. They'll tell you all of it when you're good and healed and ready."

"So I really did die. Huh." I take a moment to see if this revelation brings up any emotion in me, but it doesn't.

"Can we at least agree that something here is very suspicious?" I say.

She cuts her eyes towards the box of journals. "Mm hmm. Yeah, somethin' here is suspicious. But you can't go guessin' and fillin' in the blanks because that'll just cause more trouble. You need to wait and see."

"Wait and see if I'm really married to an attempted murderer?"

155

"That seems a little far-fetched. The man saves lives for a livin'."

"I think we need to look for more evidence." I drop the box of journals to the floor and slide it under the bed with my crutch.

Dottie follows me into the study, though I'm sure it's only because she's afraid to be left alone with the memory of the bathroom. We each survey the room and wait for the other to start, reluctant to touch anything. Beneath the back window, Jason's large wooden desk is piled high with papers. A mahogany armoire covers the opposite wall, its open doors revealing an inside cabinet stuffed with yearbooks, old pictures, and binders full of baseball cards.

I slide open a closet door and find long, wooden shelves holding massive jars of loose change, file folders full of papers, collections of old movie posters, sports memorabilia, and several boxes stacked on top of one another marked *Jason-childhood, Jason-high school, Jason-college*.

Dottie hesitates in the corner, spinning a giant globe held up from the floor by an antique wooden frame. "This boy is a pack rat. You're not gonna find anything in here."

"But where's all her stuff?"

"Did you see her dressing room? She's got tons of stuff in there. There must be a pair of shoes for every day of her life," she says.

"I mean from her childhood. Yearbooks, mementos. Just by looking at his armoire, I know where he went to college, where he went to medical school. There's a box of his treasures from middle school. Pictures of him and James. Where's Audrey's history?"

Dottie shrugs. "She probably didn't keep things like that clutterin' up her dressing area. It doesn't go with the room."

"Exactly! She must have kept her stuff somewhere else. The storage unit off the solarium?"

Dottie waves me off. "You need to be goin' through all of that stuff with Dr. Gilbert. I don't feel right about this anymore. We need to just wait and see about all that bathroom nonsense."

"Dottie, come on…"

"I mean it. I don't know about all of this; it makes me nervous."

"Fine. I don't know what I'm looking for anyway." I don't even know what I'm doing or what I want to do, not that I'm going to tell her that.

I fall into Jason's big leather chair and stare at his workspace. I pick up a framed picture of him and Audrey embracing under a trellis of flowers. His arms are wrapped tightly around her waist, dipping her backwards as he kisses the side of her neck. She's laughing, carefree and playful. I feel such love when I look at it, so much that I need to look away. I slam it back to the desk harder than I intend, and it comes apart in my hand.

"Don't break anything." Dottie looks nervously over her shoulder to the door.

As I slide the back of the frame into place, I notice a ripped-off note taped to the back of the photo.

I owe you my life. Xo, your Audrey.

Dottie reads it over my shoulder. "Was she his patient?"

"No, they met on a church retreat."

"Maybe she meant it metaphorically," she says.

"I don't know; I'm so tired of this. I'm sick of trying to live up to perfect little Audrey and everyone's memories of her."

Tears burn my eyes. I want to look through the storage spaces to see what I can find about her, but at the same time, I don't. I don't want to know everything she was that I'm not. I don't want to see how in love they were, knowing that I can't feel that for him and he doesn't feel it for me.

I limp out to the hallway and start down the stairs. "I need to get out of here," I say, turning to look at Dottie over my shoulder. My foot misses the step in front of me, and I try to grab for the railing but bang my mouth on it instead and tumble down to the landing below. I land face down on the bottom step, not wanting to get up ever again. I scream in pain and frustration, raging against the body I'm trapped in. I want to scream until my voice goes out. I want to punch something. I want to know why that happy girl in the picture did this to me.

Dottie hurries down behind me and helps me sit up. "Oh, Lord. We gotta get you downstairs, Mrs. Gilbert; this wasn't a good idea."

There's blood trickling down my thigh, and a thumping numbness spreads around my knee. The pain is making me sick to my stomach, and I cry into her shoulder. "I'm so sorry for dragging you into this."

Dottie sits behind me and positions my body between her knees, helping me go down each step on my bottom, keeping my leg straight out in front of me balanced on one of her own. Once we're in the solarium, she drags me to the bed and elevates my leg beneath a stack of pillows.

"I'm the one who should be sorry," she says, shaking her head. "I have a job to do, which is takin' care of you. But instead I'm paradin' 'round here like we're two girls at a slumber party." She secures the sheet over the rails of my bed to block my view of her examination. "Damn, lost a stitch. Looks like you twisted your knee, too."

I bury my face into the pillow and hear a wheeze in my chest. "I don't know how much longer I can take this."

"Well, you gotta take it a little longer. And you better stay put in this bed. I'm callin' the hospital."

Moments later she returns wearing an uncomfortable smile. I imagine she's hoping to erect a proper boundary between us now that she needs to reclaim her role as my husband's employee. I'm sure she'd like to forget the fact that we just ransacked his private office together.

"Dr. Gilbert's in surgery," she says. "He's gonna be backed up there for a while. Dr. Charles is on his way over. Said he can take a day or two and then go back as he's needed."

I lie in bed crying, furious at myself for trying to take matters into my own hands and frustrated with the body that won't let me. My knee is throbbing and feels like it has swollen up a few sizes.

"Dottie?" I say weakly, watching her break up an ice pack for my knee.

"Mm hmm?"

"Maybe you should get all of that Luminol out of the kitchen before Thomas gets here."

Her feet barely touch the stairs on her way up.

~18~

"What are we gonna do with you?" Thomas asks as he straightens my leg and then gently bends it back. The pain is excruciating.

"Poor thing," Dottie says, smoothing my hair. "It's just a setback, that's all."

"The stitches she lost are no big deal," he says, cleaning the blood from my wound. He looks at me, puzzled. "Can I ask why you weren't wearing your temporary cast?"

I wipe away my tears. "It was a stupid mistake, I guess."

He carefully bandages my thigh in layers of gauze. "Well it's a pretty good sprain, but we won't have to amputate. I'm going to wrap the knee, too, to keep the swelling down."

He hands a small packet to Dottie. "I brought a few muscle relaxers so we'll need to cut back on one of the pain meds tonight. Audrey isn't comfortable with the effects of narcotics, so I'll be staying with her."

She hurries over to the bar and returns with a tray of ginger ale and crackers for me to take with the pills.

Thomas turns to me. "So, what the heck were you doing all the way upstairs?"

"I was exploring. It *is* my house."

He listens to my lungs with his stethoscope. "But aren't you supposed to be staying off the leg for now?"

"I took a bath. Jason said I could practice using the stairs."

"Yeah, with help," he says angrily. "What'd you do, drug our good nurse here and go exploring while she was out cold?"

"She was taking a shower and I was bored," I say. When he looks away, I wink at Dottie to let her know I won't say anything about our misadventures that might incriminate her.

"And you couldn't have waited?" he says, clearly annoyed.

"Because if I'd waited, you'd still be at the hospital? You didn't have to come here, Thomas. And for the record, I'm in too much pain to do anything else, so you don't have to stay and babysit."

"Calm down," he says, his tone softening. "I didn't say that. I'm glad to see you. It's been a few days."

It's been much more than a few days, and he knows it.

Behind us, Dottie clears her throat. "Can I help with anything else, Dr. Charles?"

"No, that's all for now. Jason said to give you the night off." Thomas takes a bill from his wallet and hands it to her. "Treat yourself to dinner and a movie."

"Thank you, Doctor, but—"

"You deserve a break," he says. "It won't be long before this patient of yours gets more energy and tries to walk the roofline or something. Might as well relax when you can."

"You ain't kiddin'." Dottie laughs and turns to me. "Try to get some rest, Mrs. Gilbert. And no more explorin'."

Once she's gone, I look at Thomas. "Did Jason really tell you to send her away for the night?"

"No." He walks over to the bar and surveys the selection of beer in the fridge.

I grab my compact to check my reflection, and it's as bad as I expected. I quickly smooth my hair down. "How are things at the hospital?"

"Total chaos, just the way we like it." He flops down on the couch and takes a long sip of his beer. "But tragic as hell. A lot of casualties. Jason's dad came around to shake hands and console the families. Tough week to be a doctor."

"Tough week to have been on a bus trip."

He looks at me and smiles. "Now there's the old Audrey I know and love. Not going to let me take myself too seriously, are you? Can't complain without you reminding me it's even worse in someone else's shoes."

"How bad was it?"

"There were some kids. That's the thing I hate to see the most. Minivan full of kids coming home from an amusement park and they get trapped in a highway pileup. The mother is still in surgery with Jason. She's gonna wake up and find out that two of her children…" He sighs and rubs his hand across his stubbly beard.

My stomach tightens. Here I am feeling sorry for myself, and my husband is trying to save the life of a woman who doesn't even know yet that part of her life has ended.

"Sorry," Thomas says. "I know how much you hate to hear these stories." He goes to the fridge and returns with two more beers. He holds one up and tilts it towards me as if we're toasting something. "Gotta take the edge off somehow." He quickly drains the bottle and opens the second one.

"You drink a lot."

He shrugs and sits down my bed. "Sometimes I have to. So how are *you* doing?"

I can't tell him I've just been snooping through my house only to find a bathroom ripped straight from my own nightmares and personal journals with pages missing. "I wish *I* could take the edge off, too, I guess."

"Care to be specific?"

"Well...Daisy told me that Audrey used to cry a lot and that Jason was very angry with her before the accident."

Thomas groans and hangs his head. "Damn, Audrey. You can't get your information from a five-year-old."

"But is it true? Was Audrey sad a lot?"

He looks at me disapprovingly. "That's not a fair question."

"Why?"

"Because it isn't my marriage."

I fold my arms across my chest. "Come on, Thomas."

"Alright. You were sad a lot. You had some things to be sad about last year. Talk to Jason." He looks at his watch and points to the little cup of muscle relaxers by my bed. "Gotta take one soon. And eat something—you're a known puker."

I reluctantly take them with a mouthful of ginger ale and eat one of the crackers.

"You're going to feel kind of funky," he says with a grin. "I'm just warning you."

"Good. I could use a little funky at this point. Do you want to talk about what happened at the hospital tonight?"

He pauses for a moment. "I had to be the one to tell the dad. It's always frickin' me who has to do it. And I can never make it through without losing my shit."

I reach for his hand. "The dad from the minivan?"

"Yeah. I had to tell him that he lost two of his kids and that his wife is having a cardiac massage to save her life."

"I'm so sorry, Thomas." I open my arms for him.

Thomas folds his arms around my waist. "How can someone ever be OK again after that?"

"I don't know. I can't imagine how you deal with that every day."

"You have to see it as a job. But sometimes it hits too close to home. Nothing was as bad as the night they brought *you* in." He tightens his grip on me.

I listen to his breathing and feel his chest rising and falling against mine as I run my hand through the back of his hair. My leg doesn't hurt at all anymore. In fact, nothing hurts. I feel light and warm, like somebody pumped me full of helium. Like I could float away.

"Thomas," I whisper, giggling into his chest. "I think I understand what you mean about feeling funky now. And I know it's a terrible time to point this out, because I want to hear about your awful day, but I do feel very fuzzy."

He pulls me away and looks at my face, trying not to laugh. "Fuzzy?"

"I said finky." I grab hold of my tongue to keep it still. It feels like it's sizzling. "Funky," I say, closing one of my eyes to try to focus on him.

"Oh my God, you lightweight." Thomas stands up and hands me the stack of crackers. "Please tell me you ate something today."

"Nope." I try to put a cracker to my mouth but miss and poke myself in the cheek instead. "May I ask you a question?"

"Shoot."

"Do you know what Looominal is?"

"Luminol? You mean the stuff they use at crime scenes?"

I nod and put a finger to the tip of my nose.

"What about it?" he asks.

"I bought it. On Dottie's Amazon account. Isn't that terrible? I figured out her password and went online and bought a whole kit." I stretch my arms out to show him how much I bought, like a fisherman exaggerating a giant catch. I can't stop giggling.

Thomas looks at the little cup next to my bed. "Aw hell. You took all three of them?"

I nod. "You said—"

"I said to take one, Audrey. One. The others were for later." He smiles and puts his head in his hands. "No wonder you're acting like such a crackpot."

The way he says crackpot makes me laugh so hard I spit a mouthful of dry crackers all over the front of his shirt.

He smirks at me. "Charming, Audrey. Really."

"Can't you please, *please* just call me Jane?"

"No."

I push his arm in protest. "Why not?"

"I'll tell you some other time."

"Fine. Be that way." I put my finger to my chin. "What were we saying?"

"Luminol."

"Oh, yes. I bought it. And I sprayed it all over that great big bathroom up there. You know the one with the stained glass daisy? That's the bathroom from my dream, you know." I realize I'm babbling but I can't stop myself. "You know the nightmare I have and I wake up screaming? I know you know because you came and stayed with me after that and it was so nice." I grab his hand and hold it to my cheek. "I'd like to do that again, I think."

"You covered the bathroom in Luminol? But that stuff has to be mixed and—"

"One part Luminol to two parts peroxide." I smile and pat his cheek. "Don't look at me like that. I had safety goggles and rubber gloves and everything."

He sits back and stares at me. "Let me get this straight. You were mixing chemicals with a deflated lung, reading how to mix them with a serious concussion, and charging the package to the nurse who was here to care for you?"

I bend over laughing. "I think I may be a bit of a badass, Thomas."

"Holy shit," he says under his breath. "But why? Because you saw blood in a dream?" His face becomes serious and he takes hold of my wrists. "Audrey, whatever you saw, you need to know—"

"It was everywhere." I widen my eyes. "I think he tried to do her in. Maybe he smashed her over the head and put her in her car and pushed it over a hill. Maybe that's way you couldn't find him to tell him she'd been flown in. Because he was cleaning up the crime scene."

Thomas rubs his temples. "You didn't."

"Didn't what?"

"You threw chemicals around your bathroom because you think Jason tried to kill you?"

"Wouldn't you?"

"No. I'd ask someone before making that leap." He finishes his beer and returns to the fridge to get another.

My entire body feels light and tingly, and I love it. Nothing hurts or bothers me, and I don't care about the words that come out of my mouth. "You drink waaaaay too much."

"Yeah, I know. You tell me all the time." Thomas sits on the bed and cups my face in his hands. "Listen to me, ding-a-ling. You've got this very, very wrong. There's nothing you can say to get me to believe that Jason tried to kill you. You're his whole life, you gotta believe me. He's one of the good guys."

"What about you?"

"You mean am I one of the good guys?"

"No. I mean how do *you* feel about me? Because I'm not buying the 'just friends' thing."

"I don't think this conversation is a good idea," he says softly.

"Can I just see something?" I move my face close to his. "I just want to figure it out for myself," I whisper, my lips an inch from his.

He holds his breath and doesn't move at first. "Wait—"

I stop him by covering his mouth with mine and kissing him softly. His beard tickles my chin. I part my lips and put them to his again, feeling him respond. He grasps the back of my neck as we kiss, sending a charge to my very core.

He groans and pulls away. "Jesus, Audrey. I can't do this."

I slowly open my eyes. "I'm sorry. I shouldn't have done that if you didn't want me to." Truthfully, I'm not the least bit sorry.

"Not wanting you to isn't why I can't do that."

"What does that even mean?"

Thomas hesitates. "You're my best friend's wife, Audrey."

"I'm not her," I whisper. "Don't you see it? Don't you feel that I'm different from her?"

"Of course I do. I saw it the first minute I spent with you in the hospital. And that's why I can't call you Jane or any other name you invent for yourself. I have to remind myself that somewhere in there is Audrey, wife of the man I consider my brother. Audrey, my friend. For you this is a fleeting nothing, but for me this would be tragic."

I entwine my fingers with his and try to stop my eyes from drooping. "A fleeting nothing?"

"You have amnesia; you don't remember who you are. You don't remember that Jason Gilbert is the absolute love of your life and that your sun rises and sets to his existence. You don't remember that I'm just a friend to you."

"Just a friend to *her*."

"For you this is all new. You're trying to figure things out for yourself, but believe me when I tell you you're jumping to all the wrong conclusions. You think Jason is the bad guy, and I'm the one you want to be with." He laughs to himself. "But the only reason you're attracted to me is because you have a severe head injury."

"No. It had to be here before."

He shakes his head. "Jason's the good guy. He's the one you belong with. I'm not the kind of guy a girl can just kiss if she's feeling romantic and fuzzy or whatever. That's *Jason*. I'm not the kind of guy who's going to stop at kissing. I'm the one who's going to carry her into the nearest bedroom and then move on to someone else. I'm what they call a player.

"You used to try to help me figure it all out. You said you could see what was holding me back even though I couldn't see it myself. And I think I finally understand what you meant because now I feel the same way about you. I can see the big picture and you can't," he says.

I lie back on my pillows. "Is this supposed to make sense to me?"

Thomas gets up and begins to pace. "It used to drive you crazy that I'd sleep with a different woman every night and never call her again. You wanted me to settle down and marry. But the point is, you saw what it was about and I didn't. That's how I feel about you now. I see your blind spot, Audrey. It's Jason. Believe me, he's the one for you."

"Why do you sleep with a different woman every night?"

He laughs as though it should be obvious. "Because I can."

I roll my eyes in disgust and grab another cracker. "I mean why did Audrey think you were doing it?"

"I was a foster child. I bounced around to any families who'd have me for a year or two each until I went to college. I saw a lot of bad marriages. According to you, I was never able to feel secure anywhere. You said that's why I love 'em and leave 'em—because it would be too painful for me to latch on to anyone. You recognized what I was doing with those women before I did."

I sit straight up in my bed. "So that's the thing with you guys. I get it now."

"What's the thing?"

"They're your substitute family. You play house with Audrey and act like you have a wife when you want one. You plant things and spend time together, but you still get to sleep with all sorts of women. You get to experience intimacy without any fear because it isn't your family to lose. It's Jason's."

Thomas spins around and looks at me. "Holy shit."

"But that's the past; that's Audrey. I'm not her, and Jason doesn't love me anyway." I point my finger at him and turn it around in the air. "Also, just so you know, you say 'holy shit' a lot."

He scratches the side of his face. "Let me tell you something about Jason. When we were in medical school, women would hear his name and practically undress on the spot, but he never used it to his advantage. If I were a Gilbert, I would've been out there meeting every woman I could. But Jason would never exploit his family name. By the time I met him, he was already so in love with you he couldn't even look at another girl, so when we'd go out, I'd get the girls that collected around him and take them home. I got to exploit the Gilbert name, and I had no problem with it. I'm not the kind of guy for someone like you. *He* is."

"So what I think I'm hearing," I say very slowly, trying not to slur my words, "is that you were in love with Audrey."

"No. When did I say that?"

"Well maybe you didn't even realize it. The point is you would never want the girl you love to be with 'a player', right? Because she deserved better than that. But the thing you loved most about her is gone now, isn't it?"

"What thing?"

"The part of her that was unobtainable. For a commitment-phobe, she was the perfect girl."

Thomas grabs one of Jason's mini basketballs and squeezes it in his hands while he walks. "Son of a bitch." He turns to take a shot and sinks the ball into the hoop over the bar.

"Are you OK?" I close one eye to steady myself, feeling like I could pass out at any moment.

Thomas sits on my bed again and pulls me close, his strong hand on the back of my head. We hold on to each other without saying anything.

"Audrey would never have been able to say it like that," he whispers finally. "Thanks for doing it. Somebody needed to."

"What do you mean?"

He pulls away and exhales heavily, as if he's just put down a thousand pound weight. "I can't continue like this. I'll be a grown man with no family of my own living half a life. Playing house. I've been trying to decide what to do about San Diego…"

"You're a grown man already. And what do you mean San Diego?"

"Before your accident, I was offered a ten-month fellowship at a hospital in California. I was thinking of every reason not to go, but none of them are really *my* reasons."

My eyes cloud with tears. "You're going to leave? What if you love it and don't come back?"

Thomas puts his hand on my cheek. "Now you sound like your old self. Always scared of 'what ifs'. You were right before—you're a bit of a badass now. So give it to me straight. Should I stay?"

The trust in his eyes tells me he'll do whatever I want, but I say what I know is right. "I want you to stay, but you should do what's best for *you*. Go find a life for yourself and bring it back here."

He wipes tears off my face. "You're not so bad, Jane. I think I could get used to you."

My throat closes as I try to swallow back the astringent taste of rejection. Another first for me in this new life.

Thomas puts his hand on mine. "I forgot who I was once, you know, but in a different kind of way. I was struggling with who I wanted to be. Back in medical school, I got an earring and started introducing myself as Tomás. I started sleeping around. I mean *dozens* of different women. And sometimes multiple—"

I cover his mouth with my hand. "Gross."

He pushes me away and continues. "I was worried I was hiding repressed homosexual tendencies or something. I drank way too much, and my grades started slipping. One night Jason took me out to a bar and got me drunk. Walking home, he leaned in like he was going to kiss me. I totally freaked out. I was completely disgusted."

I laugh. "Was he really going to kiss you?"

"No, he just wanted to see what I would do."

"But what if you kissed him back?" I snuggle into my bed. "And by the way, I really love these pills."

He rolls his eyes and continues. "Well that's the thing about Jason. He knew me so well, if I were gay he would've known it first, and he never would've done that."

"Just because you don't want to kiss your best friend doesn't mean you aren't gay."

"It was a good test and it worked. Leave it at that. Anyway, then he punched me in the face and ripped out my earring." Thomas leans in and points to the scar. "He told me to get my shit together because he wasn't going to go into private practice with some wannabe pirate gigolo."

"And then?"

"And then I was better."

I can barely control my laughter. "How's that supposed to help me?" I ask when I can breathe again. "Unless you think punching me in the face would solve my problems."

"Of course not. I'm saying I was cured. I mean I still slept around, but I didn't overthink it."

"So as long as someone doesn't overthink something it isn't really a problem?" I ask.

"Oh, no, I'm not getting pulled into one of these discussions. But I will say that letting your mind run wild and playing crime scene detective isn't going to help you, either. *Luminol*," he says, shaking his head. "God, you're a trip."

"You should've seen the place. It lit up like fireworks in there," I say sleepily. "How can you be so sure I'm wrong about the blood?"

"You're not wrong about the blood. You're wrong about Jason. But he needs to be the one to tell you why." He plants a kiss on my forehead before standing up. "Goodnight, my loopy friend. Enjoy your drugs."

"Thomas," I say, as the room spins, "remember in the hospital when I asked why you're so nice to me and you said Audrey always asked you that? What was the response you'd give her?" Although my eyes are beginning to close, I see him smile, and I try to hold on long enough to hear his answer.

"I'd always say, 'Why wouldn't I be?'"

~19~

"Jane." Jason gently nudges my arm. "Are you awake?"

"I am now." I try to sit up in bed, shielding my eyes from the blazing afternoon sun that shines through the sliding glass doors. "What time is it? I think somebody drugged me last night."

He gives a half smile. "You took two extra muscle relaxers."

"I had a dream that Thomas wore an earring and called himself Tomás."

Jason grasps my hand and pulls me up. "He really did that once, so you didn't dream it. Heard you had quite a night." He looks over the wound on my leg and frowns. Without saying a word, he walks over to the window and looks out over the yard, shaking his head slightly as if part of a conversation I can't hear.

"What did Thomas tell you?" I ask bluntly. If I wait for Jason to initiate a discussion, I'll live the rest of my life like this.

He keeps his back to me. "That I'm not doing a very good job of showing you who I am. And that keeping certain things from you is contributing to the problem."

"Sounds about right."

Jason turns around. "Did he tell you he accepted a fellowship in San Diego? I know that's going to be hard for you for a while, but maybe—"

"Hard for me?"

"I know you have some confusing feelings, and I can't blame you for being attached to him. He and Audrey were very close. I'm beginning to wonder if she felt as strongly for him as you do."

"I don't have feelings for him." As I say it, I realize that it's the truth. "It was just easier for me to get to know him because the only responsibility I have to him is that of a friend."

A relieved expression crosses Jason's face. He smiles slightly and sits down again. "Luminol, huh?"

I put my head in my hands. "Oh God. Please know that anything I said or did last night was the result of some weird pills."

"I would have found that box of crap in the garage, even if you didn't confess. It's not like you hid it well," he says. So Dottie left it out for him to find. I should have expected that. Well played.

He shakes his head. "The thing that upsets me is you believing I'd hurt you."

"How would I know any better? You haven't exactly made things easy for me to understand," I say.

"I'm walking a hell of a tightrope here. There's a lot for you to digest, and it's hard to know what to tell you and when. Plus, I'm trying to keep you healing, keep Daisy in the dark, *and* keep hoping that the woman who forgot she's my wife will look at me the same way she looks at my best friend." He throws a basketball into the hoop above the bar. "And on top of all that, I'm harvesting a heart out of a kid who was killed on the highway for a sixty-five-year-old transplant patient. So, sorry if I seem like a prick."

174

"What can I say? I was having horrible nightmares. Somebody could have explained their origin to me before I discovered that the scene of the nightmare was my own bathroom."

"I didn't realize it was our bathroom in the dream. I suspected it might have been, but it's not like you gave me details. I didn't know that someone with amnesia could dream about events from their life that they don't remember when they're awake. I was trying to buy some time until I knew for sure that was happening to you."

I roll my eyes. "I hate that you'll only tell me things once we get to the point where you're certain I have most of it, and you only need to fill in the rest."

"I'd rather not dredge up horrible memories if I don't have to," he says.

"Well you *don't* have to. Apparently my subconscious is doing that for you. What you should be doing is explaining things to me to keep me from being terrified."

Jason sighs heavily. "C'mon. Follow me."

He leads me to the stairs and follows me up to make sure I don't fall. When we get to the second floor landing, I lean on my crutches to rest before going up the next flight.

"No, Jane, we're stopping here," he says.

He guides me down a corridor past Daisy's room and playroom to a closed door. He feels around the top of the trim and finds a key, then slides it into the lock and holds open the door for me. It's a nursery. Bright white beadboard wraps around the bottom half of the room under a thick white chair rail. The top half is painted light blue. A large rocking chair occupies a lonely corner. The crib has been taken apart and is leaning against a wall; a matching changing table stands across from it with only a white blanket folded on top embroidered with the name "James" in blue stitching.

"Was this your brother's nursery when your parents lived here?" As soon as I say it, I remember that his parents never lived here.

Jason swallows hard. "No. This would have been the nursery for our son. Your nightmares were about the night you were hemorrhaging after delivering him stillborn. We lost the baby in October. At full term."

"I'm sorry for you," I whisper. "I'm so sorry." There's nothing more I can think to say. There are no feelings attached to the memory for me.

"It happened to you, too," he says.

"Did you ever find out what caused it?"

"We don't know. Audrey wouldn't allow an autopsy. One day she went in for a checkup, and there wasn't a heartbeat anymore. Her doctors had to induce labor so she could deliver him. He was so beautiful; we were going to name him James. That's probably the worst thing I've ever been through since my brother died. Until your accident, of course." Jason wipes tears from his face. "Audrey didn't take it well—not that anyone would. A few days later, I found her in the bathroom screaming. She was hemorrhaging, just like you described in your dream. I grabbed her from behind and dragged her out. She was completely detached from what was going on; she didn't even know the blood was hers. I had to call 911 and get her back to the hospital."

I link my arm with his and rest my head on his shoulder. "How horrible, Jason. Was that when the problems started for you two?"

"Yeah, pretty much. Audrey experienced bad postpartum depression with Daisy, too. But it went beyond that after we lost James. She became a shell of a person and blamed herself. She was a zombie."

"Why?"

"It's complicated. It's just how she was." He shakes his head. "God, I'm talking about her like she's completely gone now. Sometimes I can't believe how much I've lost."

"I'm sorry I've been so much trouble, Jason. I really am."

176

"She wouldn't let me change anything. I kept telling myself I'd give her another month and then take it all down, but this was the only thing she had left of him. I wish I'd done it sooner. Maybe if I did, she would've been able to move past it."

"Have you moved past it?"

"No, but I have work to keep me busy. Audrey was here in the house with Daisy and the memories. She couldn't go forward anymore."

I run my hand along the crib rail. Blue teddy bears stare at me from their perch on a shelf as I pick up the soft white blanket and hold it to my cheek, trying to conjure a memory. "I can't remember anything."

"You know what? For once I'm glad. I don't want you to remember this." He guides me out of the nursery and locks the door behind him. "I keep it locked so Daisy doesn't go in here. It was hard for her to understand. Since the accident, I've been coming in here at night and taking things apart when she's asleep."

"I can't imagine how hard that must have been. I'm sorry for suspecting you. I'm sorry for your loss." The list of things I'm sorry for seems never ending. How could I have gotten things so wrong? All I've done for this man from the moment I regained consciousness is cause him pain. It occurred to me while we were in the nursery that Jason and Daisy would have been better off if I'd stayed in the hospital to recuperate instead of coming home. They could have gotten used to being without me, and we could have decided what to do once I was healed. I want to ask him about the journals with the missing pages and the things that Daisy said to me, but I feel I've already put him through enough.

"I feel horrible," I say.

"Don't. No more feeling bad, OK? There's been enough of that around here lately. But does this tell you what you need to know?'

I force myself to smile. "Not everything, but it's a start."

"I have to go back to the hospital in a while, and I'll be away for another day or two. My mother planned a surprise for you while I'm gone. And once your leg heals, Daisy and I would like to bring you to her favorite Mexican restaurant. Maybe we can try to be a family again for her."

"Sounds fun," I say. It would be so much easier if he told me what he wanted for himself rather than always making it about our child.

"Maybe we can find a way to meet in the middle here, Jane. I'm not expecting you to jump in where Audrey left. I know you don't know me well enough to feel safe with me. But maybe we can learn to be friends."

If I were his friend, I'd probably hug him after what he just shared with me, but I'm left not knowing what to do.

Jason slowly guides me down the steps to the kitchen where his mother and Daisy are sitting at the counter doing a puzzle. Vivienne looks at her son with palpable sadness on her face. Her eyes dart between Jason and me.

"Maman," he says, kissing her on the cheek. "I need to go back to the hospital for another two days. I hope you'll be able to keep her from getting into any more trouble."

"Of course I will." She pulls him into an embrace. "Ne désespère," she whispers in his ear. *Don't despair.*

Jason scoops Daisy up from her kitchen stool and turns her upside down, causing her to shriek and laugh. "Be good to Mommy while I'm gone." He sits her back on the stool and tells her a secret behind his hand.

"Can I do it too?" she asks.

"Ask Mamère," he says. He crosses the room and puts his hand on my back, helping me into the hallway. He leans towards me and hesitates before reaching out to tuck a piece of my hair behind my ear. "So I guess I'll see you in a day or two. I'd like us to spend some time getting to know each other better."

I can't imagine how we'll ever come to that place, but nod my head and manage a smile to show I'm willing to try. I close the door behind him and head back to the kitchen.

Daisy bounces up and down, shaking the stool she's kneeling on. "Are you ready for your surprise?"

"It depends what it is," I say.

"Can I tell her, Mamère?"

"Of course, my darling," Vivienne says.

Daisy throws her arms above her head. "Pampers!"

Vivienne tries to stop herself from laughing. "No, no. *Pampering*, my bichette." She turns to me. "I though a spa day might be just what you need."

"Wow, thank you. That's so thoughtful," I say. "Would it be OK to invite Dottie? I've put her through the ringer these last few days. She could use a break."

Vivienne pats my cheek. "Of course. My dear, sweet Audrey, always thinking of everyone else. It's a lovely idea."

The solarium is transformed in front of my eyes. Women carry in pedicure baths, manicure and massage tables, baskets of soaps and lotions, towels, makeup, giant hair driers, and tackle boxes full of supplies. Daisy is the first to have her nails partially polished before deserting the process to see the teenage babysitter who had conveniently been dropped off for the day.

"Here you are, Mrs. Gilbert," a young woman says as she helps me up onto a long massage table. It takes a while to get situated on my stomach without reinjuring my leg, but soon I'm completely relaxed into the massage, listening to the sounds of falling rain on the sound machine next to me.

Dottie is stretched out on a table next to me. "I forgive you now for being such a pain in the rump," she says while face down in a hot towel.

I'm too relaxed to respond. The masseuse works all the kinks in my neck and shoulders until every ache is soothed away. She kneads her way down my back and takes special care with my wounded leg. The smells from the hot oils are intoxicating. Every time she takes her hands off me I'm afraid it's over, but then she moves to another spot until every single muscle in my body is loosened and restored.

Once that's over, I'm helped into a chair by two assistants who submerge my hands and feet in hot bubbling baths. They give me manicures and pedicures while another woman gives me a facial. It's pure heaven. Once I'm polished and dried, Vivienne comes down the stairs with a gentleman I've never seen before, but who obviously knows me.

"Audrey, darling." He holds out his arms and kisses both of my cheeks.

Vivi looks at me with a wink that lets me know I shouldn't tell him I'm not Audrey. They sit me down and discuss what to do about my hair.

"Work your magic, Henri," she says as she heads outside to visit Daisy. "We want to knock somebody's socks off."

Henri cuts and shapes and highlights my hair. He styles it, stands back to survey his work, and styles it again. When he's done, he snaps his fingers, and a woman comes over with more makeup containers than I ever knew existed. While they work, they talk to me about what I use on my skin and what I should be doing to cover the last of the bruises and scars left behind by the accident. They show me how to use the many brushes and liners and shadows that are piled up in front of me, and when they're done, they call Vivienne in to get her approval.

"Oh, look at you, my beautiful Audrey," she says, beaming.

Henri spins my chair around to show me a large mirror. I look like Audrey, only a better, sexier version of her. For all the makeup they used, it's tastefully done. My hair has been cut several inches and parted on the other side, hiding the patch of shaved hair beneath long layered bangs that cross over my forehead and tuck behind my ear. Waves curl around my shoulders. Toffee colored highlights brighten my face. I like the way I look for the first time in as long as I can remember. I look up at Vivienne. "Why did you do this for me?"

"Because when a woman feels beautiful, she acts beautiful. And it is time for you to feel beautiful," she says.

I understand she's trying to give me a present, but it's fairly obvious she's trying to give Jason one, as well. She'll stop at nothing until her son and I are in love.

"Are you trying to get him to fall in love with me?" I ask. "If so, you'll have to make over my personality, too."

"Jason loves you just the way you are, dearest. I wanted to do this for *you*. But if that happens to make you feel extra confident and sexy and he is able to see that side of you, I do not think it would hurt anyone, do you? Perhaps you both need a reprieve from this doctor-patient thing. Maybe it is time to see each other as a man and a woman." She stands behind my chair and puts her chin on my head so I can look at her in the mirror. "I knew you were having trouble looking at yourself, and I wanted you to see how beautiful you really are," she says.

Her gesture is so thoughtful I don't want to point out that this is not at all how I really am. I'd been poked and prodded and brushed and scraped and glistened for hours to look this way.

"Shall we find you something cute to wear? There is a great big closet up there waiting for someone to enter it again," she says. We venture upstairs and I try on several of Audrey's outfits mostly consisting of flowing skirts, simple fitted t-shirts, and flat sandals.

Vivienne clasps her hands under her chin and smiles. "Don't you look lovely."

Everything is simple, lots of khaki and crisp white button down shirts. Plain and understated. Like a nun.

"Audrey was pretty conservative with her clothing, wasn't she?" I say as tactfully as I can.

Vivienne grabs Dottie's leg with a look of hopeful anticipation on her face. "Whatever do you mean, dearest?" she asks.

"It's just…I'm not sure that my style is the same as Audrey's. But I don't even know what my style is."

Vivienne yelps and jumps off the bed, nearly tripping over her own feet trying to run and hug me. "Je ne croyais pas que ça allait jamais arriver."

Dottie shakes her head. "What did that woman just say?"

"I thought this day would never come," Vivienne says laughing. "Oh, we are going shopping, my darling. I can take you to Paris! I have always wanted to dress you. Such a cute little figure to be hidden in such boring clothes."

Dottie snorts. "Paris? Dr. Patel won't even let her go on a weekend getaway yet."

She's right. I see him twice a week, and he always reminds me that I need to take it easy. He still hasn't even signed off on me watching TV or reading books. I didn't have the heart to tell him that I already watched a movie with Daisy and snuck a magazine or two.

Vivienne clicks her tongue and sighs. "Oh, that is a problem. And probably no to the city as well. I can take you to the mall, perhaps, just for now, and then we can go to Paris when you are recovered. The mall is such a disgusting place."

"I'm sorry, Mrs. Gilbert," Dottie says to Vivienne. "But if she goes anywhere and gets an infection in that leg, she's gonna be in lots of trouble. We'll all be."

Vivienne tilts her head and eyes me thoughtfully. "Do you trust me to pick out some lovely things for you, just for now? I will bring them home to you and that way you do not have to go anywhere."

"Absolutely. I'd love anything you'd choose for me," I say.

It occurs to me a moment too late that I've just given a French fashionista free reign over my wardrobe.

A few hours later, Vivienne returns with enough packages to fill the bedroom and then some. Dresses of all lengths and shapes hang from every knob in the room, artfully displayed amongst shoes, skirts, tailored pants and blouses, jackets, scarves, accessories, and a heaping pile of lingerie. Vivienne holds up a lace bodice with matching thigh high stockings, pretending, for my sake, that she's requesting my approval. As if I have a say.

"You're like her own personal Barbie Doll," Dottie says under her breath.

"Where am I going to wear all of this stuff?" I ask. I barely have the energy to look through all of it, let alone try it on.

"Edmund and I want to throw a party to celebrate your recovery," Vivienne says. "And I am sure that you and Jason will be getting away together for a few days as soon as your doctor lets you go, so you will need a few outfits for that as well. And…I thought it was time for you to drop in on your husband at the hospital and bring him lunch like you used to. Perhaps your next visit with Dr. Patel can be in his office instead of the sunroom?"

I nod my head in agreement. I'd like to go back to the hospital. I want to stop being a shut-in and get the ball rolling on my recovery. And I'd like to meet the other doctors' wives and figure out why Jason didn't want Audrey to be friends with them.

"I'll tell Dr. Patel when I call in tonight to update him on your progress," Dottie says. "He's ready for you to start with the physical therapist and counselors any day now. It'll be a lot easier to plan it all if you went there."

As they walk out of the room, I hear Vivienne whisper to Dottie about making sure ahead of time that Jason will have a nice long break to see us during our visit. She isn't going to rest until she has us happily married, and I can't help but wonder how much she knew about Jason and Audrey at all.

~20~

I wake up trembling. Even though Jason has explained the origin of the bathroom dream to me, I've had it again. Like always, the floor turns into a deck, and the blood pools around my feet until there's nothing left but red. But this time I leave the bathroom, running, and end up outside at night. Jason chases behind me, yelling Audrey's name. I fall into the dirt and pick myself up to keep going. To get as far away as I can.

I've learned to control myself during the nightmares. I no longer wake up panting and crying. I no longer need to use the oxygen mask. I peek over at the clock on the bar; three thirty am. I lie in the darkness listening to the whir of Dottie's fan in the next room and try to force myself back to sleep. It's been more than two months since my accident, but at times like this, it feels like years.

At Vivienne's suggestion, we're going to the hospital today to see Dr. Patel and drop in on Jason. I remember when I first woke up in my room there, how long ago it seems. How strange it felt when Jason came to see me with pictures of a life I didn't remember and then climbed into my bed. How confident he was that night, walking in and handing me flowers, telling Dr. Patel he couldn't be kept away from me. Now he seems so unsure of what he wants from me, if he wants anything at all. I picture his face when he left two days ago, so conflicted, so pensive. I think about the green and gold flecks in his eyes and the way he's always sweeping hair from them.

The next thing I know, the sun is bursting through the blinds, and Daisy climbs into my bed telling me it's time to get dressed. I pull on a figure-hugging coral wrap dress that Vivienne bought for me and a pair of light brown sandals since I can't wear heels until I can walk without assistance. Because it seems so important to her, I let Vivienne do my hair and makeup however she wants as consolation for my uninspiring footwear.

She hands me a pair of earrings to put on. "There. I think you're ready."

I take a look in the mirror. I have to hand it to her; she knows what she's doing. I didn't even realize I had a figure like this, and I've been living in this body for over two months. If it weren't for the ugly pair of crutches I need to drag with me everywhere I go, I'd feel pretty spectacular. I survey my reflection from head to toe, wondering what Audrey would make of this.

"Mommy, you look pretty." Daisy holds the side of my skirt and gazes up at me. She's wearing a dress so we can be "twins" and her tap shoes in case any of the nurses want her to demonstrate her newest abilities.

We pile into Vivienne's town car and head back to the place where I was born as Jane. Much to my mother-in-law's dismay, the first person I have to see is Dr. Patel since Jason is in surgery and can't be paged. Vivienne decides to take Daisy to the cafeteria for lunch while I get examined.

Dr. Patel asks how I'm feeling, and I report the same thing as always: I don't remember anything and I'm incredibly bored having to sit around and do nothing all the time. We talk extensively about how I feel about Audrey, and I follow along with what Jason suggested to me on my first day home

186

and tell Dr. Patel what he wants to hear in order to avoid having to spend hours with therapists. He checks my eyes and has me look into a machine that blinks wildly and then back at him.

"The concussion is healing, but I would still like to be conservative about television and books." He scribbles in his notepad. "So, you aren't angry with her anymore?"

"Who?"

"Audrey. You once thought it was her fault that you were in this predicament."

The last thing I should admit is that I still think of myself as someone else. "Well...I've been home for a while now and I've bonded really well with Daisy. I think it's going to take some time to get to know Jason, but if someone *did* put me in this predicament, she sent me into a very happy life, so I guess I should be grateful."

"But you still feel you are a separate person from Audrey, do you not?"

"I guess," I say with a shrug. "I'm frustrated by not having her memories, but I know there were some unfortunate events before the accident that Jason is concerned about me remembering. We decided to live life day to day for now and deal with memories as they arise."

I have no idea how to answer these questions anymore. I don't know who Audrey was or if I even want to know. If Jason were helping me recover memories and I knew a thing or two about Audrey, maybe I'd be able to decide. But I can't admit to Dr. Patel that he isn't.

He nods approvingly. "It is a good idea to do that. You sound like you're coping remarkably well. But tell me...these unfortunate events that you have discussed with Dr. Gilbert, do you find yourself feeling overwhelmed about them? Do you think you have strong feelings about these events that you'd rather not remember?"

"Are you asking if I think that somewhere in my mind I'm choosing to not remember because it's easier than facing feelings I can't handle?"

He begins to speak but then stops himself.

"That's what you meant, right?" I ask.

"It would be up to a professional to decide if you are experiencing a dissociative state. I am asking what your feelings are about the events that you and Jason discussed and if they produce any anxiety in you."

I smile at him. "You don't have to keep saying 'the events' like that. I'm not going to flip out if you mention the baby we lost. That's the benefit of not actually remembering."

Dr. Patel flinches and opens his notebook.

"I'm sorry it happened to them, of course. I can have sympathy, right?"

"Yes, of course you can have sympathy." He reads through his notes. "I didn't know that you and Jason lost a child. He told me there were some unfortunate matters in your history, but he never gave me specifics."

"That's not possible. Jason told me he shared the specifics with you, and you both thought I shouldn't be told certain things until I'm ready."

Had I dreamt that? I don't know how much more to say. Why would Jason tell me that Dr. Patel knew everything?

"You would have heard about it last year. I'm sure it was no secret," I say.

"I was on a sabbatical until April. Are you saying that Jason told you he and I decided to keep upsetting information from you until you remember it on your own?"

My mouth goes dry. "Isn't that what you told me when I first woke up in the hospital?"

"Yes, when you were in critical condition. But not now that you are strong and trying to regain your life." He closes his notebook and looks at me sternly. "Perhaps I wasn't clear with Dr. Gilbert the last time I saw him. When I specifically said he should be reacquainting you with your history to see if, in fact, you are purposely blocking anything."

"Oh, you know what?" I shake my head a little, trying to look mixed-up. I hate to lie to him, but I'd rather not let on that I'm still in the dark. "Jason did say that to me the night we discussed the situation with the baby. I was talking about way back when I first woke up. He told me about the baby they lost and suggested I keep a journal to write my feelings in like Audrey did. He said if anything came up, I could discuss it with you."

Dr. Patel's face perks up. "And have you written anything down?"

"Not yet. I haven't felt the need to. I'm just enjoying Daisy and rediscovering that I cook French food and getting to know the man I live with."

He nods to himself. "It sounds like you are getting on very well, Audrey. There's a good chance that once your head heals fully, your memories will return to you very suddenly. It can be quite a shock for some people. You may experience head pain and dizziness when that happens, or just before."

"So the people who never get their memories back..." I say casually. "Do you think it's because they had a psychological block that was preventing them?"

He folds his glasses and slides them into his pocket. "I cannot say because they weren't my patients. There could be many reasons why someone never recovers their memories."

I wonder if any of those reasons have to do with their own family members not wanting them to.

I leave Patel's office and make my way to the elevator. I'm supposed meet the physical therapist next and set up our sessions for home care. I press the down button, wondering how I'm going to find Vivienne and Daisy who are somewhere in the hospital eating lunch or tap dancing for nurses. I still don't own a cell phone, and Audrey's was destroyed in the crash. This was not a well thought-out plan.

The doors open and several doctors step out of the elevator. Jason is among them, but he walks right by me and down the hall, engrossed in conversation with a colleague. I follow behind for a few feet, but there's no way I can keep up on crutches.

"Jason, wait." I lean against a wall, exasperated by my limitations.

He turns around, his expression unchanging as he tries to figure out who's calling him. Then his eyes grow wide with recognition, and astonishment blooms in his face. He looks me up and down, shaking his head and smiling. "What are you doing here? My God, you look amazing."

"Your mother did this." I have to admit it feels pretty good knowing that I was the one who put that look on his face.

He leans in and kisses my cheek. "You look incredible. God, your hair…" He takes a piece that has fallen from behind my ear and tucks it back in place. "You're stunning."

"They're in the cafeteria," I say, staring idiotically at his perfect face.

He smiles at me. "Who is?"

I notice a little dimple by his mouth that I don't remember seeing before, and have to keep myself from smiling. I can't understand what's wrong with me, unless the change of scenery has helped us step out of the cycle we've been stuck in. The elevator doors open again. As the hallway fills with people, Jason takes my arm and gently guides me to a wall, leaning against me for a moment so they can get by. When he steps back, I feel a pang of disappointment.

"Who what?" I ask, trying to remember what we were talking about.

"Who is in the cafeteria?"

"Oh." I stand up straighter and shake myself to my senses. "Your mother and Daisy."

"Did you see Patel today?"

"Yes. I think I avoided the therapists again."

"Good," he whispers.

I don't know what's come over me, but I'm unable to take my eyes off him. He looks so handsome with his lab coat over his dress shirt and tie. I bite my lip, trying once again to stop myself from smiling like a maniac.

The corner of his mouth twitches. "What?"

"Nothing. Just something funny Daisy said this morning," I say to cover myself.

"Oh." He sounds disappointed. "Do you want to go find them?" He texts his mother to tell her we're on our way down then smirks, holding his phone up for me to see her response.

Merde. I wanted to be there when you saw her.

"She isn't going to rest until we're in love, you know," Jason says while we wait for the elevator. "The woman is a maniacal romantic. She's going to make it hard for you."

"Why will it be hard for me?"

"Because you seem determined not to like me." Placing his hand on my back, he guides me in and selects the button for the ground level. Once we get to our floor, he guides me out of the elevator and down a long hallway past a security desk. I hobble alongside him and wonder how much longer the walk will be.

I stop to adjust the pads on my crutches. "God I'm tired of this."

"I can get you a wheelchair if you'd like."

I glare at him. "Absolutely not. Your mother bought me some pretty magnificent heels—among other things—so I need to get strong enough to walk in them."

He grins. "What kind of other things?"

"All sorts of things that shy Audrey apparently would never think of wearing that actually suit *me* pretty well."

191

Jason's eyebrows lift. "Well that would certainly make getting to know you as Jane a lot more interesting."

~21~

I'm finally cleared to go away the last week of August. After weeks of painful daily physical therapy, my leg is finally strong. An ugly scar remains, but I keep telling myself I can deal with that later. I've become reinvigorated from the weight training and have begun yoga with my physical therapist. After many months of being confined to beds and crutches, having the freedom to walk slowly around the neighborhood with Daisy or go gently from floor to floor in the house is nothing short of miraculous to me. I miss having Dottie here every day, but she visits twice a week and sleeps over sometimes during Jason's long shifts.

Jason and I have settled into a much better place. Though I'm still living in the solarium for now, we've managed to find a way to get to know one another during his off weeks. Having him home for seven days and then away at the hospital for seven days has been an interesting way to begin dating. Just when we begin to get close enough to start feeling things for one another, off he goes again for a week.

We always spend the evening before his shift drinking wine together on the back patio, red for him and white for me. It's become a little tradition for us, and I'm getting more and more used to being part of an "us".

Seeing the way Daisy reacts to Jason and me being together fills my heart with more joy than I'm able to understand. There are times when she'll sit between us during a movie holding both of our hands, repeatedly asking if we're going to stay that way. She needs me to tell her more and more that I'm never leaving, that I'm still her mother, and that there aren't going to be any more disasters. Her reaction to my accident reminds me of how one views a Monet painting. The farther away she gets from it, the more she can see the complete picture, and I think she's just now realizing how serious it was.

Sometimes when Jason is away at the hospital, Daisy stays in my bed and we greet in the morning giggling and singing. I don't remember ever knowing happiness like this could exist, so when the voice inside my head wonders about all the secrets Jason has yet to tell me, I shake it away and tell myself that I'm happy, and that's all that matters now. It's easy to do when I'm with her.

I've begun to realize I'm falling in love with Jason and wonder if he feels the same way about me. He never mentions anything about our relationship. He holds my hand and lets Daisy see us kiss and hug one another, but aside from that he's been a perfect gentleman, waiting, as he once told me, for me to look at him in a way that will show him how I feel. I try to make myself look that way, try to let him see that I'm beginning to accept whatever life we can make for ourselves, but so far he either hasn't seen it or hasn't wanted to.

I find I can go days without thinking about Audrey, without wondering what secrets could have been written in the journals with the pages missing. I know I could search for her boxes and find the memories to investigate, but I don't want to. I'm too busy enjoying living, as my mother-in-law would say.

And so it was decided that Jason and I would take a weekend away. Decided by Vivienne, of course, who was still clicking her tongue at the idea of me sleeping in a guest room and concocted an excuse to take Daisy for a few days. "Take her to the inn, Jason," she had said one night over dinner. "Teach her to sail again." And that was it. Jason and I were packed for a long weekend and booked in adjoining rooms at the Hawthorne House in Massachusetts, favorite local getaway of the Gilbert family, where I would get to sail and walk and shop and, if Vivienne got her way, finally wear the lingerie she'd bought me.

Now he drives us down the expressway as I choose the music, and it occurs to me I have absolutely no idea what he likes. I don't remember the preferences of a man I've been married to for years, and I haven't even tried to figure them out before now. I stare at his playlist and begin to panic.

"It's not a hard decision, Jane. Pick something you like."

"But I don't know what I like."

"Then pick something you think you could like."

The problem he doesn't understand is that I don't want to pick the wrong thing, something that jogs a memory for him, and have to see him get that forlorn look in his eye. Something that he and Audrey may have listened to on their way to the hospital when they were having Daisy. This is the kind of thing Dr. Patel never explained to me. How to cope with the ghost of the person you used to be. Watching Jason grieve the wife he lost and wondering if he'll ever forgive me for taking her place. I sigh and click on a random artist.

"James Taylor. Good call." Jason turns up the volume, singing along with every word. After a few songs he turns it down again. "Sick of this yet?"

"Are you?"

He smiles. "Yeah."

"Maybe we could just not listen to music for now."

He shrugs. "OK."

He seems so boyish to me sometimes. I often wonder if the problem between us is that he doesn't pick up on cues very well—which could explain why he hasn't tried to get any closer to me. Then again, it's also possible that he simply doesn't want to be closer to me. I look over at him drumming on the steering wheel and realize I could be severely overthinking things about a person whose only concern for the long trip we would share was whether or not I packed enough Oreos.

"Tell me about your mom," I say. "About how your parents met."

"You're pretty captivated by her, aren't you?"

"She's the most wonderful person I've ever met." I really have to stop using phrases like this since I don't remember meeting many people.

Jason nods. "Everybody says that about her."

"I'd imagine they do. She has such a life force. I want to be better every time I talk to her."

"She and Audrey were very close."

I'm so tired of hearing things like that. I want to have my own relationships with people without wondering if I'm as important to them as Audrey was. I decide to shelve it but let him hear my frustration. "How nice for them."

Jason looks over at me and clears his throat. "She and Dad met in France. He was married to his high school sweetheart when he was young, and it didn't work out. They divorced before they were twenty-five, and Dad traveled around Europe for a while trying to find himself."

"Your father was divorced? I'm surprised his family would allow something so scandalous."

"What's so scandalous about divorce?" he asks but continues talking before I can answer. "My mother was a television actress in France. Soap operas. He fell in love with her instantly. She wasn't as sure of him, though. It took him a long time to woo her."

"What didn't she like about him?"

"She liked him a lot. It was love at first sight, actually. But once she learned he was recently divorced, she decided he needed to work on being alone for a while."

"Wise woman. So she was always that way? I got the impression she became really introspective after your brother died."

"No, she was always that way. She had a difficult life; it can make you pretty introspective. Her father was an alcoholic, not a good man, and her mother left them when she was young. She had to raise five brothers and sisters in a terrible environment with very little money. Sometimes she had to steal things so she could take care of them." He glances over at me. "I know what you're thinking; it doesn't fit the image, right?"

"I wouldn't have expected that of her." I immediately realize I've botched what I was trying to say.

He looks at me quickly. "Of *her*? The way she was raised isn't her fault. You can't judge someone on the terrible circumstances they were in."

I want to explain what I mean, but he keeps going.

"And that's the best thing about my mother. She doesn't consider any of it her fault. Not anymore, at least."

"Did she at some point?" I ask.

"She had a hard time after she married my father, once she knew everything was going to be OK. She told me that there's something terrifying about getting a fairy tale ending because you suddenly have everything you ever wanted and you're scared to lose it. So when she finally got a decent life for herself, all of the issues from her past started bothering her. She'd been so busy surviving she couldn't look at her circumstances objectively until she met my father and her life calmed down. Then she was forced to survey the damage and process it, and it was hard for her."

I think about the Monet paintings again. How once you step back from something, you can see it more clearly.

"So what was the damage?" I ask.

He shakes his head. "I don't really know the specifics. Things kind of backed up on her; she had problems. But being the person she is, she took action. She volunteered with kids who were raised in similar situations. She helped out in treatment centers so she could better understand her father's perspective. She takes advantage of my father's career to help others."

"She's an amazing person." I imagine that Audrey probably went to her for help a lot. I wonder what Vivienne said to her after she lost the baby and why, with someone like that at her disposal, Audrey was unable to overcome it.

We travel in silence for a long time. Every so often Jason's cell phone rings and he has to deal with hospital business. I find myself nodding off and rest my head against the seat.

I wake to Jason singing quietly and turn to the window to stretch my neck. I nearly jump from my seat. "Oh my God, Jason, look!"

He yanks the car over to the side of the road and stops.

"The ocean," I say, putting my hand against the glass. "I can't believe it."

"Holy God. You scared me half to death. I thought we were about to get in an accident."

He sits holding his chest as I unbuckle my seatbelt and run from the car down a grassy hill, taking care not to put too much weight on my bum leg. My heart pounds excitedly. I just have to see it up close; I have to touch it. Large waves rise into foamy white peaks, roaring as they crash onto an empty beach. Seagulls circle overhead, squawking at one another.

"Jane! This is private property!"

I kick my shoes off at the edge of the grass and walk over the gritty sand to the water. Salty air blows in my face and sends my hair flying out behind me. I stare out at the horizon in complete awe. The ocean goes on forever.

Jason comes up behind me and bends down to catch his breath. "I can't believe you ran the entire way. What kind of physical therapy did they have you doing?"

"It's so beautiful! I've never seen anything like this before." I turn to him. "Have I?"

Jason looks down at the sand with the same lost expression that he always has when something like this comes up. "You have."

I dip my toe in hesitantly and laugh, gathering my skirt in a knot at my knees so I can wade in. "It's not that cold."

"Don't go any farther. The tide's rushing in, and you aren't a great swimmer."

I continue to walk deeper. The pebbles at the bottom feel rough on my feet. "I love the way you can feel it pulling you when the waves go back in." I let go of my skirt, not caring if my clothes get wet. It's very Vivienne of me, I think, to jump right in and experience the magnificence of the sea. When I'm waist deep, I turn to face him.

"Seriously, can you please come back to the car?" Jason has to yell over the sound of the crashing waves. "It's getting dark, and we need to check in. There's a storm coming."

I spread my arms out wide and throw my head back, thoroughly enjoying my first experience in the ocean. I look back just in time to see a look of terror cross Jason's face. Before I know what's happening, I'm knocked forward by a tremendous force of water and pinned down as the wave rushes over me, turning me over and over again beneath the surface until I don't know which way is up. I flail around, struggling to find the bottom to push off from.

"Audrey!" In an instant, I'm yanked to the surface. Jason has me by the back of my shirt. He secures his arm around my chest and drags me from the water and onto the beach, cursing the entire way.

I lie in the sand trying to catch my breath, smiling from ear to ear. I feel so *alive*.

Standing above me, soaking wet, Jason furiously removes his watch and shakes out his cell phone. "What's the matter with you?" He kneels in the sand next to me and rips my skirt all the way up to check my scar.

"Stop it." I yank a piece of fabric back over me.

He pulls me closer to him and puts his ear to my chest.

"Jason, what are you—?"

"Quiet!" He takes my wrist and measures my pulse.

"I'm fine," I say, pushing him away as I try to stand up. My leg gets caught in the ripped material, and I stumble backwards to the ground.

He leans down and grabs my arm. "You're disoriented."

I yank myself away. "No, I'm not. I'm fine. I tripped. On the skirt you just tore to shreds. I'm sorry about your fancy watch and your phone."

"Screw my phone! You can't swim. Is it not enough that you nearly severed your femoral artery in a car accident? When are you going to stop these antics?" He looks up at me and I see it again. The resentment in his face.

"My antics? Screw you! My leg is healing, and I've never seen the ocean before. It amazed me, so what? I wasn't going to drown in waist deep water."

Jason opens his mouth, but I roll my eyes and put my hand up to stop him. "Spare me the doctor knowledge about how many people drown in waist deep water," I say, trying to catch my breath. Up to this point, I've never unleashed my anger on him.

"Screw *me*?" He tries to hide a smile.

"Yeah, screw *you*. You think you have it so hard because you're stuck with me, don't you? Poor you, having to bring home this disaster into your pretty life. Having to babysit her and take care of her all the time. How do you think it feels to be me?" I kick a pile of sand and march back towards the car. "I'm trying to take over for somebody I don't even know. With people I don't remember."

He follows behind me and grabs my arm. "Jane."

I pull away from him. "I know you're just humoring me by calling me that. I heard you call me Audrey when you thought I was drowning. You'll never get used to me. Admit it."

He bends over to pick up my shoes from the sand and hand them to me. "I was scared, OK?"

"Scared of what? Of the weirdo living in your wife's body who doesn't remember ever having seen the ocean? Scared of me acting like an idiot? Scared at the thought of having to put up with my antics for the rest of your life?" I almost feel guilty for yelling at him like this since it's clear by the look on his face he has absolutely no idea what to do with a furious woman. I laugh at him. "So you thought poor little Audrey was going to drown? God, was that girl made of glass or something?"

Jason sucks in his breath, looking like he's just been slapped. I've somehow hit a nerve.

"Honestly, I feel like poor Audrey was just this sweet little thing that everybody loved and tiptoed around all the time. Poor Audrey was so sad, poor Audrey had two nice doctors taking care of her so she was never alone. Poor Audrey!" I realize I'm getting to a point where I'm not going to be able to restrain myself. "Well, guess what? After poor Audrey smashed her fancy car into a tree, she couldn't handle her life anymore and she checked out, leaving *me* here to deal with her crap. I'm *not* poor Audrey. I'm the one she called in to deal with everything she couldn't. So you don't need to worry about me drowning anytime soon, because unlike Audrey, I can take care of myself."

Jason stares at me in silence as I turn, shaking, and walk off towards the grass. The sun has gone down and I'm soaking wet. There's a breeze coming in with the looming storm, and the temperature seems to have plummeted. On the road above us, cars whiz by with their headlights on, oblivious to the scene taking place below.

Jason clears his throat. "I just can't lose you again. I'm always terrified of that." The pain in his voice cuts through me.

I suddenly get it. "Is that what the problem is here? Do you not want me because I'm not Audrey or because you're afraid to want anyone again?"

"When did I say I didn't want you?"

"You don't need to say it. You make it pretty clear."

He bows his head. "Then I'm more of a fool than Thomas said. I thought I was giving you time to see if you wanted to accept me or not."

I blink back tears. "That's what I was doing with *you*."

He takes a deep breath. "Did you really mean what you said? That Audrey was weak and needed you to take over?"

"I don't know. I'm sorry. I didn't mean to insult your—"

"She *was* weak." His eyes begin to fill. "It kept her from being able to see what she meant to me. Maybe you have some of that in you, too."

"Maybe instead of telling me, you should start showing me. You seem to forget I'm starting over from nothing. So do you want to start with me or not? We have three days. Three days to block out the world, three days away from the daughter we have to pretend for. Maybe what we should be pretending for next three days is that we just met. We can start over."

202

"Three days," he whispers, turning away from me. "Give me a minute." Clearly I've set off another precious memory for him to grieve.

"Can you put the past down for a day? Or two or three? You can pick it up again when we leave." I hold out my hand for him to take before we walk back up the hill. "Can you put down all the heavy stuff, the fact that I was injured, that I need to be watched every minute, that I used to be Audrey? Just for now?"

Jason turns and takes my hand. "I think so."

I smile mockingly. "No more hovering? No thinking I'm going to be mortally wounded if I get a splinter?"

He smiles back. "No more suspicions? No more accusations? No more Luminol?"

I laugh to myself. There's no way anyone is ever going to let me forget that.

~ ~ ~

A large plaque hangs in the foyer of the inn, inscribed with a quote by Nathaniel Hawthorne.

Happiness in this world, when it comes, comes incidentally. Make it the object of pursuit, and it leads us a wild-goose chase, and is never attained. Follow some other object, and very possibly we may find that we have caught happiness without dreaming of it.

Something about it stirs me, and I read it over and over again while Jason gives our name at the front desk. I have the oddest feeling that Audrey is trying to tell me something.

"Here we are, Mr. Gilbert." The woman behind the desk adjusts her glasses and looks at the computer screen. "Two ocean front—"

"I'm sorry," I say, stepping forward and linking my hand with Jason's. "But we'll only need one of those rooms."

I realize now, after many firsts in my short life as Jane, that the one I love the most is feeling Jason's bare skin against my own. With no clothes between us and his arms wrapped tightly around my back, I can feel the beating of his heart against my own and his warm breath on my neck. We've been tangled together kissing for at least an hour, and he's been so patient. Every time he attempts to move or change position, I pull him back to me because I can't stand for there to be space between us for a single second. I want this moment, this feeling of desperate wanting, to last forever. How naïve I'd been to consider a shower a thing of ecstasy when there was this to experience.

Jason kisses me while slowly dragging his hands through my hair, and I melt into him. I ask if this is how it was with her, but all he'll say is that it's been a very long time since he felt this way. There's an incredible storm rolling through, and every so often a burst of lightning brightens the room and I can see the conflicted look on his face. I imagine he's torn between his dedication to Audrey and his feelings for me. I feel his mouth spread into a giant smile beneath my lips, and I roll myself on top of him, prepared to do anything I can to take his mind off Audrey.

I kiss his chin, his neck, his chest, gathering my hair so it spills over him and drags down his stomach after me. Jason grips the sheets in anticipation, and my insecurities about Audrey dissipate the farther down his body I travel. He whispers my name, entwining his fingers in my hair, and I realize that yet another first for me is this thrilling sensation of complete empowerment.

~22~

"You're sure you don't have a history of asthma?" Dr. Patel listens to my chest and scrawls some notes in his pad. "Tell me again how this started."

"Well..." I try to take a deep breath but end up coughing instead. "We went away for a long weekend a few weeks ago, and ever since we've been back, I can't catch my breath. It started little by little, but it's gotten worse. I feel like I can't fill my lungs all the way."

"Were you exposed to any strong chemicals or mold perhaps?"

"No. Could I be allergic to wine? I've developed a taste for it lately, white mostly, and I know I didn't drink much before." I struggle to take a deep breath and hear wheezing in the back of my throat.

"Not likely." He listens to my chest again and then flips through his notebook quietly. "I see that when you were recovering from your accident, you often complained that you couldn't catch your breath. You had periods of wheezing and asthma-like symptoms. We attributed it to your deflated lung."

"And what do you think now?" I ask.

"Now I think it is most certainly anxiety driven."

"But I don't have anxiety." Things couldn't be better between Jason and me. Our weekend at the inn brought us together, and we returned very much in love with one another. Daisy is happy; she just started kindergarten. There's nothing going on that could explain anxiety-related attacks.

Dr. Patel chews on the end of his glasses and then points them at me. "Audrey, have you retrieved any memories at all? Seen anything that was familiar? Experienced déjà vu?"

"Not really," I say. "Once in the bathtub I got a picture of Jason and me bathing Daisy."

"And did you feel connected to that memory?"

"Yes, very much. I wanted more."

"And what have you been doing to recover other memories? I assume that Jason has been showing you old picture albums and newspaper clippings and telling you stories about the life you used to have to help you jog something."

I stare back at him and shift uncomfortably in my seat. The wheezing in my chest continues.

Dr. Patel hands me an inhaler. "Two puffs. Exhale between." He folds his arms as I inhale. "Are you still having him call you Jane? And before you lie to me, consider the fact that I may already know."

"Yes."

"And the nightmares?"

"Still having them."

"Are they getting worse?"

I nod and try to take a deeper breath. "I still see the floor fill with blood and hear a woman screaming, but now he's chasing me."

"Who?"

I look away. "Jason. But I'm not afraid of him if that's what you think."

"Perhaps you're being chased by memories and they appear in your dreams as Jason."

"I doubt it," I say. Goosebumps cover my arms.

"This is a dangerous game you're playing, Audrey. The subconscious mind is not to be trifled with. There is residual anxiety under there that keeps you from being able to breathe. You must try to discover what is blocking you from remembering."

"But I'm finally happy."

He puts the stethoscope to my chest and places the listening ends in my ears instead of his own. "Does it sound to you like you're happy?"

I shake my head.

"There is a hospital psychiatrist I want you to see. He can help you start to uncover the roadblocks you are setting up for yourself and why you may be doing it. I know Jason said you are absolutely against it, but I think it's time," he says.

Jason said I was absolutely against it? He hadn't even told me about it.

Dr. Patel picks up the phone on his desk and makes a call. "Yes, I can send her right down."

I open my mouth to ask him a question, but he holds up his hand, expecting an argument.

"Those memories are trying to push themselves back in, and the way you are breathing tells me that you will not be ready for them. What will you do if you are in the car driving your daughter somewhere when it happens? The first part in taking care of a family, Audrey, is keeping yourself well. Otherwise how well can you care for them?"

His suggestion that I might be putting Daisy in danger sets my teeth on edge. I snatch the psychiatrist's card from his desk and walk out to the hallway, my inhaler in hand.

Dr. Jefferies sits in front of me pressing his fingertips together. "So in your opinion, Audrey was unable to cope with either the aftermath of her accident or the stresses of her life, so she summoned you to take her place?"

I frown at him. "When you say it like that, you make it sound like I'm just an alternate personality."

"I'm intrigued by your use of the phrase 'just an alternate personality', as if you would resent the idea of Audrey being the primary one."

"I'm not an alternate personality."

"That's how you describe yourself."

I force a smile. "Then I'm not explaining it very well."

"And you feel that you're in competition with Audrey for Jason's affection?"

I look at him and throw my hands up in frustration. "I don't know what to say. It isn't easy waking up in a life you don't know. Being married to someone you just met. Jason and I have been able to connect to each other as we are now and make a new life. I don't know what's wrong with that."

"What's wrong is that you're experiencing psychosomatic ailments brought on by repressed anxiety. That you have renamed yourself because you seem to not want to *be* Audrey Gilbert at all. That you are experiencing jealousy towards the person you used to be, as if she's another individual entirely. It's incredibly uncommon for an amnesia sufferer to resist remembering and to create an alternate persona in defiance of the person they were. Unless there's something they are bound and determined to forget."

I feel my chest tightening. "I'm not doing it on purpose."

"But you'd rather be Jane than Audrey."

"Audrey sounds like a bit of a wimp to me."

Dr. Jefferies smiles smugly and taps his pen on the table. "I understand. But if you take pride in thinking you're stronger than she is, then wouldn't you be able to handle knowing the information that you seem to think Audrey couldn't?"

I tear out of the hospital so fast I'm surprised I don't get pulled over. As soon as I get home, I call Jason to tell him what they said. When he doesn't answer, I stomp into the house and slam the door.

Nobody has even considered what happens to me if Audrey flitters back into my brain. Where do I go? Do I float off with the wind?

My chest is caving in on itself. I dump my purse out on the floor to find the inhaler, and I put it to my mouth with shaking hands. Dr. Patel told me not to use it more than twice a day or else I could have heart problems. How am I supposed to breathe?

As soon as I can exhale again, I make my way downstairs to the storage room and start rifling through giant plastic storage bins. Daisy's baby clothes and toys take up almost every box. There are wedding presents still in their packages, old silk flower arrangements, shelves of tools, bins full of batteries, and a stack of fishing poles propped in the corner. Jason and Audrey's winter jackets, skiing equipment, and cardboard boxes full of magazines. Even a neon blue surf board with Thomas's initials etched into the side. But nothing that can tell me anything about Audrey. I search the cabinet against the wall and find a metal box containing their birth certificates, passports, and marriage license. No yearbooks, no childhood pictures, no wedding album. It occurs to me that I've never seen a picture of the grandmother who raised her. Wouldn't Audrey have kept it?

I head upstairs to the master bedroom, barely making it the two flights before I need to stop and sit down. I retrieve Audrey's hatbox of journals from beneath the bed and open it, hoping to find clues in the remaining pages.

The journals are gone.

The box is now full of gardening magazines. My throat begins to close. I race into Jason's study and call Dottie on her cell phone.

"Hi, honey. I'm just leavin' work, can I—"

I wheeze into the phone. "Dottie, I need you. Help me."

"I'm on my way."

I take another short puff from the inhaler and stumble into Jason's study. He saves everything; there has to be something in here that can help me. I look through the shelves of junk, the baseball cards, the boxes of old movie stubs and dozens of matchbooks that he's collected from God knows where. Piles and piles of photos, signed vintage record albums, and old picture books from his childhood. I sit at his desk and carefully go through every drawer, one piece of paper at a time.

Where is *her* life?

Dottie runs into the room breathless. "What's happening? I've been lookin' all over the house for you."

"I need to find *something*." I try to shove a drawer back in its place but it gets stuck. "Damn it," I say, struggling to pull it free.

She crouches down next to me. "You OK, honey?"

"No. I can't breathe anymore."

"We gotta get you downstairs and see if the oxygen machine is still here," she says.

I tell her about my visit with Dr. Patel and the psychiatrist while I yank on the drawer. It won't budge, so I get down on the floor and slide a letter opener into the track and pull as hard as I can. The drawer pops out onto my lap. I run my hand along the empty well and find a small, leather bound booklet and a white envelope held together by a rubber band.

Dottie sighs. "Looks like you mangled his checkbook."

I open it up. "This isn't a checkbook; it's a balance register." A piece of paper slides out with a name written in Jason's handwriting.

Viki Dupree- 212 Diamond Wood Road, Deacon Hill, West Virginia.

"I thought we were done with all this," Dottie says.

"The journals are missing. They've been replaced with magazines." I point to the register. "Look at this. He's paying this woman every month." I flip back a few pages and check the dates. "He's been paying her for fifteen years."

"What?"

"He was paying her fifteen years ago for about eight months. Then the payments stop. They begin again this past June and go through last week."

"June?"

"My accident was in June," I whisper and look up at her.

She shakes her head. "Oh, Lordy."

I open the white envelope and scan the letter inside. My blood goes cold. Someone, presumably Jason, requested an information search on a Wyatt Montgomery.

Dottie reads over my shoulder. "Wyatt Montgomery, alias Spencer Rudnick. If I were gonna make up a name it wouldn't be Rudnick. Looks like he's been arrested quite a few times. Known addresses are several places in Alaska; Sante Fe, New Mexico; Boulder, Colorado; Deacon Hill, West Virginia…"

"I've heard the name Wyatt, but he couldn't have been arrested. Jason said he's a police officer." I put the paper down and look back at the note from the checkbook register. "Huh. That's the same place in West Virginia as this woman who Jason is paying."

Remembering something I saw when I was snooping earlier, I point to the armoire and ask Dottie to hand me the bowl of matchbooks. I dump it on the floor.

"Look." I pick up a matchbook and hand it to her. "The Hornet's Nest. Deacon Hill, West Virginia."

"I don't like where this is goin'," she says.

"Please, Dottie, I need to know. Dr. Patel's right...I need to help myself or I'm no good to anyone."

"Can't you just ask Dr. Gilbert?"

"If this was something he wanted me to know, do you think it would be hidden under a drawer? And who do you think replaced the journals?"

She looks back at me in silence.

"It isn't like before," I say. "I love him now. But if he's in trouble, I should know."

I arrange for my in-laws to take Daisy for a few days. I tell Vivienne I'm treating Dottie to a girl's retreat and text Jason the same story. With five days left in his seven-day rotation, I know he'll be happy I'm not home alone. Dottie and I pack up her car, and before she can talk me out of it, we head off to find some answers in Deacon Hill, West Virginia.

We drive all day and into the night, taking turns at the wheel. With each state we pass, I hate myself more for lying to everyone. Most of all Vivienne.

My breathing problem calms down significantly the farther we go. Once we enter West Virginia, Dottie calls and reserves a large suite at a Residence Inn a few towns over from Deacon Hill where we practically fall into our beds in exhaustion after the eleven-hour drive.

Be ready to hit the road first thing in the morning, I text her from my bedroom.

I don't know how you talk me into this stuff, she replies. *Maybe I have a head injury.*

You're the best friend I have, I type.

That you know of, she responds with a winky face.

I close my eyes and think of Jason, wondering what he's doing at this very moment.

~23~

Dottie slows to a stop in front of a hot pink mailbox spray-painted with the number 212. Beyond that, a long, white trailer slumps in the dirt, surrounded by patches of dead grass and weeds. A small, wooden porch with crooked steps and a metal roof frame the dingy yellow front door.

"You sure you wanna do this? You don't have any idea what's waitin' in there for you," she says.

"Nothing's waiting for me. Nobody even knows I'm coming," I say.

She snorts. "There's always something waitin' for somebody. Waitin' to surprise you, shock you, change your future. Call it fate or karma or what have you. But right now, you're in a place to decide if you really wanna invite whatever it is into your life." She peers over the top of her sunglasses. "There could be a whole nother family in there. Another wife, love children. Though I doubt it," she says under her breath, "because you *know* Dr. Gilbert would put them up better than this."

"How can anything change my life when I don't remember what my life is?"

Dottie wags a finger in my face. "Don't pull that with me. You have a life. That's another thing that's waitin' for you. You have a husband and a daughter who love you. But is that enough for you? Nooooo. No, you need to go diggin' in a trailer to see what else may be waitin' for you. And for what? What you find in there could ruin what you got back home."

I narrow my eyes at her.

"I know what this is," she says. "This is just what that Dr. So-and-So said the other day on TV. This is a distraction."

"A distraction? Really? Please…enlighten me on what 'Dr. So-and-So' would make of this."

"Mm hmm. That's just what the people on the show did. They made fun of the idea, too. You know, just to make more distractions," she says.

"What does that even mean?"

"You can't deal with the feelings you have about what's in front of you. You're too scared to accept Dr. Gilbert as your husband and Daisy as your daughter, so you're lookin' under rocks and tryin' to find a distraction."

"Well, isn't *that* surprisingly insightful for information gathered from a talk show," I say. "So maybe I am scared. Wouldn't you be? Everyone is asking me to jump into someone else's life and move forward with a man I barely know. But I need to know what was going on with that person in order to figure out whether or not I *want* to be in her life." I open the door and start to get out.

Dottie grabs my arm. "This doesn't seem like the smartest thing you could do for yourself. I joined this fool's errand because you'd have found your way here anyway. But we've got no idea what's in that trailer and no plans on how to handle it. Dr. Gilbert would be furious if he knew we were here."

"Good thing he doesn't know then," I say, pulling myself away and slamming the door.

I knock on the trailer door and turn to give Dottie a thumbs up. She puts her head in her hands.

A woman's voice bellows through the door. "Who's there?"

I'd been expecting someone to answer the door so I could introduce myself. I raise my voice. "Hello ma'am. I'd like to ask you a few questions please."

"I said *who's there*. I'm not askin' what you wanna do. I know you been sittin' in that car out there, and whatever you're sellin', I ain't buyin."

"I'm not here to sell you anything. My name is… Audrey Gilbert," I say, tripping on the name. "I was hoping that you could help me with some information I've been looking for."

Someone lifts a corner of the curtain to peek at me through the window. "Who's with you out there?"

"My friend. She's visiting the area with me. I just want to talk to you. I don't want to cause any trouble." This isn't turning out at all the way I planned.

The door is pulled open by a woman much older I am, maybe in her early fifties. She's definitely not a mistress or the mother of Jason's hypothetical love children, though she could be their grandmother. Her face twists into a sneer as she surveys me slowly from head to toe. "Whad'ya want?"

She looks like she may have been a great beauty in her time and still could be, if not for all the heavy makeup on her unnaturally tanned face. Her figure is cute, though she has it packed into tight jeans and a shirt that belongs on a teenager. She takes a long drag from her cigarette and blows smoke over her shoulder.

She's tryin' to fit ten pounds of sugar in a five pound bag. Dottie's voice echoes in my head as if she were here next to me.

"I'd like to ask you a few questions," I say, trying to appear unaffected. I don't want to scare her off and ruin my chances.

215

She runs her tongue along her bottom lip. "Jason know you're here?"

My heart jumps. "How do you know I'm—"

She gives a deep laugh and breaks into a crackly cough. "I guess not."

"May I please come in?"

"Well ain't you fancy." She extends her arm towards the inside of the trailer. "Yes, you *may* come in."

I look back at Dottie, who shakes her head, warning me not to go, and hold up my hand to let her know I'll be five minutes. I follow the woman inside to a small table next to a tiny kitchenette. There are stacks of beer cans on the counter and several ashtrays littered with cigarette butts. No sign of love children anywhere.

"You better be quick. I got my man comin' home from the night shift, and he don't like company." She lights a second cigarette with the one she's smoked down to nothing.

My chest tightens and I struggle to take a deep breath. I point to the window over the sink. "Do you mind if I open this window to let the smoke out? I've had a bit of a breathing issue lately."

"Painted shut," she says coldly.

"Oh, OK." I clear my throat. "I don't think I got your name."

She puts out her cigarette on a paper plate. "I'm Viki." The person he's been sending money to; at least I know that much.

"May I ask how you know Jason?"

"That's a question you should be askin' your husband," she says.

"Well, it's…complicated."

She laughs and taps her long plastic fingernails on the table. "Trouble in paradise?"

"No, not that I know of. I just—"

"There must be some kinda trouble or you'd be sittin' in that fancy house of yours askin' him questions instead of me."

I bite my lip, frustrated with myself for being led around like this. I didn't plan on being the one answering questions.

"There are just a few things I'd like to find out on my own before I talk to him," I say, straightening my shoulders. "Who *are* you? And why is Jason paying you?"

She sits back against the vinyl chair and chews her lip, eyeing me suspiciously. "Now ain't this interesting. What if I'm not supposed to be talkin' to you?"

"Says who?"

"Says Jason, that's who. Ain't he the one callin' the shots here?" She grabs a can of beer and forces a pen under the tab to open it without breaking a nail.

So not only does she know who I am, but she and Jason are also conspiring together.

"Calling what shots?" I ask.

"He's got the checkbook, sugar pie."

"I have money if you have something to tell me." I reach for my purse, but she just laughs at me.

"You still don't know a damn thing about how these things work, do ya?"

I summon as much courage as I can to keep myself from crying. "Look…I came all the way here to ask you a few questions. You can help me or not. If you're not going to help me, just let me know so I can stop wasting my time."

She sits back and stretches her arms out behind her head. "What's in it for me?"

"Isn't Jason already paying you?"

"Jason's payin' me. But not nearly enough. Look around, sweetie. Does it look like I'm livin' in the lap of luxury here?"

"May I ask what he's paying you *for*?"

217

She laughs heartily and slaps the table. "Haven't ya figured it out yet? He's payin' me to not talk to *you*, sugar pie."

"About what?" I'm beginning to wheeze again.

"Oh, *Audrey.*" She hisses my name like it's a profanity. "If he's payin' me to keep my trap shut, then that information's gotta be worth a pretty penny. I'd be a damn fool to give it away for free."

She's right. I have no idea how to play these games. My naivety has somehow just upped the price of the goods she's withholding. But for all she knows, I have other rocks to look under. I stand up and smooth out the bottom of my dress. "Thank you for your time. I think I need to have a long talk with Jason to clear the air. And maybe once we work through this, he won't have to buy your silence anymore." I calmly tap my finger on my chin. "Come to think of it, there were a few other names I found in addition to yours. I suppose I can see what they have to offer."

Viki looks at me suspiciously for a moment, then flinches, startled by the sound of an approaching car. Fear flashes in her eyes. "Don't you go messin' up what I got goin' with that cash cow of yours." She leans over the window to peer out. "Good thing Earl ain't home yet."

I put my hand on her shoulder and try to sound as sincere as possible. "I'd be very grateful if you helped me. Jason doesn't even need to know that we spoke. You two can carry on with business as usual—which will be beneficial to both of us."

She puts her hands up. "Fine, you got me. What do I need to do?"

"First, tell me how you know Jason." I brace myself for her answer.

"Maybe what you should be askin' is how I know *you.*"

My stomach drops. "What?"

"That husband of yours has been tryin' to erase me. Since you went and got the amnesia, he's tryin' to cut me out of your life. He never did like where you came from."

"Where I came from? What are you saying?" My legs go numb and I fumble to open my purse with shaking hands, knowing I'm going to need my inhaler.

"I'm sayin' I'm your mama."

Dottie lays on the horn, signaling me to come out.

Viki takes a step towards me. "Did ya hear what I said? I'm your mama." She yells the last part straight in my ear as if she thinks "the amnesia" has made me deaf.

The car horn blares again, unraveling what is left of my nerves. I can't process what I just heard. I reach for the counter but fall to the floor. "I need my nurse."

"Aw, shit." Viki stomps her foot and runs for the door.

The next thing I know, Dottie is hoisting me up. "Here you go, Mrs. Gilbert. This fresh air's gonna do you good." She walks me down the steps into the yard.

Viki follows behind angrily. "Hey, where d'ya think you're takin' her? We got some negotiations we're workin' on."

Dottie snorts. "Lady, I don't know who you are or what's goin' on, but I gotta get her back home where she's supposed to be restin'. This was a bad idea." She lowers me into the car and buckles the seatbelt around me.

I have to concentrate to not throw up. I grasp Dottie's hand. "Wait. I just need some air. Please, let me talk to her."

"I'm gettin' you back to the hotel, Mrs. Gilbert. It's too damn smoky in there, and you look like somebody who just saw a ghost. You need to lie down."

Viki stands near the car, nervously chewing on the side of her thumbnail. In the sunlight, her face looks like the fruit leather Daisy likes to unroll and cut into shapes.

"She's coming with us," I say.

~ ~ ~

"Well ain't this nice." Viki walks around our suite caressing the furniture and opening cabinets. "Y'all brung this stuff with you?"

"No. The suites are equipped with amenities for people who need to stay somewhere longer than a few nights. It's supposed to feel more like home that way," I say.

Dottie has reluctantly gone out to pick up lunch for us, giving Viki and me time to talk. I barely remember the drive back to the hotel and am only beginning to regain feeling in my limbs.

"Can we speak openly? I have so many questions," I say.

"Sure." Viki sits down on a sofa and takes out a cigarette. "Mind if I smoke?"

"I'd rather you didn't."

She puts the cigarette down. "You're the boss now. So you wanna know where you was born and all that?"

I think about her question for a minute. I'm not even sure what I want to know yet. "Do I have a father?"

"Nah, he ran off when you was a baby."

I nod silently. It feels like we're talking about someone else, just like every other time I'm told about Audrey's history. "Jason told me that Audrey's parents died in an accident and she was raised by her grandmother. Why would he say that?"

Viki widens her eyes. "*Audrey's* parents?" She shrieks in amusement and slaps her knee. "You don't think you're *her*, do ya?"

220

"Not really." I look away, realizing I've just given up crucial information by referring to Audrey in the third person. "I prefer to be called Jane."

She laughs. "This is like a regular ole soap opera, ain't it? Well, I gotta hand it to you for bein' a lot smarter than they probably think. You knew in your gut your name wasn't Audrey Gilbert, didn't ya?"

Her words are like a firm pat on the back; I'm not as crazy as they all think.

"Hold that thought," I say, hearing Dottie struggle with the lock. I open the door and grab some bags from her arms. "You're missing everything. I *knew* Audrey wasn't my real name."

Dottie looks at me sadly. "This is a bad, bad, terribly dangerous game, Mrs. Gilbert. There's nothin' good that comes out of sneakin' 'round like this. If you want that woman to answer questions, have her do it back home with Dr. Patel and your husband 'round."

"You're here; that's just as good. I just want to know one or two things. And then maybe we can bring her home and sort it all out together." I know deep down there's no way that's ever going to happen.

We sit down at the table with our lunch, and Viki opens one of the beers she brought with her by jamming the end of a plastic knife under the top. Dottie rolls her eyes.

I take a deep breath. "OK…I'm ready. What's my real name?"

Viki looks at us with anticipation, raising her eyebrows up and down like she's trying to build the suspense. "Dree," she says through a wide smile, spreading her fingers out in front of her face. "Dree Dupree. Don't that sound just like a movie star?"

I look to Dottie. Her face has gone completely slack.

"I guess so," I say. It hardly seems any more familiar to me than the name Audrey did. But not quite as foreign, either.

"He went and changed your name to Audrey after y'all ran away together," Viki says. "Had to change a whole lot about you before he could bring you home to meet Mommy and Daddy Warbucks."

I cup my hands around the mug of tea that Dottie made to soothe my nerves. "I don't understand."

She swats the air lightheartedly. "C'mon, girl. You don't think them Gilberts wanted anyone to know their son went and married some piss poor trailer girl from the sticks, do ya?"

Dottie thumps her hand on the table. "Now wait just one second. The Gilberts are the best kind of people, and I don't think we should be talkin' about things they can't defend themselves on." She looks right at me. "They love you. Anyone can see that."

Viki smiles at me. "Of course they love her. By the time they met her, he'd already changed her."

"Changed her how?" I ask.

"By the time they met you, your hair was brown. You learned to speak different. You was trained to act fancy. Trained to fit in."

"My hair was blonde," I whisper, remembering how surprised I was to see the brown hair in the pictures of Audrey that Jason brought to the hospital. "But why would he do all that? I thought you said we ran away together?"

"You did. He was on a trip with some friends, and they was hangin' out in this little place where you was workin'. He took one look at you, and well, you know what college boys like to do." She winks at me. "Y'all exchanged numbers, and then he went off on his merry way. You called to tell him you were knocked up, and when he came back to talk you into gettin' rid of it, you refused."

I feel the color drain from my face.

"Aw, what in the *hell*," Dottie says through a mouthful of salad. She glares at Viki. "I'm not gonna listen to this for one more second. Do you have her birth certificate? Pictures? Proof?"

"Well, I got *this*. I went and grabbed it when we were leavin'." Viki reaches into her purse and hands me a photograph. A blonde haired girl looks back at me, smiling slightly. She's young, fifteen maybe. She has my eyes.

Dottie gets up, carries her lunch from the table, and slams one of the bedroom doors shut.

Viki sighs. "She's on their payroll, ain't she? They usually are."

"So you're telling me that Jason got me pregnant and we ran away together, but he had to transform me into someone he could bring home to his parents?"

She swigs back more of her beer. "Yup."

"What happened to the baby? It would be an older teenager by now, right?" I ask.

"There was no baby. You was just a clever girl, that's all. Mama didn't raise no dummy." She grins and winks at me. "But nobody knew that till after. After you went and ran away with him, I tried to find y'all. I didn't know who he was, so I didn't know where to look. They didn't even invite me to the weddin'. But then you came back to me. You wanted to move me out there to be near y'all, but his family wouldn't have none of it. They even tried to buy me off. But I ain't blamin' the parents. Jason told 'em all kinds of crazy things to keep 'em from wantin' to meet me."

She lowers her voice to a whisper and points her chin towards Dottie's room. "I didn't wanna say this in front of her, but the reason I ain't got a birth certificate is because Jason sent some guys to the trailer one night when I was workin'. They took all your old pictures and birth records and stuff. Just in case I was thinkin' about tellin' anyone that my daughter married into the rich 'n famous Gilbert family."

I hold my head to try to stop it from pounding.

"He does love you," she says. "Ain't nobody gonna deny that. But he was brung up a spoiled and selfish little thing, and now he's a spoiled and selfish *big* thing. He saw what he wanted, but he was too embarrassed to bring you home so he changed you. And you was too much in love to see it was a horrible thing he was doin'. Wonder how many other girls he conned without anyone knowin'. Could be dozens more out there."

"So he's paying you not to talk to your own daughter? Didn't you want to see me?"

"Dree, you and me have been on the outs for a long time. You made your choice, and it was him. After the accident, he wanted to make real sure I'd never be comin' around again. I forgave you a long ago for leavin' me behind. It's been hard makin' ends meet, that's all."

"I'm sorry," I say quietly. "Does the name Wyatt Montgomery mean anything to you?"

"Yeah, he's the son of the man you was workin' for. Y'all grew up together and was pretty sweet on one another, but you went and left him high and dry for Jason."

"Is he still in town?"

"Nah. He moved to Alaska to make some money up there cuttin' down trees after he got himself arrested one too many times. Nobody's heard from him in years."

"Can you tell me the names of a few of my old friends?" I ask. There are always things that girls don't tell their mothers, and I'm hopeful a friend could sort out the missing pieces for me.

"You're not gonna to find anyone. They've all gone and married off." She bites her bottom lip. "You know what we should do? We should take a trip, just us girls. Mother-daughter spa reunion!"

"OK, sure. But getting back to the friends...I could look them up online if you give me their names." I grab a pen from my bag. "Old friends, people I worked with at that place you mentioned."

"Aw, Dree, I don't remember any names from way back when. Ain't it enough that you and I finally found each other? Besides, if you go lookin' up anyone from the club they're gonna want money from you, sugar pie. Once they know that Audrey Gilbert, daughter-in-law of Senator Edmund Gilbert, is really just ole Dree Dupree from the strip joint, the hands are gonna want greasin' faster than water rolls off a duck's back. We gotta keep this deal between ourselves for now."

"I'm sorry, what did you say?" My head feels like it's being worked on by a jackhammer. I blink a few times to try to get my eyes back into focus. "Did you just say Dree Dupree from the strip—"

"Like I was sayin'..." She leans in close to the table, looking me in the eye. "Jason was in town for a little fun, and he took one good look and that was it. You didn't think you hooked him with that pretty face alone, did ya?"

~24~

I wake up to Dottie holding a washcloth on my face. "Where's Viki?" I whisper.

"I called her a cab back to that shit pile you found her in. She left her number so you could call her and discuss the future. I swear that woman had dollar signs in her eyes," Dottie says.

"What happened?"

"You blacked out. I told you this was gonna happen."

I close my eyes to stop the room from spinning. "So apparently Audrey was a stripper named Dree Dupree who trapped a rich boy by faking a pregnancy. This has to be better than your soap operas."

"You gonna believe that piece of trash?" she asks.

"That piece of trash is my mother. Who my husband told me was dead."

Dottie fluffs the pillow behind my head. "Allegedly your mother."

"I believe her. I felt it in the trailer. She's definitely my mother." My temples are still pounding.

"Maybe she's the lady who gave birth to you. That doesn't make her a good mother, the kind you can trust. There are too many things you don't know. And there's only one person who's gonna to be able to set you straight," she says.

"Yes, but he's been lying to me. So who do I believe?"

Dottie dunks the wash cloth into the water before putting it to my cheek again. "I always go with my gut on these issues...and I went with my gut today. I think you should try to do that, too."

"What do you mean you went with your gut today?"

"You're gonna have to try and forgive me, Jane, Audrey, Dree, whoever you are. Because I really care about you. And I can only do what I know is right." Her face looks guilty. Pained.

"You called Jason." I stare up at the ceiling and feel a tear trickle down the side of my face. "But I trusted you."

"Exactly. You trust me because you know I'm lookin' out for you. And when I saw you walk into that trailer this mornin', I didn't think I was doin' the right thing for you. God only knows what could have been waitin' for you in there. She could've shot you dead, and I would've been the lady who drove a young wife and mother to her death. So I called him right then and there. It's not even a two hour flight to here, did you know that?"

"Is he coming to get me?" I don't even want to argue about her decision to call Jason. I'm back to having no one.

She sighs. "He's here. On his way to the hotel now. He flew in on his father's chartered plane."

I shake my head and stare at the wall, unable to look at her.

"You'll forgive me one day," she says. "You need to see that there's people who love you and wanna help you. And sometimes helpin' someone means doin' the opposite of what they think they want."

"Thank you. That will be all, Dottie," I say coldly.

She gets up and walks away quietly. I've never addressed her as hired help, but now it seems Viki was right.

Although she appears to be loyal to me, Dottie is on the Gilbert family payroll; she's here because it's her job.

There's no point in trying to do anything or go anywhere. Jason is on his way. Jason, who gets to control everything I do and when I do it, and what I know and don't. I'm trapped playing a game that only he knows the rules to, with pawns that are all on his side.

My hair still smells like smoke and it's making me nauseous. I pass Dottie's room on my way to the shower. She's quietly packing her suitcase. I don't stop her.

By the time I get out, I can tell Jason has arrived by the sound of a tennis match blaring from the television. Dottie is gone; I can sense it. The air feels different without her presence. Lonely. I walk into the living room in my robe, drying my hair with a towel. His back is to me.

"You didn't need to come here," I say.

Jason jumps up from the couch and turns off the TV. His shirt is untucked from one side of his jeans and his hair is a mess. "Jane, I—" He stops and takes a deep breath. "Why in God's name did *you* come here?"

There are so many things I can say, but I attempt to give the truth as simply as I can. "I was curious what you were keeping from me. Dr. Patel says I can't breathe because I have anxiety-induced asthma. Dr. Jefferies says I have repressed memories that are causing me stress. They both think I'm a danger to myself and my child if I don't get my shit together. The only person who seems not to mind that I've become someone else is you."

"I did keep things from you. But now that you know, I assume you understand why I did it."

"I understand that you were ashamed of who you were married to. I understand that you told me I was an orphan and kept Audrey away from her mother for most of her life. What I don't understand is why."

Jason shakes his head. "What the hell are you talking about?"

228

"I met her, Jason. I met Audrey's mother. Viki. She told me what Audrey's real name was and how you wanted her to change it. She told me what Audrey was doing when you met, and you know what? It's pretty much the exact opposite of a church group retreat!"

I throw a vase, and it shatters against the wall. I struggle to catch my breath as tears spill down my cheeks. "So you thought you knocked up some poor stripper and were afraid to bring that kind of trash home to Mommy and Daddy? That's it? That's the big mystery of my life? The big secret you've avoided telling me is that the man who stooped so low to marry me—or was tricked into doing so—was so ashamed of who I was that he exploited my amnesia to preserve his own precious image?"

Jason's face turns from pink to red to purple, and I wonder how many colors are left before he explodes.

I continue my rant. "I was thinking it was so much worse, actually. That you tried to kill Audrey, were having affairs, another family maybe. But it's really just a simple story of trying to hide who she was so she wouldn't embarrass you. Is this why you wouldn't let Audrey meet any of the other wives from the hospital? So nobody would know what she was?"

"That bitch." Jason hurdles over the back of the couch and heads for the door. "You stay right here, do you understand me? I'm going to bring that drunken psycho back here and make her tell you the truth."

I put myself between him and the door. "I don't trust either one of you. How do I know you aren't going there to get your stories straight? She tried to negotiate with me for her story, so for all I know she could be lying, too. Tell me your version now before I tell you anything else she said."

He stares into my eyes as if trying to figure out who I am.

"I know what you're doing now," I say in my meanest tone. "You don't know if you should talk to me as Jane, the

229

new wife who doesn't know anything; Audrey, the old wife who lied about everything; or Dree, the girl who would've done anything for you."

Jason grabs me by my robe and pulls me towards him. "If you had any idea what you were saying right now, you'd hate yourself. Everything she told you is a goddamn lie, and I can say that without even knowing what she said today because she's a drunk, Jane. She lies to get what she wants—money and alcohol and that's it. Those are the most important things in her life, other than the men she can never hold on to." He shakes while he speaks, barely holding back his fury. "She didn't deserve to be your mother."

His body is pressed up against mine, and his face is so close that when he speaks, I feel his breath on my lips. My entire body starts to tingle. It doesn't make sense for me to react this way during an argument—unless it's because he's not treating me like poor, delicate Audrey.

"So you admit you erased her?" I say.

His hands still grasp my collar but his shoulders soften slightly. "Yes, I did. For you. You have to believe me."

I want to believe him. Even though I'm angry, just being this close to him and seeing the pain in his face makes me weak. And the fact that I'm so turned on warns me I've lost all objectivity when it comes to him. There isn't much more a thin cotton robe separating us, and even that feels like too much.

Jason runs his hand down the side of my face. "I can explain it all. But you need to believe me when I tell you that everything I do for you is done out of love."

I know he feels the charge between us, too; his heart is pounding through his shirt.

"That's the thing, Jason." I stare into his eyes confidently and remove his hands from my robe. It falls open slightly, and I don't move to stop it. "I can't believe anything anyone says to me. I can only go by what I feel myself. I want someone to show me the truth."

Jason gaze falls to my open robe. "What about our weekend at the inn?" He runs his fingers slowly down my neck. "Didn't you feel me fall in love with you? Didn't you believe in me then?"

"I…" I'm unable to speak. I can't take my eyes off his mouth. I can barely concentrate. "I just don't know what's real."

"Then I'll show you what's real." He covers my mouth with his and pushes me back against the door, lifting me up so I can wrap my legs around his waist. Holding me firmly in his arms, he carries me to the bed. I tug at his clothes, desperate for the feeling of his skin against mine. He carelessly rips the robe from my body and rocks against me, clutching my hair in his fist, kissing my face, my neck, my breasts. I feel his heart beating against my own, and I cry out for him just before he slumps against me in exhaustion.

We lie there holding on to one another for a long time, reveling in our closeness. The room grows colder, and I shiver and burrow deeper into his chest for warmth.

Jason extends my arm and softly kisses the inside of my wrist. "That was the best fight I've ever had."

"Best one I can remember."

"Although I'm not sure how you thinking I lied to you worked out so well for me," he says.

"I think I just needed to feel something for myself. I still want to know the truth about Audrey's life. But in case anything you say changes things between us, I need you to know that I truly love you, Jason. I love you because I can't feel anything else, no matter how hard I try."

"What did I do to deserve you falling in love with me twice?" he whispers, cradling my face in his hands. He tightens his grip around my body and shifts himself back on top of me. We move slowly and quietly this time, our eyes locked on one another. He buries his face in my hair. "I don't care who you were. I love who you are now."

His words leave tears behind on my skin. I can't tell if they're his or mine.

As we fall away from one another, Jason reaches to take my hand. "I want to give you everything. Name something you want, I'll get it. Some place you want to go, I'll bring you there."

"Can we start with pancakes? I'm starving. I was too nervous to eat with Viki here."

He kisses my forehead. "I'll tell you everything you need to know over pancakes. And I'll even make them myself."

~25~

Jason slides another pancake onto my plate. "Will you let me tell you the entire story from beginning to end without stopping me? Because I want to give it to you exactly as it happened so you can decide for yourself about Viki." He searches through the bags he's brought back from the mini mart down the road and pulls out a bottle of beer.

"Don't worry, I'll try not to put my two cents in," I say with a mouthful.

He looks at me skeptically but sits down at the table and takes a deep breath. "My senior year in college I traveled cross country with some fraternity brothers. We stopped for the night in West Virginia and ended up at a little dive called The Hornet's Nest. A strip club, as you probably know from Viki."

I remember the matchbook I found in his study and nearly gag. "The Hornet's Nest! What a horrible name for a—"

Jason smiles. "What happened to not putting your two cents in? If we talk about what you think is a good name for a strip club, we'll be here all night."

I pretend to lock my lips with a key and throw it over my shoulder just like Daisy.

"Anyway, I wasn't exactly comfortable going to a strip club, but I also wasn't very good at standing up to my friends. Even if I'd wanted to be there, my parents would've murdered me if they knew. My mother raised me to be extremely respectful of women, and I'm sure you can imagine what it would do to my father's career if I were the kind of person who frequented strip clubs."

I nod at him. "Right, the Confederation for Moral Living."

"Exactly. So once we got there, everyone spread out. Most of the guys went up front to throw money at the dancers, and the rest of us went to a booth towards the back to drink up the nerve to join them. The waitresses were really aggressive; sitting in our laps, hanging all over us."

"Where was Audrey? Was she on the stage?" It's not exactly putting my two cents in if I'm asking a question.

He ignores me and keeps going. "There was an older waitress who kept saying I had a baby face. Saying I looked too young to be there. She kept trying to get my wallet away to see my ID. Not that she cared about my age, of course; she just wanted to see how much money I had so they didn't waste their time with us. Eventually she got my license and started screeching because she saw it was my birthday. Well, almost my birthday. It wasn't midnight yet. But she said I needed a private lap dance to celebrate."

"Was Audrey the private lap dance girl?" I almost don't want to know.

"Yes, but let me finish before you get upset."

I'm upset, but not in the way he thinks. He'd never understand what I'm feeling; a mix of regret for not being able to share his memories and jealousy towards the girl they're about, who is technically me, but not.

"The guys carried me over their heads to a room. I tried to get away, but they kept yelling 'get in there faggot' and 'don't be a puss—'" He looks at me apologetically.

I roll my eyes. "I do remember what that word is, Jason."

"They shut me in a room with only a couch and an old boom box. It was disgusting, definitely not a high end place. Across the room, people were arguing behind a large curtain. I heard a girl pleading and a man threatening her. Then he shoved her through the curtain and slammed the door behind it."

My stomach tightens. "Audrey."

He sighs. "Yes, Audrey. I swear she looked like a goddamn angel. She didn't belong there. She looked like a girl you'd want to bring home to your parents, not see hanging off a pole. Even with the bleached blonde hair, she was naturally beautiful. I'll never forget the first words she said to me. *But you're so young.* As if she'd expected a dirty old man to be there waiting for her. She backed away, telling me there'd been a mistake. Before I could say anything, the man banged on the back door and demanded she turn on the music. I turned it on just to shut him up and signaled for her to be quiet. Then I locked the door behind the curtain in case he tried to come in, and I remember thinking it shouldn't be able to lock from the inside. What if some pervert was in there trying to attack her? How would anyone get in to help?"

He says the last part quietly, as though the thought of her locked in there with the wrong person still bothers him. Even after all this time.

"Outside the door, my friends were laughing and asking if I was scared. Teasing me about being a virgin." He looks up at me quickly. "I wasn't. But I wasn't very experienced, either."

I take his hand. "It doesn't matter to me."

"Audrey could tell they embarrassed me, and something in her changed. I think she looked at me and recognized the lost soul looking back. I asked what her name was, and she said, 'It's uh...Dree.' But with her thick accent and the music blaring, I thought she said Audrey, and I called her that the entire time. She didn't correct me."

I hug my arms around my knees. Who could blame her? If I were in her position and someone this perfect called me the wrong name, I would have answered to it as well.

"I laid my jacket down for her to sit on since that couch was undoubtedly covered in DNA left behind by a hundred perverts. She seemed self-conscious about the way she looked and kept pulling her skimpy robe down over her thigh high stockings. She had little jeweled things stuck around her eyes, but she didn't have a ton of makeup on like the other dancers. She looked a like a kid playing dress up in her mother's clothes."

I want to be her so badly my heart aches, simply because of the look on his face when he describes her.

"We talked for a while. She told me she'd been working there for months. Her mother was in debt to the owners for a 'great sum of money' and they were letting Audrey work it off washing dishes in the back. But they'd been pressuring her more and more to get out and dance. The night I came in, her boss had come at her in a rage, drunk and high as a kite, demanding that she dance or he'd throw her out and have her mother arrested. He'd been really rough with her." Jason pauses for a moment, clenching his jaw. "The other dancers had tried to help her by doing her hair and face to make her look older, but before they could finish or find her anything to wear, she was pulled away and thrown into the room with me. She still had the marks on her arms from that bastard."

I begin to regret all the insulting things I ever thought about Audrey.

"After a while, the guys started pounding on the door again, calling me names. Audrey smeared her lipstick across her mouth and tousled her hair. Then she opened the door and said, 'You boys need to give us some time in here. This may take a while,' before slamming it in their faces." He shifts in his chair uncomfortably. "She defended me to elevate my reputation with my friends. And they believed her. They cheered and argued over who would be next. Once she realized what she'd started, she panicked. I wasn't going to let a single one of them in there with her, of course. I wanted to tell them the truth; I hated for them to think of her like that. But she made them think it. *For me.*"

He turns towards the window, lost in his thoughts. "Why would she do that for me?"

His face is filled with pain, and I can see he's wrestling with the burden of knowing just how little she thought of herself.

"We talked about my family, about me applying to medical school," he says. "She told me her only ambition was to get out of Deacon Hill, but since she didn't have any skills she didn't know where to go." Jason leans back in his chair. "Then her boss started pounding on the door and told her to hurry up because there were paying customers lining up for her outside. He said she was finally about to pay off. I couldn't stand the thought of it, so I handed him all the money in my wallet—a thousand dollars—and told him she wouldn't be entertaining any more customers."

Jason looks at me. "I know what you're going to say. It's a lot of money for a college kid. I'm not trying to look like a hero, and she didn't want me to be one anyway. She told me to meet her outside. Somehow I got away from my idiot friends who were pouring beer on my head to congratulate me. By the time she came out, she'd taken all that stuff off her face and was wearing jeans and a t-shirt. She was even more beautiful than before. She could barely look at me, but she handed me back the money I'd given her boss."

"How'd she manage that?"

"She had a key to the safe. She did their books because most of them were too stupid to add. While the manager was attempting to control my frat brothers with his

237

dancers, she stole it back. He would've killed her if he caught her. But she was fearless.

"I didn't want the money back, but she insisted. She told me she wasn't for sale. I hadn't meant it that way; I tried to explain, I tried to get her to keep it, but she wouldn't take it back. And then she said something which took me years to understand. She said my money was too good for a place like that. But what she really meant was my money was too good for *her*.

"We heard my friends calling my name. Audrey kissed me on the cheek. 'Find some new friends. Yours are assholes,' she said and then ran off into the woods. Right then I knew I wasn't going to leave that place until I saw her again."

"So how did you get her back?" I ask.

"The guys and I had planned to spend the night in a local motel. I called my father's campaign manager once my friends passed out and told him I was in trouble. That's all I needed to say, really. The last thing they want to hear during an election year is the son of their candidate calling from spring break to say he's in trouble. His aides showed up before dawn with a briefcase full of money and asked only enough questions to assure themselves I wasn't going to be arrested or in the newspaper or the father of anyone's illegitimate baby. While my friends slept off their hangovers, they drove me back to the club. The manager lived in a trailer next door, so I went to see him to offer to buy back her freedom.

"Three thousand dollars. That was it. The 'great sum of money' she was paying off by subjecting herself to that horror was only three thousand dollars." Jason looks away, blinking back tears. "That amount of money was nothing to a kid who grew up like me. With what she was earning, it would've taken her a lifetime to pay it off. And even worse, the manager told me Audrey's mother was in there drinking herself silly every day and adding to the debt. So it would never have been paid. She was a hostage, Jane, and she had no idea. Her mother was into drugs and gambling and was bartering it all off with her daughter. It was only a matter of time before they escalated Audrey's job description."

I'm beginning to see now why he wanted to erase Viki from his life. I'm surprised he let her live this long.

"So I paid the guy his three-thousand dollars and offered two-thousand more for her address. He threatened to kill me. He said she was in training, that one day she'd be his most valuable asset, so there was a price on her and he wasn't going to let her go without it."

I can't stop myself from asking. "What was the price?"

Jason shrugs. "I don't know. My father's guys got out of the car and told the man that his business would be investigated with some unfortunate consequences unless he gave me what I wanted. The idiot took one look at their suits and sunglasses and thought they were in the mafia.

"I told my friends there were some family issues so they'd have to go on without me. Then I rented a car and drove to Audrey's trailer. She wasn't exactly happy to see me. She was embarrassed about where she lived, angry at me for coming, for not listening to her the night before. I asked if I could take her out for a burger so we could talk.

"At lunch, I told her about the deal I made with her boss, and on the way home, I told her about the deal her mother had with him. She didn't believe me at first. She cried and begged me to stop the car to let her out. She was ashamed that I put money down to help her. She couldn't understand why I'd do something like that. I told her it was because I was able to and that I wanted to do more if she'd let me. I knew if I left her there, not only I would never see her again, but at some point those lowlifes would break her spirit and whittle her down to nothing. But it was no act of charity. I needed her, too, somehow. I felt alive next to her. More alive than ever before."

"And of course she took your help. You were her ticket out of Deacon Hill," I say.

Jason looks at me sharply. "It wasn't like that. She was too proud. She said if I helped her, she'd always be indebted to me, and that wasn't much different than being indebted to her boss."

So Audrey was tougher than I thought.

"I said it was her choice, and she should only come if she wanted to, not because she felt she owed me anything. I told her she was too good for the world she was living in—an angel, really—and she just laughed and called me a blind little boy who had too pretty of a life to understand what he was getting himself into. But that was just her fear talking. She was worried about what her mother would do to her if she tried to leave.

"I told her where I'd be staying. That entire night and all the next day I waited in a motel outside town. It was pouring rain, and I took it as a sign that she wasn't coming. I told myself I was an idiot for asking some girl to run away with me. I tried to convince myself I was better off, that she'd done me a favor by not coming. Because what would I have told my parents? Where would I have taken her? Eventually there was a knock at my door, and I ran to answer it so fast I don't think my feet ever touched the floor.

"She had a black eye, and her hair was stuck to her face from the rain. She had a broken suitcase and a backpack full of essentials in case she never found me and had to hit the road alone. She looked at me and said, 'A fish and a bird can fall in love, Jason, but where would they build their nest?' I grabbed her and didn't let go. I told her how brave she was for making the right decision, and I promised her that nobody would ever hurt her again.

"She'd been walking and hitching rides in the backs of pick-up trucks, so even the clothes in her suitcase were soaked through. I gave her a t-shirt and a pair of my boxers, and I swear I'd never seen that shirt look so good. There's something about seeing the girl of your dreams in one of your t-shirts that can really kill a guy. I still have it; I had it framed."

I smile at him. "I've seen it in your study."

"Anyway, she sat on the bed eating pixie sticks from her bag and talking like we were two kids at sleepover. She asked if I believed in happy endings, if people could really change their destinies. I'll never forget the trusting look in her eyes as she waited for my answers. She told me she hadn't wanted to come at first because she didn't want it to seem like she was using me as a way out. But then her mother showed up drunk, calling her names. Viki had heard that some guy bought her daughter away from the club, and she accused her of selling herself to the first yuppie college boy 'meal ticket' that drove through town. Then she smacked her and threw her into a dresser."

I shake my head in disgust. Viki conveniently left that part out.

"I think it bothered her more than I understood at the time," he says. "Her mother said she should wait for a bigger, older, richer fish to swim along, one who could take care of them both. She wanted to know where all the money was. She thought I paid Audrey to leave. That's what finally made her go. Her mother was more concerned about the money than she was about who her daughter was thinking about running off with or where she was going. She never even asked what my last name was."

I put my head in my hands. Poor Audrey. And stupid me for listening to Viki.

Jason continues. "I think when she said it out loud she realized how bad it was. She cried for hours. When she felt better, we watched old movies and ate vending machine junk food, which she insisted on paying for with a plastic bag full of change. I held on to her all night. By the time the sun came up, I was completely and utterly in love with her and knew I'd never feel right again if she wasn't next to me.

"We stayed in that motel for three days. I watched her sleep. She looked peaceful, even with the black eye. Every now and then her face would crumple up like she was having a bad dream, but then she'd open her eyes and smile at me with relief. I never felt like more of a man in all my life than I did when she looked at me like that."

He stops his story and looks at me. "Do you know that once a year, Audrey and I still go away together to a cheap motel and spend three days in the room eating junk and watching TV and making out? It was her idea, so we'd never forget the way we fell in love. That's why I was so blown away on the beach before we went to the inn. As soon as you said we had three days, I knew we had a chance. It was as if Audrey was speaking through you, telling me to embrace the idea of you and me."

"So you just brought her home with you?"

Jason gets up for another beer. "We made it work somehow. She came back to school with me; I only had a month or so left. I put her up in a small apartment off campus and moved in with her as soon as I graduated in May. She washed the bleach out of her hair and went back to being brunette for the first time since she was ten so my fraternity brothers wouldn't recognize her from the club. And honestly, she looked even better that way.

"I slept on the couch that entire summer. In the fall, I went to Chapel Hill for medical school and brought her along. We got a place off campus and lived like roommates for a while, sleeping in separate rooms, taking it slow. When I had time off from studying, we got to know one another. We had dates in our pajamas in front of the TV. If things ever started to go too far, she'd just ask me if I could wait. I thought it was because she was shy, or afraid, or maybe not as interested in me as I was in her.

"She got a job waitressing and insisted on paying back the money it cost me to get her out of The Hornet's Nest. Then one day she handed me all of the rent money for the first apartment. That night she crept into my room wearing the t-shirt and boxers she'd worn in West Virginia and crawled into bed with me. She told me she loved me. If I wasn't half out of my mind with desire for her, I think I would've cried with relief. I didn't really understand, but afterwards I put it together. She would only sleep with me after she no longer owed me anything. She didn't want her mother to be right. She thought she had to prove she was worthy of anything I did for her."

Jason lowers his eyes. "I couldn't understand it. In all our years together, I just couldn't make sense of her feeling so…undeserving."

I can't bear the look on his face. I take his hand and guide him over to the couch to sit down. "I guess it makes sense in a way," I say gently.

"Not to me. I got to appreciate so much through her eyes, things I'd always taken for granted. Life was amazing to her, and she was amazing to me. She'd never been out of Deacon Hill, never gone anywhere, never been able to afford anything. When I took her to a museum for the first time, she stood in front of a Van Gogh and cried her eyes out. I'd seen those paintings thousands of times; my family owns an original. It never impressed me until I was with her. She marveled at buildings, inhaled all the books she could get her hands on. The first time she saw the ocean she went berserk just like you did. She sat on the beach and built sandcastles and chased waves for hours like a little kid. She taught me how to appreciate the world around me. I'd become a spoiled, closed off, resentful person after my brother died. She taught me how to love life again.

"But sometimes she'd wake up crying from a bad dream, the same one for years and years. Even after Daisy was born. She'd dream that she never came to find me in the hotel. She'd cry into my arms and ask what would've happened if I never saved her. But the truth was she saved me, too, she could just never see it.

243

"She never felt she was good enough. At first I thought it was because she grew up so poor, but it went beyond that. She wanted more than a transformation. She wanted an *exorcism*."

Jason drops his head into his hands and hesitates before continuing. "She dedicated months to erasing her accent by working with speech pathologists at a local community college. She took classes in art history and political science and cultural studies just so she could keep up with things my family talked about. She nearly burned our place down trying to teach herself to cook. Then she legally changed her name to Audrey Pratt, and I got her a new birth certificate through one of my father's connections. With me, she was friendly and captivating and funny. But when we went out, or if we met up with other people from my program, she would shrink into herself, always so afraid that someone would realize that she wasn't the right kind of person.

"What kind of person was that?" I ask, though I think I already know.

"The kind of person who deserved someone like me." He looks away and steadies his breath. "She was so broken. She had a terrible upbringing. Viki did nothing for her. Nothing. She stole from her and tormented her and never taught her a thing. Audrey may as well have been raised by wolves."

"So she was pretty lucky to end up with Vivienne then," I say.

Jason nods. "She was the mother Audrey never had. They had a lot in common. She raised Audrey in her likeness and taught her how to overcome the damage done to her in her childhood. It was working...until we lost the baby."

"What do you mean?"

"Audrey believed there was something inherently bad about her. During both pregnancies, she thought her body would hurt the baby. Then when we lost James, she had the proof she needed. It was some kind of pregnancy psychosis or delayed PTSD. I should've gotten her help, but I thought I could manage it myself. She went off the deep end, and there was no bringing her back."

Jason leans back against the couch, looking exhausted and drained. "And that's what happened. That's the truth. Everything Viki said to you was a lie."

I stare at him for a while, and he waits patiently as I absorb everything. His eyes are red-rimmed and glassy from all the tears he's cried. Viki hadn't shed a single tear when she told me she was my mother. She'd been more interested in the negotiations than she was in me.

"And Wyatt? Can you tell me the truth about him now?"

"Her ex-boyfriend. A misogynistic, abusive creep. Son of the man who owned The Hornet's Nest. Supporter of her having to strip to pay them back. Apparently he'd blown into town between jail stints, and Viki spilled the beans to him during a drinking binge about who Audrey married. He contacted me online looking for her since she wasn't on social media."

"Viki left that part out. I asked her if she knew of him."

"I can't believe I'm about to defend her, but I doubt she remembers. She gets pretty loaded," he says.

"What did you do when he contacted you?"

"I completely ignored him, that's what I did. He's a dirtbag drifter who's probably in a jail cell right now. He's no threat to my family. If Audrey heard me say his name on the phone when I had him investigated, that would explain why it was on your mind after the accident."

I put my head on his shoulder. "Why isn't there anything of Audrey's in the house? Photo albums, yearbooks."

"Viki burned it all. After a year or so, Audrey started feeling guilty for running off, so we went back and offered her mom money to go to rehab. We found out she'd burned everything Audrey owned in a drunken rage. Audrey didn't want any of it anyway, but the funny thing is, without any of that stuff as proof, Viki can never convince anyone that her daughter is a Gilbert."

Tears sting my eyes. "I believe you, Jason. All of it. It's such a romantic story. Audrey was lucky to have you."

He exhales resentfully. "Audrey would disagree with that. She didn't think it was a romantic story, she was ashamed of it. That's why I invented that church group story. I would tell it to her at night when she was crying. Over and over again. Eventually we started pretending it was real, and when people would ask how we met, that's what we'd tell them. Even Thomas got that version, though he thinks she moved in with a grandmother because her mother was abusive. He knew her too well not to be able to spot that there was trauma in her past.

"I'm glad you like the true version, but Audrey would've given anything to forget it. That's all she ever talked about. What a better person she'd be without the bad memories," he says.

Are you glad that Dr. Patel is a brain man, Mommy? Daisy's voice rings in my ears.

And just like that I finally understand.

"Oh my God," I whisper. "You did it all for her, didn't you?" Jason had spent so much time and energy covering tracks, just so I wouldn't feel the way she did. "Oh my God, I'm so sorry."

He pulls me in close and sighs deeply. I can only imagine the weight that's just been lifted from his shoulders.

"Remember in the hospital when you said you'd give her up if it meant we'd be happy?" I ask. "You were talking about Audrey, weren't you? You'd give up the wife you loved just to give her a chance at a new life."

He wipes the tears from my face. "It occurred to me in the hospital that maybe I should let you forget. As long as

Daisy had a mother who loved her, I thought I should give Audrey what she always wanted."

"I was so wrong about you, Jason. You didn't keep her away from the other wives at the hospital, did you?" It's all very clear to me now. Audrey wasn't able to be around other women.

"Of course not. I hoped she'd make friends. But she hated being in those groups. Eventually the women would talk about their childhoods or—"

I put my hand on his face. "You don't have to explain. I understand. She was ashamed of who she was."

"I don't even know how the rumors got started that I didn't let her socialize with those women, but I never cared what people said about me. We just let them think whatever they wanted."

"You're a good man. Dottie tried to tell me." My stomach turns over on itself. "I was so awful to her. I need to call and apologize."

Jason tightens his grip around me. "You'll have time for that later. I'll help you explain."

I hug him back and dry my eyes on his shirt. "Why did you start paying Viki in June?"

"When that article hit the paper after your accident, I was afraid it would make national news because it was damaging to my father. If she'd gotten wind of it, she would've showed up with her hand out. I wanted to be on the offensive."

"What are we going to do about her now? She'll be expecting me to contact her. She thinks we're going away for a mother-daughter trip. She thinks you're still paying for her silence."

He kisses the top of my head. "Let her wait. There's nothing she can do to us now."

We lie huddled together on the couch. After a while I realize Jason has fallen asleep. I listen to the rhythm of his breathing and try to silence the voice in my mind that wonders just how far Audrey would have gone to forget and what will become of me when she remembers.

~26~

Jason rakes up another pile of leaves as Daisy waits patiently by the side of the house for him to give her the go signal. She's been jumping in the same pile for an hour. I hear her squeal before she lands and watch as a flurry of leaves flies into the air.

"Can I do it again, Daddy?" she asks.

"Of course," he says with a smile. "I live to rake the same pile of leaves over and over."

I sit back on my heels and take a break from my planting to watch their game. "Do I get a turn?" I ask playfully.

He laughs. "Only if you can do it without another injury."

So much has changed since our trip to West Virginia. I understand Jason in ways I never thought I would. Knowing what he went through to create a past I could be proud of instead of the one that shamed Audrey makes me regret so many things I did and said. It fuels my desire to just be without overthinking *how* to be. Dottie is helping me make friends with some of the women from the hospital, and I've been so busy with committees and fundraisers that I don't have much time to wonder about the missing pieces anymore, though sometimes I still do.

I drop another sedum in the ground. I feel so alive working with my hands in the dirt. It's a little late to be planting, but I don't waste my time on trivial worries like that anymore. It will grow if it wants to grow.

I walk across the yard to get a load of dirt. The wheelbarrow is leaning against the garden shed, unused since the day before Audrey's accident. I still catch myself measuring my time according to the last thing she did or said. I hope to eventually stop keeping track of how much more time Audrey got to spend with my family than I have. It seems like forever ago that I came home to this house for the first time, yet there are still many firsts to be had. Yesterday Daisy and I picked out her cowgirl costume for Halloween. In a few weeks I'll cook my first Thanksgiving turkey, and after that, I get to decorate my first Christmas tree.

I balance the wheelbarrow carefully, walk it over to the pile of dirt we just had delivered, and go back to look for a shovel. The inside of the shed is dark. I feel along the wall for the light switch and accidently knock a stack of recycled boxes to the floor. As I hastily pick them up and toss them back on the shelf, a slip of paper falls from a box and flutters lightly to the floor. I recognize the light yellow lined paper from her journals, a scrap ripped from the bottom of a page with a note scribbled on it.

Wyatt - 6/1 3pm Radisson, Glennbrook.

The date noted is June first, three days before my accident. I stuff the note in my pocket along with my mounting unease and quickly walk back into the yard to finish my day.

250

Later that evening, Jason carries Daisy upstairs for her bath while I stay downstairs to preheat the oven and make dinner. By the time his footsteps reach the second floor landing, I can no longer stand my curiosity.

I open the laptop to search for Wyatt Montgomery. There are too many people by that name to choose from, so I pick the most popular social media site and enter the name. Two choices come up and one of them, I can see by the photo and birthdate, is fourteen. I choose the other, an unfortunate profile photo of a hot rod with a bikini-clad woman painted on the hood.

Scanning his "acquaintance" list with dread, I pray the name isn't there. But it is, taunting me…Dree Dupree. No photo. I search the name Dree Dupree and scan her list. Only one acquaintance, Wyatt Montgomery. But without her password, I can't see anything else.

I try Audrey and Jason's wedding date, then Deacon Hill, Daisy, and Otis. Nothing works. I try Audrey's birthday, Jason's birthday, and Daisy's birthday. Nothing. Above me, the happy sounds of Daisy's bath time echo through the house as I pace the kitchen, trying to think of a password. Then it hits me.

"Audrey, what did you do?" I say out loud. I lunge for the computer and type *Hornet's Nest* in the password box.

The page opens up.

There's no information available on her. No photos, no birthday, no work history. I check the private messages and see several between her and Wyatt. Message after message after message. They date back to the February after she lost the baby, four months before the accident.

Audrey contacted him first after finding him online. She doesn't mention that she changed her name. She tells him that she's thinking about starting over somewhere and asks if he still makes fake IDs because the people in her world wouldn't be able to help her.

He tells her he moves around a lot, hasn't been home in fifteen years. He asks if she's in trouble.

I am the trouble, she writes.

They reminisce back and forth about growing up in Deacon Hill, about the friends they used to know, about whether Audrey should go back. She pours her soul out to this man, leaving out the details of where she lives and who she married. She tells Wyatt about losing the baby months earlier, and he responds by sending her lyrics to Lynyrd Skynard's "Free Bird" layered over a picture of a mountain in the winter. What a moron.

They correspond like this for weeks, and I scroll to the most recent messages. Audrey isn't sure anymore about needing an ID but thanks him for helping her. A month passes before the next message. Wyatt writes that he went back to Deacon Hill to collect the life insurance after his father's passing and ran into Viki who was "off her ass" drunk in a local bar.

I asked her about you, he writes. *I told her we were talking again.*

She makes things up, Audrey writes. *Please don't talk to her about me.*

I know who you are now, he writes.

Nothing about him contacting Jason to ask about her. He wouldn't need to do that since she'd already found him.

I have the papers, he writes. *I'm coming to New York to give them to you.*

Please don't come here, she writes. *Forget you ever knew me. Please don't come.*

She tells him she'd only wanted help with papers, but she changed her mind. She gives him a cell phone number so they can discuss it and offers to meet him in New Jersey or Pennsylvania—anywhere besides New York.

See you in New York, he closes his message. *I'll be in touch.*

So they must have made contact by phone and planned to meet. Now that I know the story of how Audrey was raised, I'm certain there's no way she could have missed that life—if everything Jason told me is true, that is. She must have been depressed because of the baby and thinking like a crazy person. She was looking to run away.

Jason calls down the stairs. "Mommy, here comes a very clean and hungry girl."

I shut the laptop and quickly shove the fish sticks in the oven.

Jason plops Daisy down on her stool and looks around the room, realizing that I haven't made anything yet. He gives me a quizzical smile. "Whatcha been doin' down here?"

Finding out you lied to me again. "Sorry. I forgot what I was doing. I'm just reading a few recipes your mom sent over." I pick up a stack of cards and hold them up for him to see.

After several serious games of Old Maid and Go Fish, we carry Daisy up to her room half asleep and put her to bed. I stand over her and watch her little lips purse in her sleep and marvel at the way the hair curls around her ears. Was life so bad for Audrey that she would have deserted a child and left her motherless? I can't imagine it. She'd been confused and reached out to her past, but she changed her mind. She wouldn't have left her husband and child. The only memory I've been able to recall is the one of her bathing Daisy as a baby, and it still resonates so strongly with me that I cry when I think of it. And the reaction I had when I met her in the hospital for the first time tells me Audrey was incredibly connected to her daughter; it seems improbable that she was preparing to leave her. She was just desperate to see if there was an exit.

Unless...

Unless she was going to leave *because* she loved her that much.

Daddy said if we didn't have a mommy we would be OK. Daisy's words ring in my head.

Not only was Audrey thinking of leaving them, but Jason knew it.

I touch the side of Daisy's face before I leave the room and creep silently down the stairs.

Jason is in the kitchen opening our bottles of wine, red for him and white for me, as he always does the night before his seven-day shift.

"What's all this? You aren't going to work tomorrow, are you?" I ask.

He smiles. "I just thought it would be nice. It's getting cold outside; we can build a fire tonight."

"Let me change first," I say, unable to look at him. "I still have dirt all over me from gardening." I tiptoe up the stairs, pull on yoga pants and a t-shirt, and grab one of Jason's zip front college sweatshirts from his closet door. I call out to him as I hop down the last few steps to the kitchen. "I hope you don't mind I borrowed—"

I stop dead in my tracks when I see him standing in front of the open laptop reading Audrey and Wyatt's messages.

"I knew you weren't reading recipes," he says quietly.

"Jason, I—"

"I thought we said we were going to start over."

"We did. But I found this note in the gardening shed." I feel around for my pockets and remember that I've changed my clothes. "It's upstairs, I can show you. It had Wyatt's name and a place to meet on it, and I didn't understand."

"I see," Jason says looking at the floor.

"Do you want me to get the note?"

254

"No. I've seen it. I must've dropped it in the shed when I was putting away her gardening tools after the accident."

"So you found it? You knew that they were planning—"

"Yes." He nods towards the laptop. "How'd you know how to access the account?"

"I just guessed passwords until I got one."

Jason sighs. "You're pretty smart."

"You told me he contacted you because Audrey didn't have social media accounts."

"Audrey didn't have an account. Dree did."

"What's the difference? Other than the fact it gave you a convenient loop hole to lie through," I say.

"If I'd told you that Audrey sought out this piece of shit to meet up with him, what would you have thought?"

I put my arm out to lean on the counter and accidentally knock the bottle of red wine onto the floor. It pours from the bottle, covering the tiles in front of me, and I imagine the blood spilling in my dream. I look up and see a man I don't recognize coming towards me. I double over, holding my head. "Oh God, what's happening to me?"

Jason quickly cleans up the wine and grabs my arm to lead me down to the solarium.

"My head is killing me," I say. "What's going on?"

He chews the inside of his mouth, as if considering what to say.

"You knew she was back in touch with Wyatt?" I ask.

Jason sighs and pours himself a large glass of wine. "Yeah."

"And that they were planning to meet?"

He takes a long gulp. "Yup."

"And you read her messages? I'm surprised she saved them."

"She didn't know that even if you delete messages on your phone, they still show up on your home computer."

"How did you know she even had the account?"

"Because she was acting like a lunatic. I didn't know what to do, so I was keeping tabs on her phone. I could see what she did and where she went. I could see the sites that she logged into."

A sharp pain spreads across my forehead. "What happened when she met him?"

"I think you need to hear that from her, not me."

Jason walks to the bar and slides open one of the wooden panels. A fake front. He pulls out a journal. "She wrote everything down. And I mean *everything*. A therapist she went to a long time ago taught her creative writing as a cathartic outlet. She filled hundreds of these books."

"I saw some with the pages ripped out under the bed. But the next time I went to find them they were gone," I say.

"Audrey would rip the pages out of the journals if there was anything she didn't want to look at again. She was worried that Daisy might stumble upon them one day, so she'd write to get things off her chest and then rip up the pages she wouldn't want anyone to see."

"That doesn't explain how they disappeared from under the bed."

He shrugs. "I'd forgotten they were there. After you started going up to the third floor, I realized I should move them in case you saw them and got the wrong idea. I kept them, though. Some of it was really special to her, and I knew someday Daisy would be able to read about how much Audrey loved her."

"Have you read them?"

"Only the ones she showed me. And this one, which I found in the garden shed the morning after the accident. You should read it, too. It's better for you to hear things straight from Audrey."

I open the journal and look at the writing on the pages. "Wow. It looks like she was writing a book."

"That's how she did it. You should get comfortable."

I settle into the sofa with an uneasy feeling. It seems wrong to read another woman's private thoughts, even though I know they were once my own.

June 1st

Wyatt texted the room number as I pulled into the parking lot. I walked through the lobby feeling eyes on me, wondering if the people at the desk thought I was a call girl, hired for some businessman's lunch hour. My heart pounded in my ears. Jason used to say our hearts were connected. If that were true, then surely he could feel mine breaking open. I had no idea what I was doing.

I was in front of Wyatt's door before I knew what was happening. My hands were shaking so hard I could barely knock. I don't remember walking in. He looked the same as always, tall and wiry, dark red hair and a rough goatee. Black angry eyes. I paced around the room, feeling numb. Dead inside.

Wyatt grabbed my face and kissed me harshly. I pushed him away and told him that wasn't the reason I came, but he laughed and said I was kidding myself. I tried to pretend that he was wrong, that I'd been unaware of what he wanted. But I knew him. I knew the kind of person he was, what he always expected from me. He pinned me against the wall, one of his rough, gigantic hands at my throat. I tried to reason with him between breaths, turning my head away from his mouth, but he only laughed and said, "Payment up front."

The next thing I knew I was on the floor. He pulled my dress up over my waist. He was on top of me, crushing me. He forced his knees between my thighs, pushing them apart. I couldn't take a deep breath; it's been happening to me more and more, the feeling that my lungs are going to close up. I prayed they would. Once and for all.

I could have punched him, I suppose. I could have screamed. But I didn't, just like always. I closed my eyes and drifted away, deep inside myself. Above me, Wyatt moaned and mumbled disgusting, degrading words about my body and what we were doing. Words that Jason would never use, let alone to a woman. Everything hurt. My thighs were numb where his knees pressed into them, and my shoulders ached from being clenched in his grip. His body was bearing down on mine so forcefully I struggled to breathe, and I heard myself cry out.

He reacted to my cries, misunderstanding them for pleasure—or maybe enjoying my pain. I was dizzy from holding my breath. Tears slid down the sides of my face and pooled in my ears. When it was over, I pried myself out from under him and made it to the bathroom just in time to throw up in the sink. I stared at myself in the mirror; mascara smeared under my swollen eyes, lipstick smudged across my mouth and cheek, bruises beginning around the base of my neck. I looked as if I'd never left Deacon Hill.

I dragged myself back into the room, unable to face Wyatt. He grabbed my hand and kissed it and said he'd missed the last several years. He acted unaware of what he'd just done, rambling on about people we used to know, things he did in Alaska. I was far away in my mind, waiting for the part when he'd promise to never bother any of the Gilberts in exchange for what we had done.

My thoughts drifted to Jason. How he treats me like I'm made of glass. Didn't he know my body killed our baby boy because something so beautiful couldn't grow right inside of someone like me? Daisy made it out unscathed somehow, but James…it happened as I knew it would. I need to save them all somehow, but coming to Wyatt for help is only further proof of how stupid and selfish I am. My mother was right about me.

I told Wyatt I needed to leave, I told him to go back to Alaska. But he said we weren't done. He called me Dree. I tried to argue, to tell him I wasn't that girl anymore, but I had nothing left in me.

He said he knew how much the Gilbert family was worth and how much they'd pay for the world not to know that Senator Gilbert's son bought himself a lifetime lap dance. Those words killed the last living piece of my heart. When I asked if he was trying to blackmail me, he looked confused. I offered him my jewelry to leave. He jumped off the couch and yelled, saying he hadn't traveled a million miles for jewelry. I told him I had no access to the Gilberts money and that I wouldn't do that to them anyway.

He said, "You're the one who wanted out. Think of the divorce settlement you'll get. How much they'll pay us to walk away quietly."

Us? Did he really think we could be an us? There's no way I'd ever divorce Jason.

"You don't belong with them and you know it. That's why you're here. You can't stay away from your roots." He grabbed my hand and put it on his crotch. I slapped him hard across his face. He didn't even flinch.

I ran from the room and somehow made it back to my car. Wyatt texted again, saying he'd be in touch to discuss the plans.

I tried to warn Jason once about what happens when a fish and a bird fall in love. He brought me higher than I should be, and now I can't breathe in his world. It's either drag him down with me or let him go. I'll have to find a way to save him.

Please God, help me.

~27~

I close the journal and stare into my lap.

Jason shifts uncomfortably in his seat. "Say something."

"Was she…" I don't want to say the word; I don't know what to say. I barely understand what I just read. My stomach is tied up in knots of loathing and pity and sympathy and blame, and I don't even understand where they're coming from. Unless Audrey's trying to tell me something.

I rephrase my question. "Do you think she was forced, or do you think she betrayed you?"

"She didn't betray me; she betrayed herself with that lowlife piece of shit. She was confused."

"You can't possibly be this understanding. You must have been—"

"Furious?" He drains his glass. "Yeah. I wanted to torture the guy."

"But she's the one you married. Shouldn't you have been angry at her?"

"I don't know why she went in the first place. That's the only part I still can't understand. Her betrayal to me was in showing up there. There was no other possible outcome to their meeting, and she should have foreseen that, considering their history."

"But she didn't even try—"

"Everything Audrey did, or didn't do—like protect herself—was second nature to her. Even the part where she was protecting *me*," he says.

"You? How can you say she was protecting *you*?"

"You read it. She tried to protect me from herself because she felt I deserved better. And I think she was also protecting me in another way. It isn't like she gave him her heart, Jane. That was something she only shared with me."

I do understand that part. Audrey hated herself so much she didn't feel her body was worth protecting, but she'd left her heart at home. That's why she wrote about feeling nothing; she was nothing more than a shell when she went to him. Similar to what Jason is doing right now by turning off his emotions.

"I think you need to get mad. For your own sanity. Yell. Anything. You must feel something," I say.

Jason face tightens. He grabs one of his basketballs and squeezes it between his palms as he paces around the room. Seething. "You were the one who said that sometimes it has nothing to do with love. Remember? When you thought I slept with Leslie? You said things get complicated sometimes. Well, things got complicated, and she went and tortured herself with that piece of shit."

I wonder what Audrey would say if she were here. Would she cry and beg for his forgiveness? I'm beginning to hate her again for being such a self-deprecating sap. For putting him in the position of having to excuse her mistakes. I want him to stop holding back. He deserves to vent, and it may be the only way to uncover the truth.

"But what about you? You're allowed to have feelings about it, even if you clinically understand her motives," I say. "According to the journal, she thought you treated her like glass. *Which*, interestingly enough, were the very words I used on the beach that day. Sounds like she didn't like it any more than I did." I fold my arms across my chest. "So out with it. Didn't you care that she was with another man?"

"Of course I care!" Jason throws his empty wine glass against the wall and it shatters to pieces. He starts to come at me, full of remorse, but I put my hand up to stop him.

"Talk," I say firmly.

"How can you ask me if I care? I love you, Audrey. Jane. Whoever. You're the most important person in my life. When I think of the way that he—that fucking piece of garbage who didn't deserve to breathe the same air as you—disrespected you, disrespected *me*, our marriage, and our daughter without even flinching..." He stops to catch his breath. "And you let him. What could draw you to a man like that?"

I sit back and take a sip my wine. "It sounds like she was seeking punishment."

"She is *you*! You let him treat you like you're nothing. Why? You're everything to me. I do everything I can to show you, and it's never enough for you to believe me." His voice breaks into a sob.

The sound breaks my heart. Another memory flashes before my eyes.

We're outside at night; Jason stands in front of me.

His voice breaks. "Oh my God, Audrey, what have you done?"

I blink back to the present.

Jason watches me, waiting.

"You said, 'Oh my God, Audrey, what have you done?' We were outside at night. Near the water. Was I with him again? Did you catch us?"

Jason takes my hands in his. "You've had enough for tonight. We survived it, and that's all that matters. You made a mistake, and I forgave you. Let that be enough."

My tears fall fast and I can't stop them. I remember running away.

It's dark and I'm terrified.

Jason's voice carries through the darkness. "Audrey! Get back here."

I fall into the dirt.

It's just like my dream. A chill runs through me. "Were you chasing me, Jason?"

"Please stop. You're not ready."

"I'm not ready, or you're not ready?"

He pulls his phone from his pocket. "I need to call Patel before we continue."

Probably so he can figure out a way to manipulate my memories. I slap the phone out of his hands, and it falls to the floor.

"What aren't you telling me? I deserve to know. Do you not *want* me to be Audrey?"

He curses under his breath. "I don't know how much longer I can do this, Jane. You're killing me. Either way I'm wrong."

I jump to my feet. "What do you mean either way? Please, for once just tell me the truth. I already know the worst of it. What more can there possibly be? Was I in a cult? Abducted by aliens? Was I having his demon baby? Was I actually leaving you?"

I watch his temples constrict and lower my voice to a whisper. "She was leaving you, wasn't she?"

He bows his head. "I thought so, yes. I thought she was leaving me for him. For that piece of shit who treated you like dirt for most of your life. I found the piece of paper with the hotel address. I saw a few texts on your phone. But I didn't read the journal until after the accident, I swear to you. I wish I had. That was my fatal mistake."

"What fatal mistake?"

"After I read it, I realized she was trying to spare me. She thought I'd elevated her to a world she didn't deserve.

You mistakenly thought leaving was an act of selfless love." His voice catches on the last word.

I realize we've both been talking as if I am Audrey and Jane at the same time, and I no longer know which is which.

The floor sways under me. Rocking.

"Jason, were we on a boat?"

"Jesus, Jane. Slow down." He hugs me to his chest. "You're stronger than I am. You're the strongest person I know; look what you came back from. Audrey was strong in a lot of ways, but not when it came to helping herself. She spent her life ashamed of who she was, and it ruined her. You're a lot like her, fierce and witty, but the difference is you *believe* it. I don't want you to lose that."

"Knowing the truth won't take that away from me." I can only hope this is true.

"I wish I were as strong as you, because then I'd know what to do right now." He gets up from the couch and walks away from me. "Do I say what I know would be better for us, or the truth you think you want?"

The fear creeps back into my mind for the first time in many weeks. I begin to shake. "What do you mean?"

Jason says he understood what was happening with Audrey once he read the journal, but that wasn't until *after* the accident. How had he felt before? When all he saw was a note with a hotel name and a text about a getaway? What would he have done to Audrey if he knew she'd been with Wyatt?

He stares at me with a veiled expression. "Audrey always said you can't un-ring a bell. All those years she couldn't tell people about her past because she'd always wonder what they were thinking about her. I get it now. Once you give someone the ugly truth, there's no way to take it back. And I admit I'm thinking of myself, too. You may not be able to forgive me."

"What did you do? They said I'd remember in time anyway. Wouldn't you rather me remember with you than alone one night when you're at the hospital? When you aren't here to explain things to me?"

He nods at me. "Yeah…I thought of that, too." His gaze falls to the open bottle of wine on the coffee table and then back to me. The guilt on his face is undeniable.

Every hair on my body stands on end. It makes too much sense. The separate bottles of wine that we drank on the night before his shifts. Was there something in it to keep me from remembering for short periods of time when he couldn't control the information? "Have you been drugging me?"

He takes a step towards me. "Please try to understand."

I back away. "What could possibly be so damaging that you would drug your wife to keep her from remembering?"

"You should see how you're looking at me right now. Just like you did when you first came home. Like I'm a monster. Me. The guy who loved you and took care of you." He paces and clenches his fists at his sides. "How you could look at *me* like that and not that fucking dirt bag you let assault you?" He kicks the coffee table over. Glasses smash against the tile floor. Wine pours from the bottle, a red puddle spreading across the floor.

My eyes dart around the room, planning my exit.

Jason continues his rant. "But then you started looking at me like you used to, and it made me happier than you can ever know."

My heart thumps wildly in my chest as I listen to him unravel.

Tears well in his eyes. "And before I knew what was happening, you were looking at me in a way I didn't even know could exist—with Audrey's love but without her pain. Getting you, Jane, to fall in love with me was something I never expected, and I thought we could finally be a family, with no bad memories getting in the way."

265

"You hoped I might never have to remember *what?* What did you do?" It has been a long time since I suspected him of being responsible for my accident. I've slept with him, I've showered with him. I've fallen deeply in love with him. But maybe I was right all along. Maybe he did try to kill her. His motive was clear; he thought she was leaving him for someone so decidedly beneath him. I back up against the fireplace, feeling behind me for one of the stoking tools in case I need to come out swinging. "Did you cause my accident?"

"Not intentionally." He turns and comes quickly towards me.

I pull the fireplace poker from behind my back and hold it out in front of me, my hands shaking.

"What are you gonna do, hit me?" He looks up at the ceiling in exasperation and laughs bitterly. "Oh, that's perfect. You think *I'm* the one you should be afraid of? You've gotta be kidding me."

"How do you *not intentionally* cause someone to nearly die in a car accident?"

"Put that thing down so we can talk. I realize I'm not explaining things as eloquently as you would, but you're jumping to conclusions. Put it down," he says.

I grasp the poker tighter and widen my stance in defense. "No."

In one swift movement, he turns me around in front of him and has the poker across my chest, holding me in place. "Jiu Jitsu," he says in my ear and then kisses my head. "Every week for the last fifteen years. If you want to attack me, you can't do it like that."

I try to squirm away. "So are you going to finish me off now?"

"No, but since you're acting crazy, I'm going to keep you here until I know you aren't going to take my eye out with this thing." He walks us backwards to the sliding glass door and raises the poker over my head, holding me in place with his other arm. "I'm going to throw this outside," he says calmly, sliding the door open behind him, "and then we can talk more, OK?"

"OK," I say sweetly and throw an elbow into his stomach. When he doubles over, I jump over his back and run out into the pitch black yard, past the garden shed and towards the trees. The crisp night air pricks my lungs.

"Jane! Audrey, wait, come back."

It sounds eerily familiar.

I'm driving along winding roads in the dark, looking for a lake. Wyatt is waiting for me on a boat. As I turn down the dirt road leading to his dock, I see Jason's car.

Then the memory vanishes, out of my reach. Through the darkness I hear Jason run towards me, and I hide quietly behind a tree. My head is pounding.

"Jane, please, I'm not going to hurt you," he says, standing at the edge of the woods. "I'll tell you everything. I'd rather you know the truth than have you think I'd hurt you."

There's nowhere else to go now. I come out to face him. "I drove to meet him at his boat and you were there."

He sinks to his knees in the grass in front of me. "I only wanted to talk to him man-to-man. If we can even call him that."

"Did you hurt him?"

"He taunted me. I think he wanted me to hit him. He told me flat out that you slept with him."

I slump against the tree and hold the sides of my head, trying to keep it from splitting in half.

"He said that all of my parents' money and connections wouldn't make you love me the way you loved him, no matter how much I paid for you," he says.

"But I don't love him," I say in a tone I don't recognize as my own. "Nobody will ever understand why I ran away with you. Only we know the truth."

Jason jumps to his feet and grabs my shoulders. "Audrey?"

267

Despair and remorse squeeze my heart. I'm overcome by sadness, finally understanding what it feels like to be Audrey. Knowing how it feels to be trapped under a weighted blanket of shame.

A man's body lies face down on the deck of the boat. Blood pools around my feet.

"Did you kill him, Jason?"

"What do you remember?"

"I heard you fighting," I say, my voice shaking. "You said I was too good for him." Jason had naively tried to defend my honor, unable to see I had none left to defend.

"I thought you were going with him, and I didn't think I could live without you. But if I had to, I wanted to make sure you were taken care of as you deserved. Because you deserve better than you think," he says firmly, as if trying to make me believe him once and for all.

"I know that now. I was only going to see him because I'd made such a huge mistake by unleashing him on us. I wanted to convince him to go away."

"How? You honestly think you could have gotten through to him? I wouldn't have cared if he told people about your past. I was never ashamed of it. But you handed him the ammunition to ruin us right there in that hotel room."

I recoil from him, unable to defend the unforgivable. I almost destroyed our family and his father's career. It was so much easier to discuss when I was Jane, before I remembered what an underserving fool I am. Jason is right; I created this mess, and I'd hurt the only people who had ever loved and respected me. I cry until my lungs burn.

"He threw the first punch, Audrey, I swear it," Jason says quietly. "I just fought back."

I close my eyes and force myself to remember.

I climb the ladder and see them rolling around on the deck punching each other. I scream for them to stop, distracting Jason momentarily. Wyatt takes the advantage and pins him on the edge of the

268

railing with a length of anchor rope stretched between his hands. He forces it around Jason's throat.

I suck in my breath. "He was hurting *you*? But you must have gotten away somehow." My hopeful innocence is back, but now, deep down, I know better.

Jason puts his arm around me and pulls my head onto his shoulder. "Are you sure you're ready for this?"

"I was afraid he was going to kill you," I say through tears, the pressure building in my chest. The truth is coming; I can feel it, like a painful splinter that has to be dug out in order to relieve the pain.

"Stop it, stop it!" I scream, but Wyatt doesn't stop.

I see the opened bottle of champagne near the rail, and I pick it up; it's cold and full. Wyatt must have opened it when he heard Jason's car, expecting it was me. I swing it like a baseball bat towards the back of his head and a sickening crack echoes in my ears.

"Oh God, Jason." I bend over, retching in the grass as the scene plays out in my mind.

Stunned by the blow, Wyatt leans to the side, his arms dangling, the large, rough hands that he dared to put against my husband's throat curled at his sides. The same hands he used to hold me down so many times. I raise the bottle over my head. Champagne pours over me, soaking my hair and clothes. All of the hatred and fury I'd kept buried inside since my youth erupts and surges through my veins. I smash the bottle down on his skull with all my strength. Wyatt topples, lifeless, as the blood—so much blood, dark and thick—collects in a pool at my feet.

Jason struggles to his feet. "Oh my God, Audrey, what have you done? The first one was enough to stop him." He feels for a pulse, then shakes his head silently. I back away trembling. Horrified. I can't feel my legs, but I run; I run away and fall in the dirt as Jason yells my name. I carelessly throw the bottle onto the front seat and peel out of the dirt road as fast as I can.

I drive down the road screaming. Screaming at life for giving so much pain to one person. Screaming for Jason and for Daisy and for everything I'd done to them. Screaming at myself for being everything my mother said I was. Screaming because I know I can never face Jason again. Seeing the turn coming and flooring the gas pedal, knowing I wouldn't be able to stop. Wanting to end it all.

I try to breathe between sobs. "I killed him." And I'd abandoned my husband at a murder scene. I should have died in that accident.

"You saved my life, Audrey," Jason whispers in my ear, and I realize he's carrying me into the house.

"Then why did you say I might not forgive you once I knew?"

"I meant forgive me for telling you. For helping you remember. When the best thing would be for you to forget," he says.

He lays me down on the couch and leaves the room. When he returns, I feel him lift my arm. "I'm giving you a mild sedative to take the edge off." After a while he hands me water. "You have to drink this."

"What happened after I left?" I whisper, unable to move.

Jason sits next to me and moves the hair from my eyes. "I did what I had to do to protect you. To protect our family. I drove the boat far out to some rocks and pushed his body over the edge."

"Oh God, Jason." I squeeze my eyes shut, tasting bile in my throat.

He describes how he methodically cleaned the deck and used one of the towels to leave traces of blood on the side of the boat and rocks to make it appear as if someone hit their head going over the edge. He found some beer on the boat, poured it on Wyatt's body, and left the cans scattered on the rocks. Finally, he destroyed Wyatt's cell phone before taking the boat into the center of the lake and leaving it adrift. He swam back to shore and changed in to his gym clothes. When he saw his phone in the car, there were a dozen calls from the hospital. And then Thomas called again.

"You did all of that for me?" I ask.

270

Jason lived with that brutal memory, keeping it all to himself to protect me. It must have weighed on his mind and tortured his sleep in the months after my accident. And I fought against him, accusing him of everything I could think of, worried only about what would become of me if I remembered. I now understand, for Audrey and for Jane, what he tried to protect us from all along. The bad guy of our story was *me*.

He runs his hand along my face. "You acted to save my life and then nearly lost yours. You always put more value on me than yourself."

"I'm a murderer. I thought I was bad before, but now...now I'm a murderer, too."

Jason leans down and looks me in the eye. "What you are is a survivor, Audrey. And the strongest person I have ever known."

I cry until I have nothing left and can only stare blankly at the wall. "What about the police? Dottie read me the newspaper in the hospital about a boating accident and a man—"

"It was him. When I saw that article in your hospital room, I was terrified. I was sure you were going to remember, but you didn't. That's when I had hope that you'd never remember."

"But did anyone investigate? Did they know who he was?" I ask.

"No. Wyatt was a drifter with a record a mile long in a dozen states. Nobody ever reported him missing, probably because he was always missing from someplace. And the boat he was staying on was stolen; the police traced it back to the owners, but that was it as far as I know. They couldn't even fingerprint him because he'd been in the water too long by the time he was found. I waited, you know," Jason says, tearing up. "I waited for the police to come and get me. I waited for the knock on the door, for someone to figure it

271

out. But they never did. If they had, I was going to take the blame."

"Why? Why would you do that?" I want to scream but I can't.

"Because I should've seen what was happening to you. I should've known. I'm a doctor and I didn't even notice that my wife was dying in front of me, little by little. I was an arrogant idiot. I thought I could love it out of you. But you needed something more than love," he says. "After the accident, I had the chance to give you what you always wanted by letting you forget."

I replay so many scenes from the hospital. His black eye and bruised mouth, the way he wanted to talk to me alone when I first woke up. He must have thought I was going to blurt out that I'd murdered someone. And then I'd asked him if his name was Wyatt.

All at once I realize the depth of his devotion and how far he was willing to go to protect me from myself. Jason had allowed me to forget, even though it meant sacrificing all of the things I knew and loved about him. He was willing to trade my good opinion of him for a better one of myself. The old Audrey was right all along; we didn't deserve him, then or now.

I feel myself crumble into a thousand tiny pieces and sob in his arms. He'd been right in trying to hide the truth from me. I finally have the answers I was seeking, only now I wish I didn't. But I'll never admit that because if he has to carry the secret with him, then I'll carry it as well.

"But the worst part was being able to love you as someone else and realizing you were right all along," he says. "You *were* better somehow. Different. Free. Letting go of your past changed everything about you."

He may never know the power behind his words. For the first time in my life, I feel like someone truly understands. I had everything I'd ever wanted when I was Jane—the family, the peaceful life, and none of the memories. And I couldn't even see it.

~ ~ ~

After days of crying, I go to the only person in the world who can help me move on. *Maman*. I tell her everything except, of course, that it ended with me murdering someone. There's no way I'm going to make her an accomplice after the fact.

"I forgive you, chérie," she says. "It is over. You will do better now, because you know better now."

"But how can you forgive me?"

"Do not think me to be so perfect that I cannot understand what you were going through. Edmund has forgiven me for things, and I have forgiven him for things. None of us is without faults, Audrey."

"But Jason is your son. Look what I did to him."

She sighs. "You loved my son. Twice. You loved him so much that even when you were someone else, you fell in love with him. All the other things you were fighting against simply got in the way. You were drowning, my darling, and you kicked him while trying to get out of the water. I am sorry he was injured, but I can see you meant him no harm."

"How can you not hate me?"

"Why would I hate you? Because you have sinned differently than me? I could tell you stories about my mistakes that would make your hair stand on end. There is only one person whose forgiveness you need if you want this to never happen again, my love, and that person is *you*. It is the only thing you have needed all along."

I draw from Vivienne's courage and emulate her spirit. I allow myself a few weeks to grieve it out and then pledge to be the woman Jason and Daisy need me to be. The person I should have been all along. *Jane.*

When I was Jane, I wouldn't have wasted a minute worrying that I wasn't good enough. I would have taken action to become it.

~ ~ ~

Dr. Patel sits at his desk, studying the results of my bloodwork. It has been weeks since the night my memories returned, but we're still conducting monthly tests to see if there's any lingering damage to address. He sent me for a complete work up recently since I'd been feeling so exhausted and weak after my ordeal.

"Is anything wrong?" I ask.

He smiles. "On the contrary, my dear, I would say that everything is quite right. Even better than right." He reaches out and puts a hand on my leg. "We always fear how patients will handle the anniversary of their traumas, but I think you will have your hands too full to care."

I look back at him cautiously. "Are you saying what I think you're saying?"

"If you think I'm saying that you are pregnant, then yes. But there's more." He hands me a lab slip to read. "Congratulations, Audrey."

I no longer flinch at the name.

I drop my head into my hands. Pregnant. The irony of this life truly astounds me. I laugh so hard Dr. Patel begins to look concerned.

I find Jason in his study, hovering over a mountain of paperwork. After everything that's gone on in our lives, after all the things Jason went through because of me, I get to be the one to give *him* a first experience.

As soon as I walk in, he turns to face me. I watch his expression change as I deliver the first part of my news. He jumps from his chair and runs to me, and I find myself laughing too hard to tell him the rest. Laughing as he holds on to me, rocking back and forth, laughing as he calls for Daisy and Dottie to come hear our surprise. And when our daughter runs to us, wide-eyed and anxious, followed by my truest friend in the world, I get to tell them all.

Tell them about the two miracles coming to join our lives next June.

A flash of worry crosses Jason's face. The old Audrey would have seen the date as a bad omen, a reminder of the pain I've caused. But not me, and I tell him so. I'm aware now of the rare gems hidden in the rubble that can only be found once we stop searching.

Jason takes me in his arms and dips me back, kissing my neck.

"Thank you," he says. "Thank you." He doesn't need to say more. I know what he means.

Thank you for finally choosing to be happy, because now we can all be.

~ ~ ~

I can still see the scars left behind by the accident. Sometimes when I'm gardening I'll gaze at a mark on my arm and watch it turn translucent in the sun. If I'd never been Jane, those scars would have bothered me; but they don't, just like so many things I used to worry about. If anything, they are true evidence to my ability to persevere.

I no longer care what the old me would have done or felt. I don't know when or how it happened, but I let it all go. Let it wash down the drain one day in the shower or fly out the car window while singing songs with Daisy. I released it all—the anger, the sadness, the guilt of not being good enough for them.

For as long as I can remember, all I ever wanted was to forget. But the truth is, the memories weren't the problem. The problem was the power I'd given them. For too long, I allowed my past to corrupt my future instead of being grateful for where it led me.

And I am, above anything else, grateful. For all of it.

It no longer matters to me what I may or may not deserve or who should be the judge of it. I have a beautiful daughter, two adorable little baby boys, and a husband whose love is worth more than anything I have ever known. I nearly lost my life searching for my worth, only to find the proof of it had been standing in front of me all along. Jason.

If I am to measure myself by any standard, it should be by the quality of the person who chooses to share a life with me. Because in the end, that shows me everything I need to know.

And anything else can be forgotten.

Acknowledgements

I dedicate this story first and foremost to "my girls" and all of the others like them who have trusted me with their stories and inspired me to take my own advice.

To my family-my husband David, and our kids, Beth, Kyle and Kate, thank you for allowing me to take the time away from you to complete this dream. No matter what I do, you will always be the greatest of my accomplishments.

To my editor, Margo Navage Padala, the closest thing I will ever have to an older sister, thank you for every second you have devoted to my book, my writing and my life. In truth, you have edited so much more than words and sentences, revised things much greater than intros and endings, and provoked me to grow as a person in addition to a writer. Your talents transformed this story.

I am lucky to have been surrounded by so many supportive friends-who are too many to name, but hopefully know I am thinking of them when I write thank you for your patience, kindness and love~in every situation. For my reviewers, thank you for reading and rereading, discussing, answering questions and keeping me going. Carrie O'Connell-the first person to ever know "Jane", Lauren Dassatti, Joanne Audyatis, Jennifer LaBella, Karen Prevalla, Brianna Guertin, Caryn Vincent, Beth Coltart, Fran Tetro (the best grammy on the planet), Lisa Phipps, Jodi Paulin, Nadine Savage, Andrea Butwell, Eileen Budrewicz, Karen VanDerlyn and Beth Mieczkowski, editor-in-training. Special thanks to the Nonnewaug High School Foreign Language Department for helping Vivienne's French passages make proper sense.

Lastly, to my dear friend, Karen Fiore-Green, who did not live to see the publication of this book, for taking the time during our last moments together to advise me to follow my dream and "just do it already, no matter how you have to." My dedication to completing this process is owed entirely to your example of how life is too short to wait.

Thank you all for reading.
~Theresa

Further Thought on When I Was Jane

~ Water is a prevalent symbol in this story. When does it present itself in the plot, and how does it affect the direction of the characters? What ideas might water symbolize in this novel?

~ Female relationships (or the lack of) are significant in this book. How do they affect Jane throughout her journey? How do Vivienne and Dottie each help Jane to grow?

~ In the hospital, Jane discovers that there are no female friends in her life. When writing this story, author Theresa Mieczkowski said, "I knew I could not have a best friend for Audrey or there would be no story." Why do you think she felt that way?

~ Audrey/Jane had incredibly supportive male relationships in the book. Is that surprising considering Audrey's past experiences? What does this suggest about men and women?

~ One of the themes of this story is trust—trust of another as well as trust of self. Was it more difficult for Audrey to trust because she was affected by her past or for Jane to trust because she didn't have information on people? What other themes can you explore?

~ The idea of "sparing" people comes up several times. On page 254, Jane guesses that Audrey was going to leave Daisy "because she loved her that much." Jason attempts to spare Audrey by allowing her to forget. Could you imagine giving up someone you loved to save them from having to share your troubles?

~ After reading Audrey's journal and her interaction with Wyatt, Jane struggles with whether or not Audrey could have had more control over the situation in the hotel room. Why do you think it was difficult for her to decide? What do you think happened?

~ There are many fields of psychology that deal with the different "parts" of people's personalities. Compare the "trilogy" of the main character (Dree, Audrey and Jane) using the idea of the parts of human psychology known as the id, the ego, and the superego.

~ The character of Thomas was integral to the plot as well as Audrey's life. In the original draft, Thomas returned to the story at the end. Why do you think editor Margo Navage Padala felt he needed to stay away for the integrity of the story?

~ On page 29, Dr. Patel explains with specific detail how and why people hold on to certain memories above others. ("Memory is constructive. Previous experience dictates how and why we cling to certain events and how we perceive them, which in turn determines what is stored and what is not.") Did this passage make you rethink any of your own experiences and wonder if you remember things as they really were or merely as you perceived them to be?

~ On page 240, Dree recites an old proverb to Jason, once again bringing the symbol of water into the story. ("A fish and a bird can fall in love but where would they build their nest?") Which animal do you think she identified with (or saw him as) and why? How did her thoughts about herself eventually make that hypothesis come true?

~ During Jason's story, he reveals how he really met Audrey, and the reader finally gets a feeling for the kind of man he is. Why do you think he was so bothered by "Dree" allowing his friends to think they were having sex in the private room at The Hornet's Nest?

~ On page 227, Dottie calls Jason to West Virginia and says to Jane, "sometimes helpin' someone means doin' the opposite of what they think they want." Discuss how this idea can be applied to nearly every character throughout the novel.

Made in the USA
Middletown, DE
24 February 2015